■ □ ■ □ ■

ALL THIS BELONGS TO ME

■ □ ■ □ ■

WRITINGS FROM AN UNBOUND EUROPE

GENERAL EDITOR
Andrew Wachtel

EDITORIAL BOARD
Clare Cavanagh
Michael Henry Heim
Roman Koropeckyj
Ilya Kutik

All This Belongs to Me

A Novel

PETRA HŮLOVÁ

Translated from the Czech by Alex Zucker

NORTHWESTERN UNIVERSITY PRESS
EVANSTON, ILLINOIS

Northwestern University Press
www.nupress.northwestern.edu

Printed in the United States of America

10 9 8 7 6 5 4 3 2 1

Library of Congress Cataloging-in-Publication Data

Hůlová, Petra, 1979–
    [Paměť mojí babičce. English]
    All this belongs to me : a novel / Petra Hůlová ; translated from the Czech by Alex Zucker.
        p. cm.—(Writings from an unbound Europe)
    ISBN 978-0-8101-2443-1 (pbk. : alk. paper)
    1. Women—Mongolia—Fiction. I. Zucker, Alex. II. Title. III. Series: Writings from
an unbound Europe.
    PG5040.18.U44P3613 2009
    891.8636—dc22

                                                                    2009023496

This translation is dedicated to M. H. P.

■ □ ■ □ ■

CONTENTS

■ □ ■ □ ■

ALL THIS BELONGS TO ME

■ □ ■ □ ■

1. ZAYA

HERE AT HOME WHEN A *SHOROO* HITS, PLASTIC BAGS GO CHASING EACH other round and round the *ger*. Sometimes I sit outside and watch as the sand spins in whirls, the horizon turns a golden brown, and the sun through the swirling yellow dust is dim and shaky. Boots turn gray under the buildup of dust, a dust that stings the eyes and crunches under the horses' hoofs, so the whole herd's on edge and the barking *nokhoi* has his work cut out for him to separate the in-foal mares with young from the rest.

Here at home when a *shoroo* hits and there's nothing to do—since you can't even see to take a step and if I went out I'd choke to death or I wouldn't be able to find my way back—I sit out in front of the *ger*, on the right, and wonder what it used to look like, when there weren't any plastic bags and families like us didn't have even a decent knife and couldn't earn any extra cash selling cookies and cigarettes, like Papa did whenever someone stumbled across us. Lately it's been happening pretty often.

Supposedly it's because someone in Bulgan sells good, cheap *man-jing*, carrots, and onions, so people go shopping there more than before and more of them pass by our *ger* on the way. But I don't think that's it, since they sell vegetables in Davkhan too, and only a few people a week pass by in that direction.

Maybe the Davkhan grower is an *erliiz*, same as his father, and that's why nobody buys from him. The Chinese are a tricky bunch, and no one around here trusts them.

Davja, who lives with her parents about five miles south of us, brought home a man named Liu Fu one day, and her father, Batu, reported him for being here illegally and smuggling plastic shoes and waterproof shirts to sell in the capital. It was probably true— at least that's what everyone thought, since he did look funny and he hardly ever talked—but still, it wasn't right to take away little Gerla's papa like that. Davja did nothing from morning to night except cry and threaten to leave, but there was nowhere for her to leave to. Liu Fu went to the city to straighten it out, but when after two weeks he still wasn't back, it began to be more than clear that they had sent him back home to China. Either that or he'd been taken in by relatives—which every *erliiz* has somewhere in every country—who'd found him another woman whose family wouldn't be such a problem. The truth is he never returned. Mama said she understood why Batu did what he did, she would never give me to a Chinaman either, not for a herd of well-fed camels and the swiftest spotted steeds.

Though I myself look just like one, with my screwy eyes and frail little frame. I've had a few people call me out on it too, like years ago, in the *somon* school, when I boasted about how my family's felts fetched the highest price in the *aimak*. And the whole time they had on the sickest grins.

Slandering my Khalkha purity like that. I wanted to get back at them somehow but instead I felt tears. That did the trick back then. Still, I believed them more than my own mother, because Nara's hair had been fair from the day she was born, and Papa was in the army then, just like he was away when Mama had me, so she can't really be trusted too much when it comes to these things.

When I was about five years old, a man who wasn't a Mongol came to our door. He had long, thick hair and a strange-looking *del* with narrow sleeves, and stayed the night with us. The way my mother looked when he left the next morning, I couldn't tell if she was going to hit him, jump him, or leave with him. She was making these wild gestures and her eyes were blazing red. I remember I was sick at the time with a fever, and the flames in her eyes were licking at me like the tongues of a mad killer dog. Those eyes wouldn't stop staring at me as Mama sat on the edge of my bed, feeding me sour sheep yogurt to help me keep my strength up. This was after the man who wasn't a Mongol had left.

Even before, I had a feeling they didn't like me as much as Magi, but that was the first time I saw how distant and mean my mother could be, eyeing me with hatred while she cleaned up after me, since except for the yogurt I kept throwing up everything else. Grandma said it was the end, but it wasn't.

That same spring the stranger who wasn't a Mongol appeared, we had lots of baby lambs, and then never again after that. Grandma said that he did it, that he put a curse on our lambs, and if he had taken me instead it would've been far less a loss, since I was only five then, which isn't even a Mongol yet, just a little baby goatling. Plus Mama and Papa still had three more. There's just three of us now, since Magi died, but that's still enough for our clan to blossom, even if some get stuck in a blizzard, catch a disease, or go missing.

It's really sad about Magi. She was the most beautiful of us all, and Papa liked her best from the start. Because though Mama didn't give him a boy—and I don't think he ever fully forgave her for that—she did bear him the loveliest creature in all the land. *Tsaraitai okhin,* everyone said when they came by to visit, while me and Nara just snuggled up close on the left, the women's, side of the *ger,* reassuring ourselves that the only reason Magi was prettier than us was because she was so much older, even though she was just three years ahead of me and four ahead of Nara and ever since she was little she had been beautiful and we knew it.

Whenever little Oyuna saw me and Nara whispering and cuddling up to each other, she would pound my thighs with her fists and force her way in between us to make sure she didn't miss out. To make sure we noticed her. She's seven years younger than Nara and eight years younger than me, so she got on our nerves and she always had to fight for whatever she got. Oyuna spoiled all our games, and we had to drag her around with us everywhere we went, because Mama had work to do, Papa was out with the herd, and Magi could fend for herself: she would take the basin in back of the *ger* and hide out there for hours, just messing around with the guts of the sheep that Papa had killed that day, while any of the rest of us would've had it done in no time. Either that or she'd make some excuse about how she had to go gather *argal* so Mama could heat the stove for *buuz* and Oyuna would get in her way. So me and Nara ended up getting stuck with her every time.

Oyuna was born during the most awful winter I ever remember. The wind outside was so cold that every time you blinked you had to peel your eyelids back open again, and sometimes, when I had to follow the herd and afterwards I was tired on my way home in the evening, I'd put it off longer and longer each time, till all I wanted to do was sit down on the snow and go to sleep. My nostrils stuck together too, tugging painfully at the hairs. It's like that every winter here, but the year Oyuna was born it was worse.

Animals' flanks caved in and so did people's cheeks. Even the young looked old, and grown-ups didn't let their children go outside at all. They tethered them to the legs of the bed or hung them over the stove in leather cradles, so they wouldn't have to worry when they went outside to scrape the snow away for the sheep.

So much snow fell the winter Oyuna was born that Grandma decided to die. She didn't think she could make it through such a terrible storm, so she slept on and off through the worst three months buried under a heap of woolen blankets by the stove, while Papa brewed strong, hot tea with milk so the baby goats and sheep would survive. He wrapped the large stock in old hides and shouted at the horses whenever he would see one that didn't want to live anymore. When a good horse died, he beat its rump and legs with his *tashuur*, to make it stand, and then shot it, and me and Nara came running out to watch its eyes cloud over and its flanks twitch like it was shooing off flies. Then I took off my mittens and reached in to touch its belly, in between the rear legs, where it was nice and warm.

Nara meanwhile went running home, hearing Grandma's cries from bed that Mama was giving birth.

Oyuna was an unlikely child, and Mama suffered for weeks with her. She wasn't exactly young anymore, so she wasn't too overjoyed to find out there was going to be another of us. Papa was delighted, though, confident that this time, at last, he'd made Mama a boy. He strutted around like a rooster during our visits over the summer, poking fun of our neighbor Öyunbat, who lived near Batu and Davja and who just that spring had had daughter number six, while slumbering inside Papa's wife was the child that he dreamed would be the future Chingis Khan of our clan.

My aunt Hiroko—who Burkhan knows why has a Japanese name and who some of our family went to see because she was a shaman—just gave a little nod and Papa believed his wish would come true. But after Oyuna was born, he declared that Hiroko had known all along or she wouldn't have wagged her head like that, and that he had thought the same thing when he saw Mama's pointy belly and how slowly it was growing.

As long as Mama's belly was big, me and Nara were happy. She got slower and clumsier every day and paid less and less attention to us. Papa was constantly off in the mountains with the herd, so Mama was left to manage the household on her own, because ever since Grandma had started forgetting to salt the meat for the *khuushuur* Mama had stopped counting on her for help around the *ger*.

Grandma got upset sometimes when Mama kept her from doing her chores, and swore at her in her dialect, from the western part of the country, so me and Nara wouldn't understand. But Mama got the message all right, even without any words. I could only guess it had something to do with the man who wasn't a Mongol, who Mama was in love with.

When Mama's time finally came, the cold was so fierce they couldn't send me and Nara and Magi outside, and I'll never forget Oyuna's first cries and Mama's deep sighs of relief when it was over. We weren't allowed to watch, so I only remember that night through my ears. A long darkness and crying, and then, as it was getting light, Mama and the baby asleep, balled into a tight, hard knot and covered with almost every sheepskin we owned. Papa was worried. Even though it was only a girl, he stoked the fire all night and all day and all night again, till the air was so hot and heavy and smoky that me and Nara felt faint. We weren't allowed to go outside except to go to the bathroom, since Papa was afraid the baby might catch cold from the draft, so me and Nara lay down in bed together and played.

We each had our own set of anklebones that we carried around in a pouch with us everywhere we went. Mine were red and Nara's were painted yellow so we wouldn't get them mixed up. When we were in a good mood we'd shake them out on the ground and play. When Oyuna was born, I rolled camels on all my bones three times in a row and Nara threw a tantrum, and with one broad sweep of her hand she sent the bones flying across the *ger*. The noise woke the baby, who had just finished feeding and was almost asleep, and she burst into a fit of uncontrollable bawling. Mama started patting her up and down to calm her, and Papa, shouting, Draft or no draft, pushed Nara out into the freezing cold with the dogs.

When winter was as cold as it was in the Year of the Rabbit, when Oyuna came to join us, the dogs carried on like crazy. They were constantly starving, and would scratch at our door all night long, even though they knew perfectly well the heat was just for us Mongols.

Grandma spent the whole winter Oyuna was born lying down. She shook with cold, even in her double-thick winter *del,* complaining that Magi wasn't keeping the fire stoked enough, me and Nara were useless, and Papa came home too late at night. For days and days she slept and wept, and early one morning, when I was still half asleep, I heard Mama tell Papa that Grandma wouldn't live to see New Year's and who was going to help her make the *buuz* dough then? Because every family had to make at least five thousand dumplings, so every guest would walk away with their bellies full like the livestock in July, when all they do is stand around for days on end with their heads down, chewing grass.

Papa just said, She'll make it, took his saddle off its peg, and went along his way. He didn't get mad at Mama at all, which only convinced me even more how mean and cruel it was of her to talk about Grandma that way. Grandma was Papa's mother, not Mama's. Maybe that was why they argued so much and why Mama hardly did anything right from Grandma's point of view. But there was also something else going on. Maybe Grandma had seen something she wasn't supposed to see. Maybe she knew of the secrets of Mama's heart.

Papa's family comes from the west of Mongolia and they've always been one of the most illustrious Dörvöd clans, so Grandma had a hard time swallowing the fact that her son married a girl from an ordinary nomad family with scarcely twenty horses and less than a hundred sheep and goats put together. Not to mention that Mama was Khalkha, and Grandma was never too fond of them.

Grandma used to go into the capital every couple of years—where even though it was Khalkha some of her distant relatives lived—and the grannies selling cigarettes and soft drinks on the street would always treat her with sneers. Even though the Dörvöds just say *k* instead of the softer *kh* and their speech is just a little bit more cramped than the Khalkhas' is, the ladies in the shops would sometimes pretend not to understand and refuse to wait on her.

Mama says the reason is in the west there are mountains, so the horizon is short and jagged, whereas most of the Khalkhas live on the vast and friendly steppe, which makes their speech more open.

Not that I would know, but I think I talk more like Mama, seeing as Papa didn't talk to me much when I was little. But I don't talk exactly like her either, since when I went to school they could tell right away that my father came from someplace else, because Mama had a talk with the teacher and Mama sounds the same way as everyone else in our *aimak*. I told Grandma about it, and she said I wasn't denying my ancestry and that was good. Papa just sat there listening, looking a little sad. He'd always had troubles in our *aimak* because of his language and he probably didn't want us to take after him in that. Papa never was much of a talker.

I used to think he was worrying about work all the time, since the livestock was all up to him and he didn't have any sons to help. Also, when I was little and I'd ask him to play *shagai* at the end of the day or to come and look at a den of little tarbagans I had found, Mama would cut me short. Run along, she'd say, your papa has work, and she would hand me a hide to shear or some meat to clean, so I'd learn how to do something too.

When Papa was in the mood, though, the livestock getting fat and the horses' coats glistening like a mountain pool in the sun, he could be a lot of fun.

The horses Papa picked out for Magi, Nara, and me were especially wild. We could ride them, but it wasn't easy to stay in the saddle. We each had a little wooden saddle, painted by our uncle in beautiful childish colors, so we wouldn't jiggle around too much. Papa also made us each a little *tashuur* so we could whip our horses when they got out of line, and off we went.

When we were three years old, and for a little while after that, Papa would boost us into the saddle, but eventually we could do it ourselves and Magi couldn't show off anymore.

The three of us would ride with Papa out to the horizon, urging our horses on toward the giant angry red sun as it slowly sank into the earth. We never did catch up to it. At moments like those, I felt like we were a family and that no one could ever sever the ties of blood that bound us, and the last thing I wanted was to go back home to Mama, hovering over the stove, her eyes red with smoke, boiling up a pot of soup filled with chunks of fat as she awaited our return.

Papa liked to ride fast. *Khush, khush, khush!* he'd shout. I could only see his mouth move, his voice was carried away by the wind, and afterwards his horse's back would be drenched beneath the saddle.

But most of the time I rode a few dozen yards behind him, just trying to keep his horse's tail in sight, since even though Papa liked to say it wasn't important, he always took the fastest horse in the herd for himself.

His *del* was the color of dark wine, with ornamental fastenings, which Mama didn't like too much, because nobody else in our *somon* wore one like it, and she'd already had it up to here with his and Grandma's language being different and the troubles they had with that. So she took Papa's boots and embroidered them with the *Soyombo,* our country's national symbol, saying that everyone and their dog had geometric patterns and coiling roses, but nobody would be anywhere near as politically minded as Papa.

It didn't matter to him, just as long as the toes on his boots were turned up nice and high, so as not to disturb even the tiniest speck of our sacred soil, and warm enough in winter, when he spent all day scraping snow away for the livestock, who were too weak to get through the icy crust to the sharp yellow grass underneath.

The winter my youngest sister was born was the worst winter of all. None of us died, but even with Papa's daily routine with the tea and blankets, not a single baby goat that was born that year survived.

If Mama hadn't given birth, then everything would've been different. She could've helped Papa so he wouldn't have been stuck inside the *ger* for three days, keeping it warm for my screaming baby sister.

Certainly Grandma thought so, seeing as Mama didn't have time for her anymore, what with the baby, and us little ones just ignored her. With Grandma sleeping all the time she hardly ate a thing, and in the spring, when she came crawling out of her flea-ridden sheep sty, she was as bony as Uregma, the horrid old hag who supposedly lived in the mountains near our summer camp and stole naughty children from their families. Mama used to bring up her name whenever we tortured our puppies or hid out in back of the *ger* and listened in on the grown-ups.

Grandma survived the winter, just as Papa had predicted, but nothing was ever right with her again. She didn't help Mama with anything, and got crankier and crankier with everyone except Papa. She had been looking forward to a grandson also, a little *baatar* to bring glory to the clan, and here Oyuna was, an ordinary girl baby, like the rest of us before her. It was obvious Papa was upset, and that just gave Grandma another reason to nag. As if she'd forgotten she herself had been a girl baby once. Mama swore she'd never have another child again, and so it was.

A year later, in the summer of the Year of the Monkey, we laid Grandma to rest. Oyuna was just beginning to run, and keeping track of her was a chore. She didn't crawl or hop on all fours the way she used to, and could stand up all on her own, without holding on to anything. It didn't bother her when me and Magi and Nara tried to frighten her with Uregma—she was still too dumb to understand, and besides, she was with us all the time. The week Grandma died, all of us except Papa and Oyuna were away on a visit to Munkhtsetseg's.

Munkhtsetseg was a cousin of Mama's who also had almost all daughters. She lived with them and her husband, Maidar, about a day's journey by car from our *ger*, in the next *aimak* over, and they had invited us to come and taste their *koumiss*.

Just like our family's rawhides were the finest in the region and our cashmeres were among the most highly prized, Maidar and Munkhtsetseg fermented the best mare's milk in all of Övörkhangai Aimak.

Papa didn't get along with Munkhtsetseg, plus he had to tend to the herd. Grandma was too weak to make the trip, and Oyuna stayed home too, since when it came to watching kids at least, Mama still trusted Grandma. The day we left, some of the sheep went astray and Papa had to go look for them, so the plan was for Oyuna to spend the next four days shut up inside the *ger* with Grandma. But it didn't turn out that way at all, and it ended in Grandma's death.

Nobody really knows what exactly happened. Papa was gone, so he couldn't say, and all Oyuna did was wail, clinging so tightly to Mama's *del* her collar was soaked through with tears. Our car broke down on the way back from Munkhtsetseg and Maidar's. It ran out of gas, and according to Mama, the nearest pump was too far away to make it there on foot.

At least Oyuna wasn't with us, since the thought of lugging her twelve miles through the July Gobi heat, shifting her back and forth between our backs and our arms the whole way, didn't appeal to any of us. We were all loaded down with soda bottles full of *koumiss,* which we stopped and sipped from as we walked, but after a while the milk got hot and everyone's heads were spinning. The whole twelve miles there wasn't a single tree.

When we got close enough that our home was more than just a black dot alone on the steppe like a stray black colt, and we could make out the door frame and the orange strip of decorations running all around it, we noticed a sort of crumpled heap about twenty steps west of the *ger*. The closer we got, the clearer it became that it was what all of us were thinking but none of us dared speak aloud. Grandma lay splayed on the ground like a tree torn up by the roots, which meant she probably didn't just fall but had gone into convulsions, though she'd never had them before. Where she was going was also unclear, since we didn't go in that direction to pee or to pray or to gather *argal* for the fire. None of us ever went that way, much less Grandma, who only went somewhere if she had a reason. Once we got over the shock, we all just stood there a while, looking down at her helplessly. She had already gone stiff and we couldn't straighten her out. We couldn't even unclench her fists, and all of us tried it, one by one. Except Mama, but she didn't stop us.

Then all of a sudden Mama turned white, let out a cry, and went racing toward the *ger*. We'd forgotten about Oyuna.

She sat squatting on her heels by the stove, absorbed in Magi's knucklebones, lining them up in rows and scraping the ground with them.

That's what Mama told us, by the time we got there there was nothing to see—just a harsh braying sound coming from Mama's arms, which were totally white from lack of blood she was squeezing Oyuna so hard.

Papa came home the next morning to find Grandma out in front of the *ger*, covered with a hide, and five womenfolk inside, squeezed onto a single bed.

Mama and Papa took her out to our spot on the mountainside a little to the east of us, and left her. When we went back to look after forty-five days there was nothing. That was the first time Oyuna stayed at home alone. Papa mentioned Grandma's name along the way, and she started squirming around so bad that he had to put her down on the ground, and she ran back home like a kicked puppy dog.

I asked her about it later on, and even though by then she was old enough to make sense of it, she still didn't tell me any more than she had at the time, which was nothing. How Papa got gored by a bull, though, and came home clutching his belly with blood-stained hands, that she remembered just fine. And that was only a week or two later. Oyuna can't be trusted any more than Mama can. They always stuck together too. Right up until Mama's death.

We didn't really talk much about Grandma after that. The way she left us, no one could make any sense of it. But Magi and Nara would sometimes spin the most horrible stories about it, watching Oyuna out of the corners of their eyes as she stared at the ground and pretended not to hear. Papa frowned and Mama turned white with rage, and sometimes she would give them both a whack on the back to be quiet already. Papa only talked about it once to us, a couple of months after we laid Grandma to rest at our spot and left her to the beasts of prey.

One evening he took us out on horseback to check on Magi's favorite white mare, which was due to foal any moment.

Magi kept moaning that it was too late and we'd already missed it, so we rode at a gallop, the tired, tyrannous orb sinking toward the earth in the clouds of Gobi dust behind the horses' backs, and when I turned to look at Nara she was loping through the sunlight like a

Yuan princess in a golden frame, every hair on her head aglow like the Russian girls in our *somon* center.

As soon as we got close, we could tell it was already over. A short way from the herd stood the motionless white silhouette of the exhausted mare, wet foal fastened to her teat. They looked content so we didn't disturb them, and Papa said he had something to tell us.

The last time I'd heard him sound so serious and urgent was after that awful winter, when he told us we didn't have a single baby goat left and if we didn't move camp fast we wouldn't have any more lambs either, and Mama went to pack our things and the next morning we rode. That's how solemn Papa looked and almost just as gloomy. He said he didn't want Oyuna to hear what he was about to say, since Mama had forbidden us to speak of Grandma in front of her and Mama herself didn't do too well with it either. He said Mama felt guilty for having left Grandma at home alone, and was angry at him for putting his sheep before his mother.

There was no way for Papa to know that Grandma was going to die, though. I realized that even then. So I told him he didn't do anything wrong, and I still think that today.

He said: "Though we may no longer speak of your grandmother, one of your children's first words will be the name Dolgorma. It is thanks to her and our other Dörvöd ancestors of the west that we can sit here now by our herd, feeling the warmth of the home *aimak* under our behinds. Your grandmother's great-grandmother was called by the name Chuluuntsetseg. Her father gave her that name because she was their prayed-for flower sprung from a crack in the barren rock of his wife's womb, along with her first gray hairs.

"Now this daughter Chuluuntsetseg, the mother of Dolgorma's grandmother, at the age of fifteen was promised to a Manchu prince, but on the night before the wedding my great-great-grandfather came and stole her away, and he kept her hidden his whole life, even though he was just a poor taimen fisherman and one of the few pure westerners settled around the Great Lakes, since all of the others had fallen in the Khamar wars and the rest couldn't stand the constant humiliation at the hands of the Khalkhas."

This wasn't what I called fun. I sucked a blade of grass, waiting for Papa to get to something exciting, to tell a story to make me hold my breath. I knew he could do it, though he didn't show it often. Stories like this were like the buzzing of flies on a hot afternoon. They put me to sleep. But I knew it was important to Papa to tell it to us.

"Your grandmother came from a wealthy family of cashmere moguls, since her mother had caught the eye of the father of Grandmother's father, Onon, who was a direct supplier of cashmere to the court of the khan, and the khan's exactors rode their horses all the way from Örgöö to get it, adorned in velvet caps with bird-of-paradise plumes. Onon was chief *darga* of the Selenge River region, what he said went, and not a *ger* in the region would pay levies to the Manchus if Onon didn't want it, or his nobles would take care of them and everybody knew it.

"For instance, if the khan just up and decided to lower the price of cashmere, and from one day to the next, no one could afford Chinese rice or good Russian knives anymore. With a shout of *Morindo!* Onon would swing into the saddle and change into a peerless rippling four-legged beast. As he hurtled across the steppe, kicking up a cloud of dust, his men would come running out of their *gers* in their carmine *dels,* sacks of dried meat and hard wooden saddles over their arms. Their wives and children would wave good-bye and spatter them with milk for good luck, and Onon, with his warriors at his back, overturned the khan's decision every time. So long as Onon lived, the price of cashmere never fell so low that Grandmother's family had to occupy themselves with hides, or bargain for meat, or concern them-selves with milk, unlike the others, who had to fight over every yuan with the miserly Chinese. They had no choice.

"That's why your grandmother has always scorned the Chinese. Her family didn't need them, so she never had any dealings with them."

I hadn't been listening to Papa for a while now. The ancestors' names were confusing, he'd never told them to us before, and besides, a beautiful shiny blue beetle was crawling on Magi's head, and I just wanted to watch as it skillfully wove its way through her hair and take a little nap, because the sun had long since set and a chill was slowly beginning to rise up out of the ground.

I burrowed into my *del* while Papa kept on about the Chinese and whether the Davkhan grower—that is, the father of the current one—was an *erliiz* or wasn't, since the way his mother ran around he very easily could be, even if her husband, old Dorj, treated him like he was his.

"Then again, old Dorj is such a sucker he'd probably take in any tot his old lady wrapped in a blanket and shoved into his arms. I just can't figure out what he sees in that woman. So actually maybe the Davkhan grower is really an *erliiz* after all."

Papa went on for a while still, and by then I had my eyes closed, hearing his words from a distance over the sweet humming sound in my head and picturing that big beetle, with its wings latticed like the walls of our *ger* when we helped Mama take the felt covers down before we moved camp each time.

I was ready to fall asleep, because if Papa was talking about Davkhan Dorj and his son, he was probably finished with Grandma and I wouldn't find out anything interesting, since he'd been spinning this same yarn over and over for years, when suddenly I heard him stop. Maybe I overslept and he had stopped a while ago. I snapped open my eyes, thinking what a disgrace it would be for Papa to catch me nodding off in the middle of one of his stories, given how rarely he told them. That was what went through my head as my eyelids shot up and I saw him staring straight into my face, and my sisters staring too, and I just blushed and lowered my eyes, and I suddenly felt like an outsider, like a lame calf with a split hoof, or a sheep when it's born black. Only those animals die right away because nobody wants them, even their mothers won't let them get near, and when a calf like that pushes its way to the teat, all it gets is a kick in the head and in two or three days it's gone. But me they had kept, and I felt like I was that reject calf, because that story about the Davkhan grower, that had to do with me.

Then Papa said it was late, we should go. But before we gave our horses a kick, he leaned over to Magi and said—half-jokingly, so she wouldn't get too cocky and me and Nara wouldn't feel bad since it truly was an honor—that Grandma would surely be pleased if her favorite son's first granddaughter would bear the name Dolgorma. Magi just tossed her braid. It's good being the oldest. We all knew that.

Sometimes it struck me that Oyuna had pretty bad luck, being the littlest one and nobody wanting to play with her. When everybody else would go to Munkhtsetseg's for *koumiss,* or to the *somon* center to get the radio repaired and run some minor errands, or to the Davkhan grower for onions, staying at home with Oyuna always meant boredom and a punishment for whichever of us was the naughtiest. It was almost like Mama could sense it when we were up to something. The second she heard Oyuna cry, she'd come flying in and belt us one.

We probably deserved it, what with all the things we did to her. Tying her on a lead and letting her run in a circle all day like a dog so she wouldn't be such a bother. Boosting her up on a camel and making her climb to the top of the *ger* and close the smoke hole, then laughing at her while she thrashed her arms and threw a fit till we helped her get down.

Magi almost killed her once.

Until Oyuna came along, Magi had always been the pet. She was born exactly nine months after our parents moved into their *ger,* and Mama used to say she was the most precious of us all, as she gazed lovingly at her glistening blue-black hair, thick as a horse's tail, framing the noble features of a true Mongolian face. So Magi was a little bit jealous of Oyuna, and her tortures were always the most inventive ones, right from the start.

But the time she almost killed Oyuna, that was something different.

Papa needed some looking after, so Magi went out with the herd for the day, and Mama gave her the baby too, since it wasn't really that much work. We were expecting some relatives from the City, so Mama would be bustling around the stove in a greasy cloud, and with us there too, and the baby all sweaty and crying, she wouldn't have had a moment's rest.

Oyuna was almost a year old by then, and even though it was late fall we were having a warm spell, so Magi gathered up Oyuna, a blanket, and a bowl of overcooked rice for Oyuna's lunch, and walked out to a hilltop with a nice view of the herd. She looked down, fed the baby, and then went off to see if there was any wild garlic around. Afterwards she said that she had been looking back every minute or two to make sure Oyuna hadn't crawled off the blanket, and then one time she looked back and there was a wild dog on top of her. But maybe it wasn't like that at all. I know if I was dumb enough to leave a baby alone for that long, I wouldn't admit it either. One thing for certain is we waited for Magi an awful long time that day. Papa fished the last two mutton ribs out of the basin, picked them clean, and sent Nara out with the bones, and Magi still hadn't come home.

She didn't get back until after Papa climbed in the saddle and rode out to the herd and Mama screamed her name at the top of her lungs in every direction. Magi came slouching in, her face as white as a snow leopard's, with a soft, pitiful whimpering coming from under her arm. After some convincing, she handed Oyuna over to Mama and all of us held our breath.

Both Oyuna's chubby cheeks were sprinkled with tooth marks. They weren't bites so much as the playful little scratches of a dog familiar with human young.

Mama was more attached to Oyuna than ever after that, and just like when Grandma died Oyuna didn't want to be left alone with anyone else for too long. The marks were still there for a long time to come and her cheeks were never smooth again. She still has the tiny purple scars to this day.

Magi didn't talk at all for several days, and when she finally came clean about what had happened, she stammered through every sentence, helplessly flailing her arms, as if with every word she was sinking lower and lower in our eyes, which she was.

Even Papa, to whom she had promised a little Dolgorma and who almost always stood up for her, suddenly turned hard and sullen.

And none of us yet knew that this warm and unusually rainy fall would be our last together.

It was almost as though when Grandma died our family started to fall apart, like an *ovoo* that no one goes to worship anymore, crumbling stone by stone into the steppe.

The *ovoo* we went to the most was about three hours' ride on horseback, near the western edge of our *aimak*: a heap of rough, worn stones at the foot of a mountain shaped like a woman, known as Boroony Uul. True to its name, the number of sunny days there could be counted on a horse's hoof. The whole peak was constantly shrouded in clouds of rain, streaming down in ropes.

We mostly went there to pray when it was dry and you could tell the herds from miles away by the clouds of dust. When the river turned to damp muck, with a few lone pools over which the cattle waged a daily battle for water. The newcomers and old-timers didn't stand a chance, and just stood there staring dumbly until finally their knees gave way and their rumps pulled them down to the ground.

Then Mama and Papa and all of us would make the trip to the *ovoo*. The vultures circled over our heads, eager to plunge their long, bare necks into the carcasses' moist, bloody innards, and Mama and Papa would urge the horses on until the womanly shape of Boroony Uul peeled itself out of the shimmering air on the horizon, its slope aflutter with blue *khataks*. People would bring all sorts of things to lay at the *ovoo,* and for us little ones, every step of the way was filled with excited anticipation of the new things that would be there since the last time we'd come. We could see the blue scarves flapping in the distance, and some white and yellow ones also, tied up in the nearby trees. They were ordinary scarves, like the kind we always brought along for us to tie up too, but the *ovoo* was covered with old tires, beer bottles people brought from the City, red cans with yellow designs, scraps of old wire, and lots of other neat stuff we weren't allowed to take. We would walk around the *ovoo* three times clockwise, the tattered *khataks* sailing as the wind blew through the tree stumps, and then ask for rain using the formulas we'd been taught.

Grandma liked to go to the *ovoo* more than anyone. She would dress in her special *del,* the one with silver stitching and the same special western fastening that Mama didn't like Papa to wear. Undoing her long, gray braid, she would brush out her hair and rebraid it into a skinny little tail. Then she'd fold some *khataks* into her sleeve and press a couple candies into each of her grandchildren's palms, so that later, under her watchful eye, we could lay them at the *ovoo.*

I think the reason we went there so often was mainly for her. Not that Mama and Papa didn't like to pray, but they weren't as devoted as Grandma, who was always ready to make the trip, even after only a week or two of drought. Once she died we went less and less, and Oyuna missed out on a lot, I think, by being too young to come along.

Like any proper family, inside our *ger* we had a little wooden table facing the entrance with different-sized figures of Burkhan on it, and other stuff as well. Besides pictures of us when we were little, there was one of Mama as a seventeen-year-old beauty and of Papa as a young border guard with a rifle.

Grandma kneeled in front of the figures the most, bowing her head and talking to herself. Papa and Mama would act different too. But when Grandma prayed, it was special. At moments like those I had the feeling that she was a powerful witch. I wonder if her last fitful steps weren't actually headed toward our *ovoo.* The spot where we found her suggests it, but I can't recall after all these years whether or not she had on her *del* with the silver stitching. Then there'd be no doubt. Grandma would never have gone on a pilgrimage in a dingy old house *del,* that I guarantee.

I never did tell Mama about that time after sunset when Papa stopped talking and gave me that funny look. Instead I went to Nara with it, since she was always a little bit brighter than the rest of us and could understand my feeling of loneliness better.

As a matter of fact, she knew it well.

Most of my time between my third and seventh year I spent at *khuukhdiin tsetserleg.* Nara too. We're only a year and a month apart, so our parents sent us together. I wouldn't have gone without her, and Mama was glad to have the both of us there at once.

Like most boarding schools here, our *khuukhdiin tsetserleg* was in the *somon* center, which was the closest thing to a city we knew in those days.

A handful of *gers* with fenced-in yards, a couple of light wooden huts—impossible to heat in the winter, unbearably hot in the summer—and some big brick buildings courtesy of the Russians. Besides the *khuukhdiin tsetserleg,* there was a grade school, a doctor's office, the building of the revolutionary party and the *somon* presidium, and the House of Culture, where anniversary celebrations were held, and also the grown-ups went there to vote.

The first time our parents brought us to boarding school was a sunny September day in the Year of the Snake, and from then on they brought us back every ninth month, at the end of our summer vacation, when most of the kids returned from their *gers* to the chilly school dormitories.

We drove there in our UAZ, newly acquired from Papa's brother-in-law Tsobo, a clever dealer in Novosibirsk jeeps. Papa worked for him as a driver at one point, but Tsobo was the kind of man who always promised and never paid, so one day, instead of driving in to the City, Papa pulled up in front of our *ger*. Grandma wrung her hands until Papa promised her that he would return the jeep the very next day. That settled that. Eventually Mama learned to drive, and also took us to school.

Papa pulled up directly in front of the freshly plastered school building. The tired horses of Mongols from far away snorted at the hitching posts, while grown-ups stood in quiet clusters, sticking close to those they knew, and groups of relatives mingled at random. As a bottle made the rounds and the grown-ups, high-spirited in their sparkling ceremonial *dels,* sprayed a few drops in every direction, the children skipped around, pulling each other's hair, or, like the two of us, cowered at their parents' side in dread of the separation to come.

Nara sensed something wrong from the start. She wasn't fooled for a second by all the laughing faces. She gave such a kick to one little boy who teasingly tried to choke her from behind that he sniveled all the way through the *somon* chairman's opening speech.

I liked our classroom, with its Bakelite horse and carriage, the little stuffed wolf with real fur, the building blocks from our sister school in Vladivostok, the peg racks with washcloths, the chairs in a circle all around the walls. Not Nara.

Nara sees through most things sooner than me.

The teachers sat us all in the chairs and had us cup our hands, and one of them went around the room with a bag of gray Russian chocolates, which tasted of grown-upness and smelled like all of the other things that came from our *somon* store. Then the parents left.

It was clear after a few days that Nara was being left out of all the games. Nobody but me liked the warm brown shade of her hair, the color of the sand as the sun sinks into the steppe.

Nara the *Oros,* the teachers would say when she beat the little wolf on the ground or pushed away the tea because it wasn't salty or fatty enough. Then, taking the lead from our dumpy Buryat teachers, the children started taunting her too. I told Papa as soon as I could. First he turned purple, clenching his fists, then suddenly he softened and a look of malicious glee flashed across his face, or maybe not, because in the end he just briskly told us not to make anything of it, just ignore what our teachers said and keep it to ourselves.

He said that they were the bad ones, not us, so from then on me and Nara just acted like none of it bothered us. But that didn't completely work. Something was wrong and we knew it, because normal hair was black as night, black as the braid on our Magi, who everyone loved from the day she was born.

The first time that I got a taste of it was in grade school.

The time when Dorj's dog went missing.

It was the talk of the school, because Dorj's *ger* was the first one in the *somon* center coming in from the east, from the Red Mountains, and a lot of kids in school came from that direction besides me and Nara and Magi.

The dog barked nonstop, tearing around with his fangs bared, dripping dark pools of saliva on the ground. He was also an unusually large dog, so everyone knew who he was.

And then one day he disappeared. Vanished, just like that, overnight, and was never seen again. Nara and me were in grade school by then and lived at school during the year.

A couple days later, when word got out, a message turned up in the outhouse next to our dormitory, carved on the wall with a knife: "If you want to know what happened to Dorj's dog, look on ____'s plate." And there was my name. Soon everybody was saying it.

Maybe it was a mistake that those words stayed there so many years. Bit by bit they faded, turning darker and darker, until one day they tore the outhouse down. But I wasn't in school anymore by then, and no one had any doubt that there was something wrong with my mother.

What went on in the *somon* center was pretty much useless to us at home and the other way around as well.

As time went on, the two worlds grew further and further apart. Magi and me and Nara spent most of our time at boarding school, and our parents' *ger* felt like something strange and temporary, like the *khuukhdiin tsetserleg* did on that first warm September morning.

As for me, during those years in our white felt tent wound around with ropes, with a heap of *argal* for heating, wolf dogs, and a doorway whose sacred threshold no one ever tread on that I can remember, I lived more in my dreams than in reality. As a matter of fact, it was always like that, even later on.

I'll never forget those awful nights when I was maybe ten or so, with Mama and Papa nowhere around. My dreams were filled with the howling of wild beasts, our winter camp in the shelter of the mountains was empty, and I had nowhere to go. They hadn't waited for me. And in the distance I could clearly see a rocking, like the hips of our camels when they carted all our carved orange furniture and the wooden poles and rafters that held up our *ger* and kept the heavens above us from falling, since nothing else was braced against the sky for miles around except the mountains shielding our backs, and those impassive stone behemoths could never hold up the sky on their own. I ran a lot in those dreams, chasing after something, while my family disappeared over the burnt horizon, and I sensed a connection with the writing in the shack where I went to piss, and also just to squat when I didn't want to see anybody, not even Nara. Everyone saw those words as they sat squeezing in the dark. Carved into the wall in big, easy-to-read letters.

Nara slept next to me, but on those nights I was alone. Alone with the howling of the beasts, and sometimes in their howls I heard Oyuna's pleading tears from the nights I frightened her with Uregma and she understood enough to know that she was lost without Mama, and on those nights I felt my first pangs of conscience.

Maybe Nara had nights like that too, but I doubt it, because I climbed into her bed a couple of times when it got to be too much for me, but she never came over to mine.

Magi slept with the older kids, so I don't know about her. But I don't think her nights were so bad that she had the same thoughts as I did. She never talked to us much or played our games.

I don't know much about Magi. What I remember most is her milky-white face and dark, dreamy eyes. She was the tallest of us, and probably the smartest, at least when it came to school. But I still think she was too lazy for Papa to love her more than the rest of us. She didn't deserve it. But that's what he said when she died, and we all knew it, even before.

When I brought little Dolgorma home to show to Papa, his first granddaughter and the fourth of that name in our line, he started right in about Magi and got all emotional, so I snatched her back up and left. I'm not about to feel sorry for a father I'm not good enough for.

That was years after Magi got killed at Naadam, the first and, praise Burkhan, so far only child of Alta and Tuleg, my parents, to die.

When we were really little and Oyuna's soul was still wandering the cosmos, or in a mountain goat or an old man in some distant *aimak* with one foot in the grave, Nara rode better than any of us. In those days Mama had yet to get a single gray hair, and when Papa, disguised in a wolfskin, waited at the tarbagan hole, he always bagged two or three marmots at least.

Once we had eaten our fill, if Papa didn't have to go out to the herd, he would boost us into our saddles and off we'd go, slowly in single file. Papa would lead the way and we'd ride, fingers dug into our horses' necks, breathing in their sunny musk as the hairs of their manes tickled our cheeks.

Sometimes we'd ride in twos, and then it was best to go with Papa. I could lean back, feeling his hands in my hair as he signaled the horse what and how. Mama didn't come with us often, she only rode when she had to, since any trip that didn't end with honoring the *ovoo* or a visit to Maidar and Munkhtsetseg's didn't make sense to her. In that, she was like Grandma. And also she was afraid. If it had been up to her, we wouldn't have learned how to ride till much later and Nara couldn't have come in second in the *aimak* championship for three-year-old children, and Magi might not've been killed, since she wouldn't have had the confidence to ride in the biggest horse race in our country—the Naadam.

I was always a decent rider, but I couldn't compare with Nara. When we were home on probably our fifth vacation, finished with school again for another two months at last, Burkhan knows why but Magi started improving by leaps and bounds. The next vacation or two after that, my sisters spent locked in fierce competition.

Nara wasn't about to let go of her crown, so I spent all my days with Oyuna, or gutting and cooking in the *ger* alone with Mama, while Magi and Nara galloped all over the *aimak* trying to prove who was best, even though neither of them ever said so. They were just breaking in their new saddles, or training the two-year-old fillies, or doing the shopping as an excuse to go tearing into the *somon* center and back. In the evening they'd come home sunburned and wobbly-legged, and there was no one for me to play *shagai* with, since they went right to sleep. I couldn't stand Magi even more than usual, because she was taking away the one thing in life that was mine. I wanted Nara to lose so I could hug and console her, so she would see that I wanted her for real, and not just for racing, like Magi. Then suddenly it was settled: my sisters stopped their all-day outings, and Magi slowly began to prepare for Naadam.

Naadam is a big event held every year in every *aimak* and *somon* center, on the eleventh and twelfth of the seventh month, and the biggest Naadam of all is in the City. Besides horse racing, they also have wrestling and archery, but I never cared about them.

The summer before Naadam, Magi rode every day. By that time she was sixteen or seventeen and our parents had started to talk about marriage, but the world from the back of a horse is incredibly fast and blurry, and I don't think Magi had much of a chance to look around for suitors as she went racing through the colored smear of the *somon* center every day.

Nara and me singed the ends of our hair and prayed the best we knew how, because Magi wanted to win and that was the only thing we could do.

The Naadam field, which is north of the City center, is bordered on one side by the Tuul, a river that nobody ever swims in, whose banks are always crowded with women soaking rugs and scrubbing colorful ornaments, and on the other by the meat market, a big canvas tent with lots of flies and mutton fat on hooks.

We all went to Naadam.

Oyuna wanted to be important too, so she wheedled her way into riding in the race for five-year-old children, but just before the start she went and hid among the barrels of water for the horses, and with all our hectic searching for her we almost missed the start of Magi's race.

Magi rode well. Just like Papa had taught her to. Instead of charging off the line, she let the rein dangle at first, so the horse could set its own pace. When she galloped past, Mama had tears in her eyes and Oyuna got so excited that if Papa hadn't held her she would've run out on the racecourse and spooked the horses. Magi probably would've come in second or third, but something terrible happened as she passed the *chatsargan* bush. Her horse ended the race on its own. Magi fell off and broke her neck. As the other horses leaped over her, Papa dashed out onto the course, and I remember the total silence as he rose from her body and our eyes hung on his.

In the midst of all the uproar a gateway opened. Mama started to scream, and I saw a void like the jaws of a giant poisonous flower, like an endless tunnel, swallowing my sister, leaving behind only empty space for everlasting tears, and I knew I was peering over the edge into darkness for the first time and mustn't sway.

Magi died quickly and we laid her to rest the next day at our spot among the stones. When we went back after forty-five days, there was nothing there, and all of us, even Oyuna, knelt down, and after the sun had set we returned home in silence. During those days, for the first time in my life I saw Papa too drunk to talk, and Mama got up with the morning sun to tend to all his outdoor chores, which only took him a while. She'd come home worn out and gray in the face, while Papa just sat around the *ger* or took a bottle and rode out to our spot up in the mountains. Even from a distance we could always tell it was him coming home by the wilted shape of his carmine *del,* his horse staggering under him as Papa lurched from side to side, barking muddled commands.

One day I was out gathering *argal* by myself when I spotted him sitting against a rock. He was a mess, and a colorless trickle was draining into the grass from a bottle propped at his side. He waved me away with a sweep of his arm and hid his face in his hands. I walked away. Papa didn't come home at all that night.

In the morning I was awakened by the sound of crackling twigs, and when I lifted my head I saw Papa's face glowing over the coals as he blew them to life for our morning meal of noodle soup.

Mama didn't go out to tend the herd that day, and Papa took his last bottle and flung it into the steppe.

During the time when Papa was in a bad way, Mama's younger sister, Shartsetseg, came to stay with us a while. That was one yellow flower who did justice to her name, since I don't know what we would've done if she hadn't turned up in those evil days.

Shartsetseg's face always shone with a sunny smile. She was a little bit younger than Mama, but with her sharp, thin nose and slim, wide-hipped figure you could tell that they shared the same blood. Shartsetseg managed the *ger* while Mama was out with the herd, and at the end of the day when Mama came home she would rub her legs with milk and comb out the sweat and dust caked onto her braid. She kept an eye on Oyuna and thought up things for me and Nara to do so we would leave Papa alone instead of sitting around the *ger* with him going on about Magi. A day with Shartsetseg was packed from sunup to sundown with all kinds of little chores that got on my nerves. I didn't see why we had to clean the *ger* cover, or cook such complicated meals when we'd always been fine with *khuurag* and *buuz,* but except for that, me and Nara adored our aunt.

With Mama we never went hungry or needed to be afraid, and she always made sure we changed our *dels* once a month. When we were sick, she held our heads so we could drink, and when there wasn't enough sheep and Papa was starving, she gave us her meat. But that was it. Shartsetseg knew how to laugh, and she could say such funny things that me and Nara would squirm on the ground with laughter till our bellies ached, and the whole *ger* would shake so hard that Papa got up and walked away and instead of one bottle he would take two. And at night, when the yurt was empty except for her and us, she would tell us scary stories.

With her hair down in the darkened *ger* she reminded me of Uregma, the way that Grandma used to, and I couldn't help but think how scared Oyuna must've been when we used to frighten her with the old witch. No one could make things up like Shartsetseg.

Each of her stories was totally different and every one was as wild and mysterious as the next. Outside, the *shoroo* roared, gusts of sand rippling the *ger* and rustling the canvas. As the snakes slithered out of their holes on the steppe and the sound of howling wolves came rolling down the mountains, I had a feeling that every one of Shartsetseg's stories was true. I whispered it to Mama once and she just said I had a vivid imagination. Which was one more reason why Shartsetseg was better.

Mama's sister was the first person from the City I ever met. And seeing as I was the oldest one, she promised to take me with her. One day, after Papa was back to his normal routine and before Mama sent her away, Yellow Flower took me aside. I still had three more years of school left, but I was ready to pack my holiday *del,* grab a sack of dried meat, and leave that very day. But Shartsetseg said, *Surguuliig togsokh yostoi,* so I had no choice but to wait.

Three years full of fantasies about real life, which was out there somewhere flowing along without any idea I existed. Three years spent in a daze of indifference because nothing going on around me was good enough for me. I carried that promise within me like a mission, longing to be where the dreams of every young girl from the *somon* centers collide and they burn their wings like moths.

Shartsetseg really did come that summer, just as she had promised.

She turned up out of nowhere at our graduation in the *somon* House of Culture. It was filled to overflowing. The families of the kids who were finishing school with me that year had come to extol their descendants one last time before carting them back to their world for good.

We dragged our chairs into the hall and wrote TAVTAI MORILNO on a big piece of paper that we hung over the stage, and the headmaster delivered a fiery speech about our future.

Our school had its share of distinguished graduates. Tsuuleg was a national eagle in archery, Davaa married the *darga* of Khövsgöl Aimak, and the twins Uram and Tsagaanbulag opened an auto parts shop in the City two years ago, and word was they were doing well.

The younger students wove in and out of the chairs, handing out apples and pieces of *aaruul* purchased for the occasion with public funds by the *somon* presidium. My aunt was in the first row; she must have come really early to get a seat like that. We stood onstage reciting verses by Yavuukhulan and then went up one at a time to shake the chairman's hand, and Shartsetseg kept winking at me the whole time. My school certificate was one of the best. When we got home, Mama propped it up against the Burkhan on the table, I had a little cry with Nara, and Papa gave me some words of advice so I wouldn't be taken in by anyone in the City, because he'd been there and didn't trust a soul, and that was the surest way not to go astray.

My aunt had brought Oyuna a big huge bow to put in her hair, like the kind the little Russian girls wear, and when my sister told me good-bye it looked like she had a big sky-blue bird nesting on her head.

The trip was awful. No sooner had we set out than the *Tengers* unleashed a torrent of rain, and within two hours the steppe, not being accustomed to drinking, had turned into a mud bath for as far as the eye could see, and every other minute our jeep would end up spinning its wheels and Shartsetseg and the driver had to get out in the soaking wet and push.

I just sat on my bag and looked out the window, partly because I didn't want my holiday *del* to get muddy, but also because Yellow Flower had told me to stay put.

There isn't any road between the Red Mountains and the City, but our drivers know how to find their way like animals, even when they drive drunk or at night they never get lost, so we drove hours and hours through mountains where the only reminders of life were some twisted tree stumps and the occasional camel with young, and then we descended onto the plains, where we were all alone between the horizons, and I thought there must be something coming along any minute, but it was dark by the time we came to a stop at three proud and solitary yurts, and for a couple of *tugriks* we got a place to lay our heads and a bowl of noodle soup, and the next morning we were back on our way.

My family had other campgrounds besides our favorite one in the Red Mountains: one by Baga Uul, another near Murom, and a fourth one that we called *risunki* because the rocks nearby were covered with the ancient drawings of our ancestors, which nobody understood. The Red Mountains had *risunki* too.

In the end we just called them all the Red Mountains, though if the weather was bad it took a few days to get from one to the other. But I'd never traveled as far as I did when I went with my aunt to the City. The world was so much bigger than I ever could've imagined, and it just kept getting bigger with every hill we crossed, and there was no end to it.

Part of the way we gave a ride to a Mongol woman with a baby in a pack on her back. Both of them were pretty dried out from waiting in the heat for so long, and I thought they might be a little bit different from us. By then we were less than half a day from the City, where supposedly everything was different. The woman was quiet the whole way, and when we dropped her off at her *ger* with her baby she didn't even thank us.

An hour later the first smokestack of the Ulaanbaatar power plant peeked from over a hill. I was hoping to see the airport, but that was farther out so that the planes wouldn't fall on the houses, so I was out of luck. But I did get to see our country's biggest department store. A tall, stern glass building, across from the concrete circus, and either side of the street was packed with little stalls selling colorful cookies and brown and green bottles of soda, and little folding tables with fruit and scales and telephones, and old ladies peddling crumpled single cigarettes.

As we drove deeper into the City, everything got thicker and the people reeled around faster and faster and more and more haphazardly, till we turned left uphill on the far side of the square and I was relieved, since the people sank away until there were only about as many as when the Mongols come together in our *somon* center for Naadam, and I was used to that.

Shartsetseg's *mikrorayon* is called Sansaar. It's a nice part of town. Respectable families live there, who've been in the City a long time, and there aren't too many Chinese or other nationalities, which is good. My aunt paid the driver with the money my mother had pressed into her hand before we left. I suddenly had an uneasy feeling that it had been some sort of payoff, but only for a second, until the Mongol who'd driven us walked away, and Shartsetseg thrust a piece of goat from Papa into my hand, and pointed to her door.

We stood in front of the concrete panel building that was going to be my new almost-home—that's what I called it in my mind, since at the time, the thought of not going back to our *ger* for years would've killed me. I was newly sixteen, it was my first time in the City, and the only thing I was sure of was my dream had just come true.

I guess I thought I'd do the rounds of the shops, gorge myself on jelly doughnuts, buy myself a soda or two, take a quick run through the Museum of the Revolution, and go home. I don't know what I was thinking back then, what was floating around my head. But it definitely didn't include work or money. There was no room. Every day I saw new things; there were just too many of them. One thing I hadn't expected, though, was Shartsetseg had a man. She'd never told me that. I thought it would just be the two of us, and Mergen hardly moved from the kitchen during the day. I don't think my aunt ever mentioned him. The look on his face was so blank, it was like I didn't even exist for him the first few days I was there.

Shartsetseg quickly saw that I didn't have any notion what grownup life was like, and after I'd spent most of what I had from my parents on sugary triangle wafers and hadn't done a thing except for shower my aunt with praise and thanks, she realized someone needed to show me how to get on in life. So one day, after a week or so, we were sitting over our morning meal and I was picking at the leftovers of our goat, what with my stomach being ruined from all the City's temptations, when Shartsetseg started to speak. It reminded me of Papa, telling me what I already knew. How the City's a dangerous place and I'm young and inexperienced, and don't be taken in by all the movie theaters and canned franks and tiny little radios and silky scarves—in other words, all I admired and wanted—because maybe this world looks happy and grand, but you see the flash of a blade here a lot more than you do at home.

Back in the Red Mountains, a knife's for cutting a cow's throat, but here in the City it's for stabbing you in the back, my aunt said. I don't know whether she thought my knees would start to shake or I'd jump in the saddle and go dashing back to my *aimak,* but I'd heard this talk before. A lot of grown-ups do it, especially in front of young people, it lets them show off, since you haven't lived through anything yet, so you don't have any smart remarks that you can come back at them with. So I just muttered, Mm-hm, and went on poking at my goat. But then Shartsetseg started back in on me, and this time she was right.

It hadn't even crossed my mind to think about money, so I just sat there nodding my head to everything she said. I admitted that I was an irresponsible child and said I'd take a look around about getting some work as soon as I could. Shartsetseg threw the goat out the window and said, Get a move on, we're going to look together.

Yellow Flower wasn't like other grown-up women. As far as my mother went, there wasn't even any comparison. Shartsetseg talked more, laughed more, thought about things more. At least that was the feeling I got. My aunt was constantly full of ideas, she was interested in all sorts of things, and she never gave me that blank nod like Mama did when I told her a story. It always felt like my aunt was listening, which was new for me, and I appreciated that from the moment we met. Maybe that was the reason why I was so drawn to her, since it wasn't just the wide streets and bright shop windows that made me want to go to the City, but also her. It hadn't occurred to me before, when Magi died and Yellow Flower came to our rescue. I didn't realize it until three years later, as I got up from the table and went to get dressed so we could go find me a job. I didn't know a thing about looking for work in the City, so I put on some clothes and tagged along behind her. After all, she knew about life.

On our way downstairs we ran into Mergen, teetering slightly, and in the few days I had been there I had quickly gotten used to the fact that it wasn't just Mongols who lost a child that drank themselves senseless, but ordinary people too, people who wanted for nothing, who had families, a room of their own in a panel building, and lived in the City. How many people in our *somon* center would've given half a herd for a room of their own in a building like that? Every day I saw people who were unhappy. As far as I was concerned, they were fools. I didn't understand about vodka till much later on.

Mergen clutched the banister, a vodka glaze coating his eyes. His arms, stiff as blocks of wood, lifted toward me as we squeezed past him on the stairs.

All of a sudden it hit me. This wasn't the first time I'd seen him. I remembered those outstretched arms.

Maybe he wanted to grab hold and just hang on and rest, or maybe he really did want a hug, but either way he was mistaken: my aunt was behind me. I ducked away from his fingers and he dropped like a sack of flour. Shartsetseg lifted him up, helped him back to the apartment, unlocked the door, shoved him inside, and slammed the door with a sigh. I noticed he gave me a strange look as she helped him to his feet. I could've caught him, but I didn't want him to touch me. Somehow I could tell it wasn't my aunt he was after, but me. He hadn't made a mistake. His grasping hands had been meant for me, and in that certainty was disgust, a feeling that reeked of his bad breath and weighed me down like a man's body.

I didn't know what Shartsetseg had in mind; I didn't have any notion what it was like to work for someone; I only knew she could arrange it somehow. So we walked the streets and I stared at the people crammed on the buses, at the Russians and the Mongols who dressed the same as they did—it was all still new to me. We stopped in front of a *guanz* and Shartsetseg told me to wait. She went in and after a little while she came back out with a Mongol who stank of boiled mutton, wiping his greasy hands on a grubby apron. The head cook, I guessed, expecting my aunt to introduce us. But he just looked me up and down, nodded, and slipped back inside.

Over supper that night in my new home, Shartsetseg mentioned casually that tomorrow I'd start my new job. It was obvious where.

I already knew what a *guanz* was from before. There aren't too many things in the City we also have in the country, but *guanzes* are one.

People everywhere have to eat.

But while our *guanz* was a *ger* at the halfway point between the Red Mountains and the *somon* center, where we'd stop in for a cheap bowl of soup or a cup of cool strong tea, in the City there was at least one steamy lunch bar on every street. Everywhere it was the same thing: *buuz, khuurag,* soda, and tea, just like ours back home.

Four tables in front, a counter, and Erka and Purev cooking in back. They both knew my aunt, so they treated me nice, and even when I messed things up they weren't mean to me.

The first few days, I wiped the tables and floor, washed dishes, poured tea, and only stirred every once in a while, so there wasn't a lot to ruin. But then there were times I was all alone in the *guanz,* and I'd stumble around covered in sweat, mixing up the pots and pans amid the clouds of steam, while the people on the other side of the counter bellowed at me and the noodles boiled over. But eventually it straightened out, I had a job and some money, and Shartsetseg had her peace.

What she did for work I had no idea. Mergen mostly sat at home or out in the street and drank.

He was that man who didn't look like a Mongol, who'd come to our *ger* when I was sick as a child. I've got a memory for faces.

That was the first time I realized my mother didn't have only me and Magi and Nara, but other concerns and worries as well. Which was why Mergen's shaky, trembling affection was so disgusting to me. He belonged to Mama somehow, and I'd seen her frantic and confused over him. Floating in his eyes I saw the reflection of my mother's as the two of them stood outside flailing their arms, and I needed my mother to sit at my bedside and hold my hand, and I was afraid she would run away with him and never come back again.

That was what ran through my head whenever I felt his gaze, while I was cooking, or at night after supper, when Shartsetseg had gone to bed and I'd sit with him in the kitchen and wait till his head sank to the table, then pick him up by the armpits and stuff him into the next room, where my aunt was already breathing deeply.

Only after I shut the door to their room and tidied up the kitchen did I finally feel at ease.

Then I'd stretch out on the sofa across from the table, and next thing I knew it was morning again.

Every day I would come home tired from the *guanz,* my legs heavy and my hands hot and red from doing dishes.

The days flowed one into the other, and everything else but my worries at work was washed right out of my head—my family in the Red Mountains, my school, my fantasies about life in the City—all of it had drained away, and I knew it, but what could I do? I was here and I needed money.

Erka and Purev were both really nice. Purev was an enormous man, and his starched apron was constantly covered in noodles and grease from wiping his hands on it. He looked like a huge khan from one of our winter stories. At the end of the day he would always give me the leftover *khuushuur* to take home with me, so Mergen and my aunt had their supper all taken care of. Erka was tiny and worked so fast the dough just flew through her fingers. On top of that, she also kept an eye on me, chatted with the regulars, and helped Purev bring in the meat, which he was in charge of. There were months when I was happier in the kitchen with them than I'd ever been at home. Purev would sometimes take me along to help him pick the meat, since I was from the country and knew about these things. Actually I knew more about animals than about meat, but to him they were the same.

Back home in the *ger,* I cooked whatever meat Mama gave me. Papa killed the animals. He was the only one who knew how and he was an expert at it. Laying the sheep on its back, he would gently kneel on top of it, then slice open the belly, stick in his hand, feel around till he found the heart, squeeze it between his fingers, and wait for the sheep to fall asleep. Its hoofs would shake a tiny bit, just a little sort of quiver, then its eyes would turn glassy and sad and its whole body would droop. And that was it. It went off almost every time without a drop of blood.

There was plenty of blood at the meat market. Women stood at long tables with skinned cuts of cow, sheep, and goat, talking them up as the best in town and massaging and flipping the meat so the nicer side always faced up. Men in aprons with cleavers and long knives hovered around their hooks, ready to hack off whatever you wanted.

The meat market was in a huge tent and was always crammed full of people. I kind of liked going there with Purev and pretending I understood, and once I got my courage up, after about a week or two, I could spend a whole hour arguing with a stingy saleswoman to get a good price. Then me and Purev would hurry straight back, because swarms of Mongols came to our *guanz,* and Erka could barely keep up on her own when noontime rolled around.

Some people came only once and other people came often. We served good food, we didn't pad our *khuushuur* with flour like other places did, and our *buuz* were well seasoned and not too gristly. I never would've guessed that the reason Biamkhu came in so often had nothing to do with the food.

He was a couple years older than I was and had a crush on me.

By then I was seventeen, but I was still a little girl as far as those things went. I knew how it worked; I'd even had crushes myself, but never anything more. For three months every day Biamkhu came to our lunchroom, cracking jokes left and right and buying double portions. Whatcha got cookin', he'd always ask, and he hung around the counter so much it was obvious to everyone. I didn't catch on myself until Erka started to tease me, and later that day, for the first time, Biamkhu asked me out.

Biamkhu was the real thing, he was serious about me, and he showed me all over the City. He lived near us, with his parents and two brothers, and every day after work he would walk me back to my building and talk about our future together. Some nights he would take me out to the Tornado for a tiny glass of vodka and a glass of yellow soda. Whenever Purev asked him, he'd go with him to buy the meat, and every time a regular got drunk and smashed up all the chairs Biamkhu would help put in new ones. But even after several weeks I didn't invite Biamkhu home, and then my chance was gone.

Shortly after one Sunday when we sat down by the riverside and I confessed to him that I'd never been with a man before, a hideous thing happened.

Mergen and I were up late playing dominoes one night, and I kept winning and he kept saying congratulations and pushing the bottle over to me and I would just wet my lips. But after a while, I started taking little gulps, and it wasn't nearly as bad as I'd thought and I was feeling good, because Erka had told me just that day that she knew a shoe repair shop that had closed that if things worked out we could rent and set up another *guanz* there, and it would be sort of like mine, since she and Purev would stay where they were, and I could take one of the cooks with me, and the meat and flour and salt and the rest I'd have to round up on my own, and I would be in charge of it all. Right away I thought of Nara, and through the light vodka haze Mergen actually looked kind of nice, and I saw her in a cap and apron, disappearing into the steam and reappearing again as she stirred the pots in our new *guanz,* which we'd decorate together, and we'd put pink washable tablecloths and daisies on every table, and a vase of fresh flowers on the little fringed cloth on the counter, and all of the tea bowls would match and they wouldn't have any scratches, and Biamkhu would bring us the best meat in the City and crates full of soft drinks, and at the end of the day we'd lock up and the three of us would go for a stroll on the main square, and soon it would be four of us, because Nara would catch someone's eye right away.

I rested my chin in my hands and thought of the happiness that awaited us, and I felt grown-up and independent for the first time since I had come to the City. Then that heavenly feeling melted into a warm embrace and wet kisses, which weren't too hard to put up with. Mergen toppled me off the chair onto the sofa, yanked up my skirt, pulled down his pants, and rocked inside me a couple of times. Then he collapsed by my side and the two of us slept there like that until morning, squeezed in on the couch.

I thought the first time it was going to hurt like hell. That was what Dulma said, who at boarding school slept in the bed next to mine and knew about these things. Actually it was nothing. Just a tiny spot of blood on my panties, like when Papa slit a sheep's throat and it didn't come out perfect, and there were moments at the *guanz* when I felt like I needed to sit, and I had this funny tingly feeling in between my legs. That was it.

What was worse was my aunt.

She already wasn't as nice as she'd been to me at first, and when she shook me awake in the morning, before I even opened my eyes I realized what had happened and I knew she would throw me out. Throw me out and keep Mergen for herself.

I got to work a little bit late that day.

As I walked in, Erka lifted her head from the pots and gave me a disgruntled look. But then her face turned solemn and she came over to show me where to put my things.

She gave me a hug and didn't ask any questions.

I told Biamkhu everything when he came in that evening, so he wouldn't have any surprises in store for him later on.

How he was the only one I loved, how Mergen was disgusting and there was no way for me to defend myself, and anyway, from now on I was going to sleep in the *guanz,* so nothing like that would happen again. Then I told him about the shoe repair shop and how it was going to be like our very own lunch bar, and how I wanted to introduce him to Nara since she was going to work there with us. I wanted to tell him more about how I pictured the rest of it, how our first girl was going to be named Dolgorma, in accordance with my father's wish, and how, if he wanted, I could take him with me to see our *ger* in the fall, but I didn't get that far, because suddenly Biamkhu turned to me, screamed out some filthy words, and slapped me across the face.

My head snapped around, my whole face burning with thousands of tiny needles bathed in scalding tears, and Biamkhu walked away with a quick, determined step. I wanted to run after him but my legs wouldn't move. My whole body was tingling, and I felt so dirty and empty I would've flung my arms around the neck of the first Mongol who smiled at me.

It was late in the evening and I was all alone on Ulaanbaatar's biggest square. Slag-scarred asphalt spread out under my feet in every direction. Tufts of grass sprouted up from the cracks, and a couple of homeless people were dozing on the benches nearby. One of them I knew. He would come to our lunch bar for *khuushuur* every now and then, whenever he could steal something and hawk it for a few *tugriks.* The others had their heads buried into *dels* or old sweaters, stiff as sleeping birds. A horse with a bronze rider reared up on the right of the square, a monument to our national hero Sükhbaatar, fenced off with chains so the little boys couldn't climb on it and stick chewing gum on the horse's back.

Behind me towered the mighty colonnade of the national parliament, and I saw the roof of the opera house peeking out across the way.

A few streetlamps cast dim, yellowy shadows in the darkness, swaying with the wind. I made my way toward the lights on the other side of the square, tripled by my tears and exhaustion, and walked into some sort of nightclub. I was drawn by the music leaking out onto the street through a velvet curtain. It was summer and the door was open wide.

It was dim inside, and a couple of Mongols were squeezed in at the counter, just like in our *guanz*. On the other side of the counter, covered with stains from cigarette burns, bottles lined the shelves like soldiers. Some of the chairs were overturned, broken glass crunched under my feet, I wondered where I should sit. I sensed lumps of people in every corner, couples nestled close in the dark. The only place free was under a big knitted portrait of Chingis Khan, with long fringes that tickled the back of my neck when I sat. There was nobody there taking orders or wiping tables, and the ashtrays were piled high with butts like majestic yellow *ovoos*.

I took a sip from a glass of something sitting on my table. It tasted funny, so I left it alone and waited for someone to come and talk to me so I wouldn't be alone.

He was old, older than Mergen was, and dressed like a Russian, but it turned out he was an Uzbek. Kulan by name. He introduced himself as Kolya. He plonked himself down next to me so close that I could smell his breath, and for the first time since that morning I remembered the way that Mergen had moved inside me and his quiet moan before he collapsed. Kulan brought over some vodka, but I just pretended to drink, pressing my lips to the glass. I didn't have any money and he wouldn't buy me a soda.

By the time we left, the night was turning gray with a bright strip of light shining on the horizon, and Kulan lent me his sweater. It was bitter cold. I knew what was going to happen next, but the thought of going back to that narrow little kitchen and folding out my cot there among the pots and pans and breathing in that greasy air all night long didn't appeal to me either. So I climbed in the car that Kulan flagged down, and sprawled out on the back seat, content to watch the night fade and the buildings flashing by like dots, turning poorer and poorer and smaller and smaller, until we came to the yurt district, wrapped around the City in an ever-thickening ring, as more and more people moved here from the country every day.

I thought of Papa, how he'd told me to be careful and not to trust anyone in the City and how easy it is here to come to no good, and I wondered whether this was the no good he meant and how someone could tell that sort of thing, but I couldn't come up with an answer. One thing for sure was I didn't trust Kulan. All I knew was he wanted to sleep with me, just like Mergen, who I had seen through right away, and satisfied that maybe I was coming to a little no good but I wasn't being taken in, my head started to drop to the side and a sweet sleep came over me.

The only ones who let me down were Biamkhu and my aunt.

When we got to Kolya's *ger,* he sat me down on the bed and took off his pants. I helped him with mine and let him kiss me some more and touch me on my breasts and in between my legs, which Mergen didn't do, so that was the first time for me.

I was wondering what it's like when two people are together and do it every day, when all of a sudden it was like someone was stabbing a knife into me, it was much worse than the day before, and I started to scream. Kulan covered my mouth with his hand, actually my whole face, so all I could see through his fingers was his sweaty red face rocking up and down, and now I knew for sure this was it, this was the no good that Papa was talking about.

The one lucky thing was I didn't have to go to the *guanz,* since the day before, when Biamkhu came, Erka had leaned over and whispered in my ear that if I didn't feel like it, I didn't have to come in tomorrow, she and Purev could manage just fine. Then she'd winked at Biamkhu, meaning he'd better take good care of me and treat me right, I guess.

In the morning I woke up alone. There was a strange burning sensation between my thighs, and next to the bed on the floor was a piece of paper with a telephone number on it, a greeting from Kolya, and a pot of warm milk tea he must've brought in from Burkhan knows where, the little stove was like ice. There was hardly anything there at all; he probably lived somewhere else.

I didn't feel like leaving, the tea was really good, so I lay back down again, squeezing the blanket between my knees, and watched the sky through the smoke hole, so blue and still it was as if someone had climbed up top and slapped a *khatak* over the hole. I hadn't seen the sky from bed since the day I left the Red Mountains. I listened to the rustling grass and peered up at the orange rafters, shooting out from the patch of sky above like the rays of the sun.

Summer was always the most beautiful season back home. The spring young had the worst of it behind them and fed at the side of their mothers, who didn't lift their heads all day, till the end of the ninth month, when the first timid snow came blowing in on a chill wind from Siberia.

But that was for later.

No one gave a thought to winter when it was summer.

Mama wore a light *del* when she gathered onions and garlic, and we went barefoot, and nobody's eyelids were burned with cold, and the stove was lit only for meals.

Summer was also the time of year when people would stop in the most to spend the night or have a meal. Mama put more effort in than when it was just us. She would cook up a big batch of noodles, and a layer of the finest fat would float on the soup a finger thick. After we ate, the men would drink *koumiss* and Mama would set a blue-and-yellow plate of candies out on the table, which normally she kept hidden high up where none of us could reach it. Then Nara and me would wrap pebbles in the candy wrappers and use them to play *somon* store, while Papa sat with the guests, discussing the price of cashmere and last winter and who had had children and how everyone in the area was getting on these days.

Sometimes the visitors would buy cigarettes or soda from us, since Papa had Russian cigarettes, which were better than Chinese ones, and in return for spending the night they would give us a bottle of booze or Mama would get a couple of *tugriks* to toss in the bowl on the shelf. Mama never smoked—almost none of the women where we lived did—but Papa did, when he got the urge, every now and then. In the City it's different, even women stagger around drunk, and no one even bats an eye when they light up. What would Mama say to that, I thought, and suddenly Nara came to mind. She was the one I missed most.

After she was done with school, Nara came back to live in our *ger* and traveled around with Mama, being introduced. In my opinion, she could've found a man on her own, and besides, she was only sixteen, but Mama didn't want to leave anything to chance. Maybe she was afraid that Nara would end up like her sister. On the other hand, if Yellow Flower had had kids, she wouldn't have been able to come and help us out that time and I would never have gone to the City.

That was the first time it hit me that maybe the City wasn't all good, and it made me feel sad and empty, but only for a moment. I put on my pants. The sun outside was blinding.

It was already close to noon and I was somewhere out on the very edge of the City. Instead of being all jammed together, the *gers* were in wooden enclosures here, far apart from one another with horses grazing in between. The streets of the suburbs disappeared amid the *khashaas*. The City here was a shaky thing, dwindling away until it was swallowed up by the steppe. Another twenty yards of thinning *gers* and that was it. Wolves ran here at night sometimes, and nothing over the hill even knew there was such a thing as the City.

I set off toward where the *gers* were thicker. Both sides of the street were lined with fences, the sand burned even through my shoes, and after a while I was sorry I'd left the rest of the salty tea in the *ger*. Every now and then I noticed someone sizing me up—I can also tell right away when someone isn't one of us—and naked little kids hooted and hollered at me, running from yard to yard slamming the gates shut. Instead of shops, there were just little stalls like the ones where I bought soda, only here they sold practically everything. Shoe repair, pawnshops, hairdressers, and dumpy little plank-board *guanzes,* but those are all over the place. In the part of the City where I lived, there were people who dressed Mongolian style and people who dressed like Russians, but there weren't too many Russian clothes here. There also weren't a lot of food stores around, since people here had animals, which weren't allowed in Shartsetseg's building.

Then all of a sudden there were people everywhere, streaming out of the cracks in swarms, washing away the animals, and the *gers* turned into wooden homes that grew into concrete and panels. Like the first time I had come, with my aunt. The roar grew louder and louder as I got closer to the center, then cars and buses and people crashing into each other and then, according to custom, politely shaking hands. But it wasn't the same anymore. The colors looked pale and faded in the dust and midday heat. The glittering shops and wide streets of the City's downtown seemed tired, like they were peeling away and something was peeking out from underneath, but I was too lazy to crawl in and see what it was. My legs hurt, and between them too, I didn't have money to take the bus, and when I finally unfolded my cot and lay down that night, I was glad to be back among my own, and Erka's morning pat on the cheek was the most blissful thing I'd felt since my grandma used to massage my frozen feet in winter.

Everything went back to the way it was before. Only Biamkhu went someplace else for his noontime meal, and I slept on the canvas cot in the kitchen. I also went back to my aunt's one more time, for my other pair of shoes and a plastic barrette that Biamkhu had given me.

No one was home.

I left my keys with the janitor and wrote a note to my aunt on a piece of old newspaper that Mergen used to use to roll his cigarettes at night. I said I was living in the kitchen now but except for the air it wasn't that bad, and I thanked her for helping me since I couldn't have found a job on my own, and I told her our *guanz* had really improved and she should come by and see it sometime if she felt like it.

It didn't work out with the new place, but I wasn't too upset, because the shoe repair shop got bought by the twins from our *somon* who sold auto parts, the ones that our headmaster mentioned, which was better than if some stranger had snatched it out from under us.

Me and Erka finally bought some new, washable tablecloths to put on the old tables, and I even inspired her to get some pink tassels to hang over the counter. That way at least we looked like a better establishment, even if our *khuushuur* went for the same price as they charged at the tiniest, crummiest holes-in-the-wall, where they don't even wash the dishes and the *khuushuur* meat has mice and sewer rats ground up in it.

I had my job so down pat, I almost didn't even have to think about it anymore, and grater, dishcloth, or lump of dough in hand, I found my thoughts drifting more and more to Nara and the others, and as summer turned to fall and fall into winter, I knew I had to go back to the Red Mountains, even if just for one short week.

By then I had been in the City four years and didn't have any idea what was going on at home. All I knew was that Shartsetseg had been there once and sent me a message through Erka saying that everyone was still alive and Nara had a man.

I was just waiting for it to warm up a little before I made the trip when Mergen showed up one day. He said he was sober for the first time and not to go, my mother never wanted to see me again, and he put some money in my hand and before I could say a word he yanked me into his arms like he was roping in a shy horse. I started shrieking and pounding his chest with my fists. I could tell he wasn't going to hurt me, but I couldn't stand it.

He let go, yelling at me that I didn't understand, and suddenly I saw him, blurred through my fever, standing in front of our *ger*. He was yelling something just like it, and for the first time in my life I understood my mother. Why she didn't want me now and why she had almost left that day.

Sometimes when I lay there at night, staring up at the pots and pans, waiting for sleep that wouldn't come, I'd play the box game. I would picture the dented tin box we used to keep *aaruul* and crackers in, only this one had letters in it. Letters from each of us. I knew what mine said, but the rest of them were a mystery. I came up with the game during my first year in the City, when I used to go to the post office to check for mail almost every day, and the only thing I got all year was a postcard from Mama of Choibalsan, saying they'd bought some new horses, the oldest camel had passed away, and part of the roof at the House of Culture had fallen in, so the *somon* had shut it down.

I knew it wasn't true, though, because Papa was the only one who cared about the animals, and as long as the roof hadn't killed Oyuna, Mama couldn't have cared less. The *ger* and us, that was all she cared about, and there wasn't a word about either of those. But a person gets all sorts of crazy ideas when they're cooking. I found that out when I worked at the *guanz,* and my mother must've known it for ages.

Burkhan knows how Papa was, spending all his time on his own, hunting down rogue sheep. He wouldn't come home for days at a stretch, and on nights when the black sky was full of holes that let in the sun from horizon to horizon, he would sleep alone, far away from us.

Papa's letter was about Magi and the animals. He couldn't trust Mama, so he also couldn't love her. Nara and me were both half-breeds, and Oyuna was Mama's child. It's true that Magi died a death like Chingis Khan—falling from a horse is a proud way to go, better than wasting away under blankets—but any death is sad at the age of seventeen, that was clear even to Papa.

Mama would've written about Oyuna, since when a woman has a child in her gray-haired years, she always spoils them.

Mama knew how not to think about Magi. At any rate she didn't talk about her, and whenever Papa started in she'd always cut him off. Then again, she had to look at us every day. Maybe I remind her of something beautiful too, but Nara doesn't, for sure. Munkhtsetseg told me about the Russian sardine salesman one night when I was helping her with the *koumiss*. Maidar was sitting with us, and all of a sudden he stood up and walked out without a word, slamming the door behind him.

Mama met Papa by accident. Before Grandma died, when all she did anymore was lie in her lair and hiss at us, she used to say it should never've happened.

If Grandma had known that the girl who stopped at their *ger* asking for water and rice would end up as Papa's wife, she would've set the dogs on her, and instead of a bowl of soup she would've given her *argal* porridge. But Grandma didn't know what she was saying anymore, and Mama didn't care.

The day my parents met, my mother and her brother and sisters—Onon, Shartsetseg, and Gerla—were traveling with their parents to Bayan-Ölgii to buy rugs from the Kazakhs.

Mama's parents had never been too clever and they were doing pretty badly, so they figured they'd buy a couple of rugs in Bayan-Ölgii for cheap, then take them back to the City and sell them for a profit. In the end they came back with nothing, since no one would part with a rug as cheaply as Mama's father had thought. But on the way home they stopped at Grandma's *ger* again, this time for two nights, and Mama and Papa were glued to each other the entire time. Mama still went to bed with her family in the guest *ger,* but she didn't do much sleeping, spending most of the night with Papa, sitting out on the steppe a little ways from the *ger.*

One year later, the two of them had a *ger* of their own.

Grandma Dolgorma gnashed her teeth, but Mama's father, Ogoi, was glad to have married off his daughter so well and it hadn't cost him a thing, and Mama wanted to stay with her family, so Papa left his home.

First they had Magi, then me, then Papa had to join the border guard, and Grandma moved in with us. Thanks to a herd of her finest cashmere goats, he only spent a year patrolling the borders of the Mongolian People's Republic. The lieutenant got his money's worth. But still. Twelve months in a lonely hut with a red star on it, with nothing for company but a machine gun and a permanently plastered Ivan. Barbed wire all over the place and a three-month-old baby at home.

Munkhtsetseg said it was a sardine *naimaachin* from somewhere near Verkhoyansk. Which is strange, since I went and looked on the map in the Aeroflot waiting room and there isn't any sea anywhere near Verkhoyansk. Maybe she meant Magadan, or maybe it was just another one of Mama's lies.

He came riding in from the foothills as she was nursing me out in front of the *ger.* He said he had something to sell and he could do with a drop of soup. Mama served him, then he wrestled her to the ground and he did it to her, I guess. Munkhtsetseg wasn't exactly sure. But Nara's got fair hair, anyone can see that. Not to mention, no true Mongol eats fish. Nobody in our family, no one I even know. A Mongol eats what he raises, and fish don't belong to anyone. And that damned *naimaachin* must've known it the moment that that nag of his set hoof on our sacred soil.

In the end I went home as I'd planned. As if Mergen of all people could tell me what to do. Pff. There were plenty of buses when I arrived at the station, and more than one was heading in the direction of my family's home: the southern route, through Kharkhorin.

Purev had a cousin from Darkhan who had just arrived, so he was glad to have the kitchen cot free for a while, and he brought me a sack of *khuushuur* to take along on the trip. I don't know where I'd be without you and Erka, that's what I told him through the bus window. I'll never forget my aunt for introducing us.

The driver said he could take thirteen. In the end we were eighteen, loaded down with all sorts of gifts—plastic basins and plates, shoes, balls of wire. More and more Mongols kept getting on and changing seats, and I was relieved when everyone had finally settled in.

The sky was murky, and the clouds' dark shadows glided over the steppe like wings of giant birds.

Grandma said you could smell misfortune. She said every animal could detect its sorrowful scent, and the more experienced of the steppe people too. She could do it.

It happened more than once that Grandma knew when someone in the area had died. When the sky was full of streaks and the leafless stumps in the mountains groaned, Grandma would kneel down and sputter. When a dust storm hit and tattered leaves spun in swirls and a lone wolf howled in the distance, she would raise her hands to the heavens and beg the *Tengers*. And the sky spirits would stop their quarrels and send down a crackling flash to show her that they'd heard.

I could sense something, but my arms were full of gifts and the prayers just wouldn't come. Then our *ger* peeked out and I broke into a run.

Mama's ward was on the third floor. I put on a plastic mask at the door and went to find her room. They say nothing but the best about the Bayankhongor hospital, so in spite of it all I was glad she was there.

She was asleep.

Five other women sat on their beds or guzzled milk tea from thermoses while they chatted around a small Formica table overflowing with food from relatives. Pieces of meat, tin cups with daughters' strong healing soups, other cups of half-eaten rice, strips of *borts,* and flies buzzing over everything.

I was glad the room was so nice. They even had a radio and a sash on the window. Plus a coatrack and a calendar of Russian cities on the wall.

Mama's bed was right by the door.

A bag lay tipped over on the floor next to her bed. Papa had made sure she had everything she needed. Her eyes were closed and peaceful, as though that was how they were meant to be. She had two blankets over her, pulled up to her chin, and her temples shone with beads of sweat. I rolled back the blankets a little, trying not to wake her, but she wriggled right back under them, blindly grabbing hold of my hand and pulling it close to her.

Sit, it's all right, come and sit a while, it's fine, Mama said, making room for me on the bed. It's fine, she said, feeling around for her belly under the blanket. That's good. Forget about Mergen, all right? I nodded eagerly. You have a good job in the City? I nodded again: The best. Nara's always asking about you. Oyuna too.

I watched the sunlight reflecting off the edge of the bed. The light bounced back and forth every time I moved my head. Papa should be coming for me in a couple of days. Will you still be here?

I nodded my head up and down to all of Mama's questions, and the light jumped back and forth. When she asked why I hadn't come sooner, I remembered all my useless trips to the post office, and the box game, and kept my mouth shut.

She didn't ask about Shartsetseg once—she probably got her news from her—so I told her a little about the City and the *guanz*, but it felt like I was talking about someone else's life. As soon as her breath began to slow and it looked like she was asleep, I left.

When I got outside, I realized I still had the mask on, but bringing it back would've taken too long, so I crumpled it up and stuck it under a rock.

It was simple when I played the box game with Nara. She thought the same way as I did. Sometimes it even seemed like there was just one of us. Like her voice was coming out of my mouth and my steps were carrying her body.

Now that would be something for Grandma. But I was too little when she was alive. What a pity. I can smell death too, but Grandma could call it to her like a work dog, or thrash its hide when it circled the *ger*, poking its claws down the smoke hole to try to get at the sick.

Now I know what Papa's eyes were searching for when he bent over Magi and felt for the end. They were searching for Grandma. Magi still wasn't that far gone, but none of us knew how to pull her back and Grandma wouldn't listen to us. Maybe she remembered the way that me and Nara made fun of her for wetting the blankets at night because she couldn't get out of the *ger* in time, how we hid her cane and screeched at her and imitated her moans and groans. And that's why she wouldn't help us.

Nara was always on my side and the other way around. She would go and distract Mama whenever I tortured Oyuna, and when Magi sheared Nara's favorite lamb, I gave her mine and put stinkbugs in Magi's bed. She deserved it for getting to sleep alone.

Eventually Mama put Oyuna in with her, since Papa refused to sleep with a baby and Oyuna didn't need to drink at night anymore.

But the days of our worst hostilities were over with by then.

Magi wasn't an *erliiz,* so she didn't have to be as sly as me and Nara were. I only remember the good things when I look back on her now, but it's the same as with Grandma.

Both of them are dead.

In my dreams, Nara flew through the air on a straw-colored horse, the wind blending her hair with its mane, weaving it into golden braids, and as they sailed over the Red Mountains the horse swept off their tops with its tail, and I was always afraid their jagged peaks would tear the horse's belly.

Everyone said that Nara was playing with fire.

She would whip her horse to breakneck speed, till its flanks were streaming blood and its rump was green with torn-up grass, then yank the rein and make the sharpest turn the steppe had ever seen. I just stood there gaping, gnawing on the hem of my *del,* and Mama turned and went inside to spare herself the terror.

Those were the moments when I saw Papa at his angriest. The horses that Nara rode would always have their lips torn up. She got whippings often.

At eighteen, Nara became a teacher at the *somon* school. While I was scrubbing slobber off of dishes and utensils, she was wiping the noses of wide-eyed little first graders.

I went to see her as soon as I left the hospital.

Nara had the littlest kids and taught everything from A to Z. Once a month the parents would come and meet with her, and they were surprised that this was the comrade teacher their kids had been telling them so much about. She may have looked sixteen, but the parents had nothing but praise for her. No one passed meat around the class or crunched on candy when Nara taught. She brought in small animals and flowers to show the kids, and took the ones who didn't have parents home with her on vacation.

Papa told me all this in a rush before I left the *ger* for the Bayan-khongor State Hospital.

It didn't take long to find Nara. Everyone knows the school. But the story she told was different, and made me think of my visit with Mama.

Nara talked about the clacking of children's pen cases, the paper wads they shot at her, the fat Buryat teachers who were still there from our days and spied on her teaching notes, and the mothers who had nothing else but their kids to call their own, and she couldn't tell them to take them home, because their fathers were such juicers that that little Mongol of theirs could break himself in two and he'd still never be able to wrap his head around Cyrillic.

Orosmongol, the children called her: Russian-Mongol. They weren't used to fair hair, and by that point in her life Nara was fed up explaining, and anyway it was impossible to justify herself.

When my aunt sent the message through Erka that Nara had a man, I imagined some mighty Mongol who tamed wild horses for her and waited for her after work in a big jeep in front of the school with a different gift every day. But in walked a stoop-shouldered meek little Russian, a land surveyor from Chelyabinsk. He wrapped his arms around Nara's waist while he rattled on about agricultural development and the Mongolian nomadic perspective or whatever.

He had studied in Petersburg, had never sat on a horse in his life, and was trying to lure Nara to live with him in Moscow.

Then me and Nara went out one day.

The kids were off for the anniversary of the revolution, so when Nara was done taking down the drawings of red stars hung around the classroom, she borrowed two fat, lazy mares from Anra, and the two of us went for a slow ride and reminisced about old times.

Nara loved her kids. She was teaching them to read and write, and the best ones had already started reading *Chuk and Gek.* Twice she had taken orphans back to the *ger* with her on vacation. These kids knew nothing in life but boarding school, and Nara taught them to climb up to the smoke hole and milk the ill-tempered mares, and by the end of vacation the bright ones could drive the goat herd and knew all the nomad commands. But then it was time to go back to school. They ran away to Oyuna and Papa again. Papa didn't mind and Oyuna had grown to like them, but the headmaster said something about laws and it made bad blood for Nara.

Nara also went to the *ger* on weekends now and then. During the week, she had a cramped little room in a building at school, where she shared a hot plate and a toilet with Alexei. That's how they met.

Alexei had come to the *somon* to survey a branch line for the Baikal–Amur railway. No one took it seriously, but even the *somon* chairman couldn't very well refuse. So they shunted him off into the little house with Nara and waited for him to be called back to Moscow. That's what Nara's friend Anra said, but I didn't tell Nara that. She must've seen for herself how useless Alexei was.

I was at Nara's about a week.

She told the Buryat teachers she was sick, which she was. Alexei kept insisting that they leave for Moscow together. Then his pals showed up. They stayed in the *somon* hostel and came riding with us every day. The rest of the time they sat around Alexei's room while me and Nara cooked and cleared away the bottles.

One night they announced that they were going to hunt for bears. They set out with their rifles the next day and came back with some wolf cubs covered in blood. They were rasping for breath, and Alexei finished them off in the hall.

Alexei fell asleep early that night. As usual, me and Nara brought in the bottles and kept the cracker bowls full. Then I went out with one of them to get more, and while we were gone, two of them pinned Nara down with their knees and did it. When I walked in, she was lying on the ground with her skirt around her waist and Alexei's pals were belting out Russian songs and passing shots back and forth with two hands, Mongolian style. Alexei came in, carried Nara into her room, kicked the others out the door, and did it to her again. I didn't know Nara like this. I stood in the doorway and watched. Nara was stroking his hair. She was twenty, and it was good for her to know. Most girls younger than her had already had men by then. It was getting to be a disgrace. In the morning we laid in bed whispering. She said it wasn't so bad at all, and I told her about Mergen. We both agreed that later on it might even be nice. Later on.

Grandma used to say young men rode with iron chains, gallivanting about the steppe, prowling around the *gers,* till they spied the one they wanted and snared her in their metal noose. Once she was dragged to the ground in their noose she was theirs, and bore them strong, healthy children. Me and Nara agreed that we wanted all boys. I didn't know that I was going to have Dolgorma.

A few days later, Alexei was called back to Moscow. The Baikal–Amur branch line would not be built. He left Nara his address and a short, frilly Russian skirt. For several weeks afterwards, Nara thought she might also have something else of his, but she didn't. It went away with the blood-red settings of the tyrannous sun.

A red stripe over our mountains told of good fortune.

Grandma had always loved red.

Mama stayed sick for a long time. It was her gallbladder. A lot of people here get that, so we all breathed a sigh of relief. In the City some say it's because of the thick crust of suet that forms on the top of cold soup, because of the fatty sheep rumps that everyone loves so much, but that's impossible. This is the food of Chingis Khan, of Ögedei, Kublai, Temür, Sükhbaatar, Choibalsan, Tsedenbal, and Bagabandi. This is the food of us all, and no one can claim they never got anywhere eating suet soup. These things have stood the test of time. But that was what the doctor said, so we didn't bring Mama any of that. Papa slipped something into her bag every now and then, but Mama didn't eat it, and when the doctor found out she exploded. Just take her, she said, it was no use with numbskulls like us anyway, Mama was just taking up a bed there for nothing.

Papa had never been yelled at by anyone like that and was at a loss for words, because the doctor was a young woman and he was a respected man, and shining through his plastic gown was a carmine *del* so splendid the doctor could only dream of it.

From then on, I went to the hospital instead. With the money from Erka and Purev I bought bandages and dressings, and a bottle for the doctor, and twice a week I brought meals. It was a strange treatment they gave her. They kept her lying down all the time, and she hardly ate, except for a teeny little glass of vodka twice a day from a rattly cart that the nurses pushed around. The clinking of glass every time was the signal for me to go. The only remedy I ever saw on Mama's floor was a big fridge full of vodka.

Evenings we would sit in the *ger*, Papa and Oyuna and me, missing Mama. I don't see why she can't be here, Papa would mutter into his collar while the rest of us stared at the hot air quivering over the stove. Summer came to an end and I didn't go back to the City in the fall, or the winter, or the whole next year after that.

Papa missed Mama the most. I looked after the *ger*, but Oyuna went back to boarding school in the fall, and Nara went to teach, so Papa was left with the animals on his own. It was too much for him, so he asked Ariuna, his sister, if she'd lend him her two youngest sons, Jargalsaikhan and Naima, to help him for a while.

Tsobo, their father, was always driving back and forth in jeeps. That was how he supported them, since they had little livestock to speak of, and two more sons besides those two. Every Shin Jil they would swear up and down that this year would be their last on the steppe and then they would move to the City, and ever since I was little I had been looking forward to having such close relatives there.

If Papa had known where it would lead, he would never have taken them in. Or at least not Jargal, anyway. But how could he have known? Papa needed somebody, and Burkhan didn't give us any warning when they arrived. The sky was smoky gray and smooth as glass. That day we got our first snow, and we took it just the opposite, as a favorable sign.

I can still see those soft, light, slow flakes and their two approaching silhouettes, moving toward us so slowly the dust didn't even stir. We knew they were coming, so we waited for them in front of the *ger*. I cooked a big meal, Papa rolled some cigarettes from his store of good tobacco, and the two of us sat out in front of the door for hours. I kept refilling our tea bowls, and both of us had aching eyes from keeping a constant lookout. Jargal was the older one, it was obvious right away. I'd never seen such a handsome Mongol in my life.

A few years had passed since the last time we'd been to Tsobo and Ariuna's, so for a while we just stood there staring at each other. Then they shook hands with Papa and I went off to get the noodles and all the rest.

His shoulders were broad as a yak and his arms were thick as a tree trunk. He wore soft fur boots that his mother had embroidered for him with red wrestlers. When he stood, it was like a mountain rising up from the earth, and when the three men took their seats, Papa put a cushion underneath himself, so at least that first evening he wouldn't feel so bad. Ariuna had been pregnant with Naima when Mama was carrying Magi, and Naima may have paled next to his brother, but he looked good too when he was by himself.

I remembered how I used to feel compared to my older sister, so I tried to make it clear from the start that it didn't matter to me if he wasn't like his brother, I couldn't have cared less.

That first night was a long one. Jargal and Naima sat solemnly puffing away and Papa spoke to them as if they were his equals. Jargal, especially, dragged out every word the way that serious men do, and when we were through eating he pulled out the vodka and called for the bowls himself. We were impressed.

Up until the next spring Papa was content. I was glad and Mama too. In the fall they released her, so I wasn't alone in the *ger* anymore. She'd gotten a lot grayer during her time in the hospital; her breasts sagged and her belly bulged. But meanwhile Papa was strong as ever, sauntering around like he didn't have a care in the world, and everything was going his way. The herd grew fat despite the cold, and we were happy the way we used to be, when Magi was still with us and Oyuna had yet to come.

Papa treated Jargal and Naima like sons, and I think that meant a lot to them. Their own father was always away, and Ariuna didn't know how to teach them men's things. Both of them were skilled. Naima was not only a fine rider, but when he let fly, he was always right on target or close to it, and Jargal was as strong as they come, so Papa got the idea that they could compete in our *somon* Naadam come next summer: Naima in archery and Jargal in wrestling. Naima wanted to ride in the horse race, but Papa refused on the spot.

In the end it was all the same. Everything went to blazes as soon as Nara showed up.

We hadn't expected her back so soon. She usually stayed for a few days after the end of the school year, tidying up and taking care of various odds and ends. Not this year. She also didn't bring any kids with her this time, as the headmaster had forbidden it. She just all of a sudden turned up in front of the *ger* with two bags.

Those were beautiful days. The sun didn't torture us that summer like it usually did, and even at midday we would sit out front with our work, discussing the kids in Nara's class and the finer points of cooking. Mama let us do things our way, every now and then dragging some story up from our youth, and at night she would rub our sunburned backs with suet. There was nothing to suggest that Nara was going to lose her mind.

We even made fun of Jargal together.

We would whisper about his neck. He had a neck like Baisa's bull, which was known throughout the *somon* because its neck was so short and muscular it almost couldn't turn its head, so instead it would just angrily roll its eyes to the side, till the corners bulged with purple veins and its eyes were bathed in white. Ariuna had to alter all of Jargal's *dels*. Me and Nara would picture him trying to wrestle into Papa's—eyes popping out of his sockets, face turning red as he struggled for air—he'd never be able to button it shut. The two of us would roll on the ground, laughing so hard we couldn't breathe, while Mama shouted at us that the soup was boiling over, because she wanted to know why we were splitting our sides and clawing our throats like that.

We only saw the men in the morning and the evening, and only for a while, and we really looked forward to it. Papa grew fat and began telling jokes, and Jargal and Naima were always hungry, so as soon as they had emptied their bowls we would whisk them away and then put them right back again, refilled to the brim.

Mama said it was a treat to see, since hollow stomachs like theirs were an honor to any woman. Papa would tell how their day had gone and Mama would ask if they'd seen any wolves. Oyuna's scars had never completely gone away and Mama had been cautious ever since. If Papa just grumbled or didn't respond, he could object all he wanted but she wouldn't let him leave without a rifle the next day.

I don't know what led up to it, but I started to notice that every day around noontime Nara would disappear. Then after a while I'd see her again, sweeping out the oven or mending, but something strange was going on. The days passed one by one, and Nara kept disappearing at the same time every day and coming home later and later. Between

Mama and Oyuna and me, there were plenty of us to do the chores, and Nara had always had her secret spots and hideaways, which nobody knew about, not even me, so for a long time we let it be.

That was a mistake.

Even Papa didn't do anything when Nara started turning up at the herd during the day.

Every day she'd bring Jargal his lunch, then the two of them would find some excuse to go off and sit by the boulders, and Papa would have to call them back, because Jargal wouldn't come on his own and Nara wouldn't dream of moving from his side. After a few days of this, Papa turned sullen and Nara and Jargal also started going out after supper.

Just like that, the two of them. Like it was nothing. Nara almost didn't even talk to me anymore, and Papa circled the *ger* at night like an animal in a cage. Mama just waited.

Suppers turned quiet and downcast, our shadows thin and spiky in the gloom, our words wheezing like raspy old dogs.

During one such strained silence, Papa banged his fist on the table. If quiet can get any quieter, it did so then.

The thud of the wood died away, Papa took a deep breath, and when he was done speaking, all eyes rested on Jargal. Nara's blazed hungrily, like they were going to grow right into him, to dissolve there and never return to the world again. Jargal nodded his head. Nara jumped from her stool and started showering him with wet kisses. His cheeks, his forehead, his neck—the one that we had made fun of together—then she covered his arms with her eager lips, all the way down to his fingertips.

Papa looked away, Mama started clearing the dishes, and me and Oyuna didn't know what to do with our eyes.

Jargal sat through it all unmoved, shadowed in darkness like a temple Burkhan and just as majestic, with an almost imperceptible smile on his face. He agreed to take Nara as his wife. She would teach for one more year—it was the end of summer and it would be hard to find a replacement before the start of the school year—and the next summer relatives would descend on us from every direction to see Tuleg and Alta marry off their first daughter. That was how it was supposed to be.

Papa cast a last glance at Nara and went outside to smoke.

ZAYA

His eyes said, If you aren't mine, so be it. You could be the cuckoo's for all I care, I love you just the same.

One thing for certain is it's dangerous to marry a cousin and Papa said nothing against it. On the other hand, he felt worse than anyone about how it ended up.

Just like when Magi left us.

The strangest thing was no one but Nara seemed happy. My first thought was, She could hardly have found a stronger man. Tsobo's family is rich, and that's the way it should be. But I didn't feel any joy either.

I guess we all had a feeling that the fire burning in Nara's face as she consumed his arms with her lips somehow didn't fit with Jargal's gentle, sparkling smile.

But it was much worse than that.

Nara stopped riding out to the herd with Jargal's lunch, instead leaving with the men in the morning and not coming back until night. She would bring some darning or sewing along so Mama wouldn't make a fuss, but she didn't care what anyone said, no one could keep her from going. Then she started riding around in next to nothing. Her hair was a mess, her face turned thin; only her eyes grew in strength.

Every morning she'd tag along behind the men like a wild thing, and at night she would come home with flowers and hang them up around the *ger*. Wedding flowers, she'd say. Mama and Oyuna and me would tear them down, wilted, the next day, but Nara just ignored us and came back the next night with new ones.

It's said that wild women, who leave their families and go to feast with the wolves in the rocks, can kill with their eyes.

The first time they strike—a woman out in the rocks, say, searching for a stray baby goat—the woman goes home and never again will the tiny head of a baby peek from between her legs. Nothing can help. If the woman gets struck a second time, she goes home to her *ger* to find her children sick, doubled over in cramps. Nothing can help. If she isn't careful and it happens a third time, she dies. Nara was turning into a wild thing.

Jargal tried to avoid her, but in a *ger* it isn't easy, so mornings, at least, he would ride out to the herd early, while Nara was busy with something, so she wouldn't notice. It kept getting harder and harder, though, as Nara stopped doing anything at all. She realized he was running away, and wouldn't let him out of her sight.

He would wake up to find her looking at him. He would go to sleep at night knowing she was watching every quiver of his nostrils, every little cough or snore, until just before dawn, still in her clothes, she would doze off for a while.

Gradually it dawned on us that Jargal would rather go through the rest of his life in shame than marry this girl. This wasn't our Nara anymore, and the wedding was the one thing in life she was clinging to.

There was nothing left but for Mama to pay a visit to Hiroko, her forbidden older sister. I had never heard Shartsetseg even speak her name, and Mama's younger brother, Onon, wouldn't mention her until he looked in every direction and drew a protective cloud in the air. Safe is safe, he'd always say.

Mama had nothing against her, and though she didn't speak of her often, when she did she never said anything that she wouldn't have said about anyone else. And we were raised the same. Mama always defended our aunt in front of her siblings. On that she and Grandma agreed. I don't know that Grandma had ever even seen her, but whenever the talk turned to Hiroko, she would prick up her ears, and if anyone even ever so slightly put her down, snickered, or made a cloud with their hands, Grandma would start to splutter with rage and chase them out of the *ger* on the spot.

Nara—or rather the person who used to be her—didn't notice anything except Jargal anymore. Sometimes you could hear her humming to herself, some long-drawn melody, some strange, wordless tune in which the grass rustled with forbidden things and eagles swooped from rocky cliffs.

Jargal tried to act the same, but he didn't want to do the things they used to do before. When Nara beckoned him to come outside at night, he would always find a way to wriggle out of it somehow.

After seven long days, Mama returned with Hiroko. Sometime around then Nara stopped speaking, and Papa and Naima were the only ones who went out to the herd, since Nara wouldn't let Jargal even a single step away from her. I took care of the *ger* with Oyuna, and Nara spent her time playing strange games with Jargal.

A shiver ran down my spine when I heard her loud, silly laugh from outside, as I pictured Jargal's slight smile, that awkward grin of uneasiness I saw frozen on his face whenever he was with Nara. I stayed away from them both.

Nara would come home tired and dirty, hair tangled with grass, with the look of a guilty child on her face. At night, Jargal would busy himself cleaning Papa's hunting knives while Nara sat on the bed playing with her fingers and mewing to herself. At times like those she looked just like our neighbor Oyunbat's sixth daughter, who was born the spring before Oyuna.

Papa used to tease Oyunbat that he only knew how to make girls, and ask whether he was planning to try for seven. We visited them a lot that year. Oyunbat's wife, Soldoo, had a soft spot for Mama and gave her all sorts of advice about being pregnant. Mama kept quiet, since giving birth six times is something to be respected, though if you ask me, half the thrilling tales that Soldoo told were nonsense. Then again, she had been pregnant practically her whole life, so maybe they weren't made up.

So while Papa took potshots at Oyunbat, peeking over at Mama's belly every minute or two, Mama was subjected to a nonstop barrage of advice and maybe true stories, and Magi and me and Nara took turns holding the baby. Soldoo couldn't praise her enough: she almost never cried, hardly moved, and slept a lot. We just always ended up with drool all over us.

After a month or two, she still couldn't really do anything, and the doctor said she would never get better. All she did was lie there, and their *ger* stank of urine so badly we stopped going to see them.

Her parents never called her anything but Little One. It wasn't worth it to give her a name, since the only thing she knew how to do was play with her fingers and mewl, like Nara did.

I remember how excited Soldoo was when she learned how to eat by herself. To us it seemed silly. Oyuna was already cooking by then, but we knew we weren't allowed to laugh.

Little One died the winter before last.

Soldoo wept, but everyone else breathed a sigh of relief. I think she was just too old and her belly didn't know how to make babies right anymore.

Until Hiroko came, Nara's behavior was pretty much like Little One's. She must have sensed that Hiroko was coming, because the night before, she started running around the *ger* so fast even Jargal couldn't catch her. But then she tripped and burst into tears, Jargal leaped in and grabbed her, and from then on we didn't let go.

Nobody got to sleep that night till just before dawn. Nobody except Nara, dozing on Papa's shoulder while he kept screaming that no one was taking her anywhere, just try and take his daughter away, and he had a knife in his hand. Hiroko spoke slowly and deliberately, and every time Papa started to yell she would stop. Mama chimed in with her sister, grumbling in agreement and nodding her head. Oyuna and me didn't have an opinion. Jargal started to say something, but one look from Hiroko and he shut right up. Naima stayed hidden off to the side, probably thinking about his own *ger,* where Papa never pulled a knife on anyone and Mama didn't bring back any witches.

Nara left with Hiroko just after daybreak the following day. The sky was leaden, and snow-filled clouds hung over the mountains, lying in wait. Mama was the only one of us who said good-bye. The rest of us were asleep, and by the time I scrambled out of bed and ran out front to wave good-bye and wish them a safe journey, they were gone. As the mist rolled over the steppe, I could just make out their two bundled figures shrinking in the distance.

Jargal stayed a few days more, to help Papa round up the sheep from the mountains, and then cleared out. None of us tried to stop him. Papa gave him a letter of thanks to Ariuna, saying he'd always been conscientious about his work and had shouldered a lot of the load, and I think he gave him some money too.

Naima stayed.

We needed him and he didn't mind. So he stayed on a second year with us and then a third. Nara was gone that whole time. At first, Mama went to Hiroko's every month or two and came back with scraps of news. I think Hiroko told her more, but she kept it to herself. One thing for certain was Nara wouldn't be pulling out of it anytime soon.

At the start of the new school year, I took her place.

I packed my things in her bags and lodged in her room. It's better to be around children than washing dishes and pouring milk tea in a *guanz.* Plus teaching is much more serious work. It wasn't long before everyone in the *somon* center knew who I was and looked at me with respect.

ZAYA

I was twenty-two. I wasn't running around with ribbons in my hair anymore, and if I had had children, even the old ladies would've accepted me as one of their own. As it was, I listened patiently to their long-winded speeches and kept my lip buttoned. They'd never been to the City and their advice was useless to me.

My favorite person in the *somon* center was Anra, the girl who loaned me and Nara her horses when Nara was still one of us and I came to visit that time. After they rounded up the money to get new wooden trusses and the men shored up the roof on the *somon* House of Culture, me and Anra started a singing circle there. Twice a week a group of little ones would gather, and every so often we'd put on a performance for the parents. Anra played the *morin khuur* and the *limbe,* while I wrote the words on the blackboard and saw to it that everyone sang out loud and what they were supposed to. Anra lived not far from me, so we'd get together at night and talk. Her mother wasn't home much—she had a job doing something or other for the *somon* presidium—and her father had been gone for as long as she could remember. So Anra was alone, except for her grandpa and grandma, lying in bed in the back. That's what she told me, I never saw them myself.

I told Anra about the children. The ones I couldn't stand because they never knew a thing, the ones who didn't care since they didn't have anyone to show off their grades to anyway, and the ones who were my favorites. Who came to school clean, pencils sharpened, didn't speak without permission, and whose mothers and fathers came when I sent word for them to come.

Anra told me about her mother, an ugly Mongol woman with a big bumpy nose and enormous ears. I had been afraid of her ever since I was little; everyone knew who she was. When I pictured Uregma, I always pictured her looking like Mrs. Ulantsetseg. Apparently Anra's father couldn't see for his eyes. But he didn't stick around long, and it wasn't Mrs. Ulantsetseg's fate to meet with such good luck again. Anra had always had everything all to herself, and except for the name-calling her childhood was a happy one.

She drifted off, thinking back to those long-gone days, and then tumbled out what she really wanted to tell me.

For several months, off and on, a man had been coming to see her. He wasn't from here. They met one day in a shop in the center. He said he was looking for gasoline, since Kharal from the pump was somewhere sleeping it off again and nobody else had a key. So Anra went home and brought him back some gas from her mother's car. That was it. Then, one evening a week later, he came knocking at her door. In one hand the canister, in the other a bag of candy and a bottle of vodka. He said Anra had rescued him and now she had to have a little nip with him to celebrate, so they sat and drank till the bottle was done, and when Anra's mother came home, they fled out the back door, and there, behind the building, he told Anra she was the brightest star in the night sky and threw her on the ground.

It was bitter cold. Anra described how her teeth chattered and how embarrassed she was by the hollow, bony sound but she couldn't help it. Luckily he'd been able to grab a dishcloth on the way out, so they did it on that. She said she didn't remember much of that night, but not since the days of the Golden Horde had our steppe borne a mightier Mongol. Then he kept coming back again and again, always with vodka and candies, and they did it behind the building and they did it inside of it too.

It went on like that for a month or two. No one ever saw them, except once, they were in full swing, with him like a raging stallion, mounting her from behind, when suddenly there was a crash of glass and a stone came flying in.

All they saw was a back running away. Some dirty girl with blonde hair, she wasn't one of the locals, so that couldn't have been the reason he stopped coming after that.

Anra gave a little sigh and laid her head on my shoulder.

She hadn't told anyone else, she sobbed, throwing her arms around my neck.

"When he held me, I felt like life was glorious. Colors bloomed like sedge buds and the steppe smelled sweet as freshly drawn milk. Now I'll be alone for the rest of my life. Men like that are born only once. And me, oaf that I am, I didn't know how to keep him."

She lifted her head like she was asking me a question. Every word of advice here was precious. Amber Warrior, she called him. She was surprised I was curious what his real name was. She'd never asked.

As long as I'm talking about men and how the women I cared for—and still do, since with Nara it can't be otherwise, and Anra hasn't left this world yet either—have been tangled up with them, there's one other thing I remember.

It was a little bit later on.

Another three winters flew by, and three magnificent springs, with Mama getting sicker and sicker from her gallbladder, our herds growing a little bit bigger, and our cashmere fetching such extraordinary prices that Papa traded in our old car for a new one. To everyone's surprise, Anra's mother scared up another man, so Anra stayed mostly with me. Li Po was shacked up at their place, and Mrs. Ulantsetseg was expecting an *erliiz* with him.

And just as little Baldam was first seeing the light of day, a celebration was held in our *somon* House of Culture. There wasn't actually anything to celebrate, but the presidium had decided the building wasn't safe anymore, since even after the men repaired it, a piece of the roof fell in again, so it had to be torn down. But first, to keep people from being too sad about it, the presidium organized a farewell celebration there.

Me and Anra had the children practice "My Steppe Stretching into the Distance," "Good Altan's Horse," and other favorites from our *aimak*. Anra played the *morin khuur* all night, and the women cooked pot after pot of *buuz* and pailfuls of velvety milk tea. Two of the girls in my class had been doing *nugaralt* since they were little, and snake women are always a big favorite with everyone, so we went back and forth between our singing and their routines. It was a great night. The little girls twisted and bent themselves all around, grown-ups and kids alike watching them with bated breath, and a lot of *somon* business got taken care of to boot.

I was one of the VIPs of the whole affair. I put almost the whole program together, so most of the time I was onstage, watching over the kids and just generally keeping an eye on things.

There was no way Oyuna was going to get away from *me*.

I didn't think anyone from my family would come—they aren't much into this sort of thing—but then I noticed her, all the way in the back, on a bench in the corner. She had to have seen me, so I knew there must be a reason why she hadn't come up to talk. And there was.

Oyuna sat all bunched up in the corner, Naima's arms around her waist, the two of them whispering back and forth. I pictured Nara and the way that she had ended up, and purple spots danced before my eyes. It was all I could do not to go running over and yank Oyuna by the hair, but I caught myself in time.

I might've spoiled something and she would've clawed my eyes out. No. I let it be.

Two months later, when I went back to the *ger* for the summer, Oyuna and Naima had already told everyone. Papa gave his consent, and Mama hugged them and started right in with the wedding plans and practical matters like housing and so on. All was well with us again.

It was obvious that Nara had to be there. Oyuna insisted the most. I'd never really thought much of her, but now I saw her fight for her sister like a tiger. It was agreed that Oyuna and Naima would set up a *ger* by our parents for now. Naima liked Papa so much, I don't think he felt any pull to go home, and we were glad to have Oyuna stay with us.

She had grown up to be beautiful.

Papa said she looked something like Magi might've looked. But he only said so to me, and he whispered it in my ear, so that Mama wouldn't hear.

He was right.

She was the only one who took after him, so he had a right to be proud.

Naima could also brag. A young, beautiful, stately bride like her was a sight to behold. Naima was the same age as Magi would've been. In two springs he would be thirty.

Grandma always said that young bucks weren't for any woman who was serious. Maybe for fun, for a start, but when it comes to marrying, a woman needs someone of substance. Same goes for a man. Let him bide his time. Then he can look forward to a young maid for the rest of his life. All of Chingis Khan's wives were much younger than he was, people these days have got it all wrong, Grandma complained. She would've been happy for my sister. Though Oyuna had nothing on her: Grandpa was older than Grandma by a good twenty years.

I never knew him. Neither did Mama. Even Papa only knew him from Grandma's stories and a few vague memories.

It was a joyful summer. Naima and Oyuna were always fooling around, racing horses and whatnot, but they also put in a lot of work.

Oyuna embroidered Naima's old *dels* until they shone with color like the flowery steppe in spring. Like a true wife, she took over the job of taking care of his clothes from Mama, and got up in the morning before him each day to make sure he had everything ready, and for his part, Naima wouldn't let her do any hard work. If she carried so much as a pail of water, he'd yell at her to put it down.

In the evening they would sit and whisper in each other's ear, like that time at the House of Culture, and go on and on about what it was going to look like in their new *ger*. Sometimes I caught them necking, but they never did it in front of us. After everything I had been through, I saw that it could be different.

Those two are going to love each other all their lives, Ariuna said once when she came to visit Mama.

And Burkhan knew, even then, it was true.

Nara was there for the wedding in the end. By that time she was no longer living with Hiroko. Shartsetseg took her to see Purev, and he and Erka had taken her on.

After their great success, the famed brothers from our *somon* had gone bankrupt, so in the end the former shoe repair shop turned auto parts outlet became a *guanz* after all.

Apparently Nara was doing as well as I had done. Shartsetseg wasn't about to put up another girl again, so Nara had a little room of her own behind the kitchen in Erka and Purev's new *guanz*.

I couldn't wait to talk to her.

I'd never been so curious and excited as I was on the day she was due to arrive. I couldn't even stay in bed, so I put on my fanciest *del* and fixed myself up nice.

Papa teased me that just in case I spotted a groom, one girl was all he intended to marry off today. But Nara was closer to me than anyone else in the world. Who else should I get dressed up for if not her?

It was an awkward homecoming.

Nara just stared at the ground, then rushed in to Mama's side at the stove. The whole festive atmosphere went flat as a camel's hump in a hungry year.

All the revelry meant nothing in comparison to a single word of Nara's, a single glance from her. But she didn't give me a thing. Until that evening.

The first thing she asked about was her children at school. Some of the ones she taught were gone, but most of them I had still, so I tried to tell her as much as I could without leaving anything out. Then she asked if the headmaster let teachers bring orphans home on vacation now, but that I didn't know. I told her about Anra, and how Uregma Ulantsetseg had had a baby with a Chinaman but nobody held it against her since that was the only man she could dig up, and about the celebration and how I'd seen Oyuna in the corner with Naima. Nara gave me a sly grin and asked if I had anyone. I shook my head. What a disgrace, Nara said, tossing her head toward Oyuna. The two of us broke down in laughter. We were both older than the bride.

The wedding was magnificent. People talked about it for weeks.

We cooked for several days and for several days we ate. All of our uncles and aunts were there, except Hiroko and Shartsetseg; all our male cousins except Jargal; every single one of the female cousins begat by our clan; and lots of others besides. Anra came with her mother and little Baldam; all of Oyunbat's family was there; Batu, Davja, and Gerla; Maidar and Munkhtsetseg; and people kept arriving the second and third day as well.

The young couple got plenty of gifts, so Oyuna had an easy time setting up the household. Then they raised the *ger,* the guests slowly drifted off, and a blessed silence settled back over the steppe.

No sooner did Mama's worries about the wedding arrangements end than she went to work sewing little boots and a *del* for the baby, till Oyuna started scolding her that she was going to jinx her. But that was the only thing keeping Mama afloat.

We could all see how yellow and bent she'd become. She was in and out of the hospital constantly. They wanted to keep her there, but we knew that that would kill her, so we only let her go when the pain was at its worst. After the wedding, she was laid up for several weeks. She was hardly allowed to eat anything, and all of the food we ate in the *ger,* except for dry noodles and rice, was off limits to her. Papa couldn't take it anymore, and so one day we climbed in the jeep, lined the back with blankets so she would be able to lie down, and drove to the hospital to bring her back.

The doctor just said it wouldn't be her fault if Mama didn't make it.

She thrust a sack of pills into Papa's hand, and I held Mama up as we walked down the stairs.

Oyuna had worries enough of her own and Nara was back in the City now, so I was saddled with Mama. At least she could eat by herself, unlike Grandma, but otherwise it was the same. The same not moving, constant sleeping, and nagging reminders. Papa would come home early and head straight for Mama's bed, but death was just prowling around. It would still have to wait a long time before it could come for Mama.

What finally snapped her out of it was Oyuna's baby.

It was a boy. Everyone congratulated Naima, and Oyuna too, for not inheriting Mama's bad luck. Mama caught a second wind when she became a grandmother. She sprang to life like a jack-in-the-box and began to take charge like the old days. She was young again.

She had the whole *ger* under control, including the baby, and for the first time in my life I felt like I was just taking up space. Everyone in my family was important somehow except me. I was the only worthless one in the bunch, and the years when the gossip starts to spread about unmarried women were just around the corner.

I knew I had no choice but to try again. Try again and trust that this time things would work out.

Waiting for a moment when I was alone in the *ger,* I lit two candles, and, holding our cool stone Burkhan in my hands, I made a wish.

I left a note on the table and took some *khuushuur* in a sack.

Then I rode to the *somon* center.

Sooner or later there's always someone heading to the City. I didn't want to have to explain. I was twenty-four years old.

I slipped a letter under the headmaster's door telling them to find somebody else to teach their kids. I wasn't going to end up an old maid for their sake. I already knew every spinster in the *somon.*

And so for the second time in my life I saw the two majestic towers of the Ulaanbaatar power plant rising out of the haze, and an hour away I could already smell the intoxicating stench of smoke, born in the stoves of thousands of *gers* and the boiler rooms of hundreds of proud Soviet prefab apartment blocks. I stepped out into that huge gray dusty pot and went to where the market was.

My feet took me there on their own. My head wasn't thinking.

It was filled with the sounds of metal and skin, the market's sounds of men trying out saddles and chains while boys ran pieces of wood over the corrugated metal that surrounds the asphalt lot, dividing it from the City, because whoever wants in has to pay, you've got to give a little something to the women bundled up at the gate for that pink admission ticket.

I had to walk a ways through the outskirts of the City. Towering girders and concrete ruins with twisted rusty wires slashed through the mist like wolf fangs. I clambered over pipes with people dozing inside them. It was still morning. Right about now, Erka and Purev would be starting to chop the carrots and cabbage for *baitsaani* salad. If I had gone back to them then, back to their warm, cozy lunchroom, there's a good chance I wouldn't be sitting here now. Probably I would be somewhere else. With somebody else.

People from Russia don't like our City. They say any City where there are years when not a tree turns green and there isn't a single street without cracks and treacherous drops in it is no City at all. I met a Russian man in our *guanz* once who said he'd never seen anything like it, and he had been to Europe and knew Russia like the old-timers here know their *aimaks*. He tossed me three hundred *tugriks* extra on top of the price of his soup, pulled me onto his lap, and said if I wanted that he'd get me out of this place. Then I had to go back to the kitchen, and by the time I came out with his milk tea he was gone. I told Erka. She just laughed. He said he was from Petersburg. That was my first time in the City.

The market was just opening, the vendors unloading cars crammed with boxes of T-shirts, jackets, knife sheaths, combs, dishes, gloves, smokes, horse harnesses, televisions, you name it. They set up their stalls, filled them with stuff, and stood beside them, rubbing their chilly hands. An old lady doddered around selling *khuushuur* out of a box, the vendors passing her on from one stall to the next.

I got tossed around like a hot potato too. Nobody had any work, but everyone kept slowing me down, trying to make conversation.

When evening came I gave Kulan a call. I hadn't forgotten the man I'd sat with under the fringe of the woven Chingis Khan, or that milk tea the morning after. By the time I got my nerve up, the paper with his number on it was so crumpled up I could hardly read it. I bet he was surprised I still had it. At first he just sort of mumbled and didn't really want to talk, but eventually a man came to the market gate for me, saying Kolya had sent him and I should come with him. He barely talked the whole way. We came to an old apartment block and he rummaged around for the keys in his satchel for a long time. It was dark and I was scared. As he unlocked the door I heard voices shrieking from inside. It turned out he had three little kids.

I said hello to his wife, lay down where he showed me, and fell fast asleep. At the market the next day they put me to work.

I stood by the entrance selling ice cream, and for another few *tugriks* a day I carried food and drinks to the vendors. It was just enough to survive.

I couldn't have eaten my fill for that much even in our *guanz*.

After a week I was skinny and filthy, since there was nowhere for me to wash, and Kulan slammed the phone down on me every time when he heard it was me. I never would've thought it would be so easy to steal.

After noontime, when most of the people came, I could get away with hanging around for a pretty long time by the stall that sold bread rolls and cookies with icing. Long enough for me to swipe a couple of bags, two or three rolls off the counter, and something to give the little girl who was holding the ice cream for me. But I wasn't doing all that well.

At the end of the day, the people went off to their cozy prefab apartment blocks with their bags full of purchased goods, and the stallkeepers drifted off in twos and threes to drink.

I lingered by the gate. The stalls' covers slapped against their bare frames, crumpled papers fluttering in the wind. I slept out among the boxes by the rear gate. Crawled inside some bags and pressed my chilly hands between my thighs. There were always other people from the country who were homeless too. We'd chat a bit before going to sleep—who came from what region and that sort of thing.

I often got offers to go with men. I was young and at first glance obviously from the country. Runny-eyed, they took me by the hand with trembling fingers. Their crusty lips all asked for the same. Sometimes I would just say no and sometimes I'd have to wrestle free and run away. Their shameful words carried to me on the wind.

I was there about two weeks when I ripped one of my *del* sleeves all the way down its length. I had a nice little stash of cookies up my sleeve, when suddenly I felt fingers snatching at me from behind. I started to run and that's when it happened. My sleeve tore open, the cookies flew out, and I fell into the vendor's clutches. Then a few more people joined in, and by the time I untangled myself, I had blood bubbling out my nose and drops streaming down my head onto my tattered *del.* I didn't sell anything that day or the next. No one wants to buy ice cream from a blood-covered slob, and I couldn't steal anymore either. I had to come up with something else.

Nara had never ceased to be my dearest sister, and the only reason I didn't stop in on her right away was out of awkwardness or whatever.

That's what I kept telling myself all the way to Erka's *guanz*—she would know where Nara was. But even that wasn't certain. Strange rumors had started to spread since I saw her at Oyuna's wedding. Mama probably heard them from Shartsetseg, and Burkhan knows where she dug them up. Supposedly Nara was running around with men. Everyone at home acted like they didn't believe it, but I could tell it was eating away at Mama's and Papa's insides.

I think Papa blamed himself for letting his knife lie that night. They had taken his daughter away, and all he did was wave his blade at them over the stove. Nothing was said aloud. I didn't believe it either. But I didn't want to walk into the *guanz* and not find Nara there. Maybe that was why my feet took me to the market first. But now I needed help. I only hoped the whole thing was just jealous talk on Shartsetseg's part.

Nara wasn't there. Erka gave me a number for her, then yelled at me for just disappearing like that for five long years, and for being all rumpled and smelly now. She said Nara had been a very conscientious worker, and asked if I wanted to take her place. I could have her room, she said, and the little girls would wash the pots, all I would do is supervise. I needed work. I needed money. Someone who wasn't me said no. It was me and it wasn't me. I regretted it right away, but Erka considered it settled and I sensed it was time to go. Outside it had gotten cold and the lights on the buses shone in the dark like human eyes.

Seeing the City at nighttime is like seeing innards at work. A few lamps flicker up and down the street, but the main square is the only place with any real light. There's always action in the City. The fancy jeeps of the rich jostle with dozens of beat-up secondhand cars. Pool tables outdoors, even at night, are thronged with men who never sleep. The bumpy sidewalk is covered with gaping black holes and open sewers, sighing with heat and the deep breathing of sleepers. Bundled figures huddle under overhangs and in alcoves.

I walked along the main road, avoiding the shadows with clenched fists. I walked with the wind, which pushed and shoved me, smelling of gas and oily grit. I walked along with the wind, which didn't smell anything like it did in the Red Mountains.

Where else on earth is there this kind of wind? Where else is there a city so fierce it strips *gers* of their felt covers and dresses them in cracked concrete? So high it touches the clouds and so vast it stretches into the endless sacred steppe? A city whose dawn is bloody with the spears of endless ranks and whose dusk is crimson red with a five-pointed star. That night was one of pride. The City of Khans was raining dirt and hurling stones. Nara's house of ill repute was nowhere to be found.

I gave Nara a call with the phone from the little boy in front of the *guanz*. Day after day, he squatted there on the sidewalk, trying to push his crackly phone on everyone who passed. The voice on the other end cut off and then went looking for Nara, I guess; the line was quiet a long time. I peeked nervously at the little boy, adding up the minutes with a look of satisfaction as he waited for my coins.

Nara spoke fast and confusingly. When she said five minutes, I didn't know if she meant on foot, by horse, or by car. I forgot to ask. After an hour of trudging around, I finally found it. I was back on the main road, in sight of Erka's *guanz*.

One look and it was obvious what it was. The doorway glowed red, with a big, painstakingly lettered sign over it that said DIVAAJIN, and some fancy cars sat in front with women milling around them: two in friendly conversation, one frantically throwing herself at a man strolling slowly past, paying her no attention, and another two, under a neon sign, gripping each other by the hair and tugging savagely back and forth. Their lipstick was smudged across their faces like battle scars, their eyes shrunken to tiny black dots glittering with rage, their legs spread in fighting stance, luxurious lace spilling out from under their short skirts.

Nara stood hidden in shadow next to the doorway. We hugged. She took me by the arm and the two of us stepped inside. Then up a steep flight of stairs, a woman's shrill laugh stabbing into my temples; the banister writhed like a red-hot snake, the lights receding into the distance, then merging into a starry sky sprinkled with shiny pebbles, and then again swelling larger and larger, and I thought I was going to burn up, my *del* was starting to burn me, baking into my skin. I wanted out. Out of my skin, down the stairs, I couldn't breathe, and Nara's fingers were cutting into my arm like chains, and they kept dragging me higher and higher, into the loud, bright, heavenly light. Then I said to myself, Enough. I remember a regular *click click* of feet on stairs. There must've been two of them dragging me. Their footsteps thudded on the floorboards like a countdown, the lights and noise turning murky, sloshing together, the ceiling sinking lower and lower, dropping on me like a hammer. Then the sound of a click. The light switch in Nara's room, I guess.

When I woke up, Nara was gone. From the other side of the wall came the regular creak of a bed and a grunting like the animals made when Papa didn't shoot them right and the blood ran into their lungs. Other than that, it was totally quiet. Then slowly the sounds started coming to life. One by one, like the lights coming on in the City at night. I heard the chattering voices of women, then cars outside, then the tinkle of music from far away, then creaking stairs, someone going up or down, and then the door handle rattled. I shut my eyes again. Nara said I must've been at the market more than just a week or two. I was sure I hadn't, but for me to be that wiped out, she said, it must've been a month or two, at least. She insisted. I was too weak to argue. For a few days I just laid in bed, counting the spiders and the cracks like spider webs fanning across the ceiling. They were different every time. My dreams were full of nets. I trapped animals in them.

Gradually I learned to recognize all of Nara's men. By the slap of their bodies, their breathing, their whispers and violence.

Some got it over with fast. No words, no long creaking. Those were the ones Nara liked. Some of them would talk first, swearing and showering her with abuse, and Nara had to take off her clothes and show them her stuff for a long time before they got down to business. Then the room next door would thunder and the two on the other side of the wall would get mixed up in my dreams. The ones with requests were the worst. Most men didn't have any, they just came to do their thing and walked away satisfied, with a quiet grin on their face. But some did. Those were the ones that kept coming back, and Nara knew how it would be and what worked the best and the fastest, and didn't have to bother with any guessing or experiments.

Volodya, a sweet Russian man, like the ones who used to stop by our *ger* a few times a year and who sat at the table in back in our *guanz* around noontime, would lose his temper every time. I don't know why, but he'd always get really rough and Nara's back would be all bruised. He was the worst. Afterwards Nara would have to sleep on her stomach for weeks, which she couldn't stand since she was little, and the other men would get turned off by her back being such a mess and go to another girl.

Ravdan was just the opposite. He always came with a bag full of all sorts of gadgets and props, and afterwards Nara would tell me about what new things he had brought this time and we would have a laugh. Ravdan wanted to be tortured, so Nara tortured him.

Nara hated the work at the *guanz.* She said Erka butted in all the time and wouldn't let her do anything her way.

Plus she slept on the ground floor and at nighttime the street men would come and bang on her window, so every day she lived in fear of the night to come. She couldn't get to sleep, so she'd lurch around like a drunk at work, and when darkness fell and Erka left, the shadows of the night traffic and the men outside her window would flicker across the walls of her room. She could hear the clink of bottles and the vodka swishing inside. That was if she had the window open a crack, so she could breathe.

As for Erka and Purev, she tore them to shreds. She couldn't stand it when Erka ran her greasy hands through her hair. Me, I adored the motherly touch of her soft, open palms. Going to the market with Purev to pick out the meat was a pain in the neck for Nara. When I went I felt important, and haggling was fun for me, but to Nara it just stank, and whenever her elbow brushed against the meat dangling on the hooks, it made her feel sick to her stomach.

Nara sat on the bed with me, talking, and every once in a while she would stop and stroke her hair, and I couldn't take my eyes off of her.

I wondered about Hiroko. When Nara left with Mama to stay with her, my sister was a wild thing, and no one could say any different. What went on with her and Jargal was one of the strangest things that ever happened in our family. We had always been a sensible clan. People were born and grew up, the men went with the herd and the women's duties were in the *ger,* and the winters went by, and people stooped lower and lower and then went to sleep for eternity, and the clan continued to blossom on through its descendants, who went racing around the grown-ups until then they were divided into the ones who followed the herd around and the ones who cradled their babies in their arms.

Growing up, I only ever heard stories about wild women. Maybe Grandma was a witch—at least that's what we had come to believe more and more since she had died—but she never did anything that didn't make sense. She could be mysterious at times, since she knew more than we did and she had the power, but until she got old and started forgetting to salt the *khuushuur* meat, she carried out all her domestic and other duties as expected.

Nara was mysterious in a different sort of way. Whatever it was got into her, she ceased to be one of us—one of us women who knew their place: when it was proper to speak and where the driest *argal* was, what to do with a child who screamed all the time, and how to make milk tea as smooth as a newborn camel's tummy. Nara knew nothing of any of that.

I don't know what went on at Hiroko's, or even where Hiroko lived, but one thing for sure was the person she returned to us wasn't Nara. I realized that as Nara sat there on the bed with me, talking about all those awful years wiping Formica tabletops and slopping rice into chipped bowls, and Purev, who was so fat there was no room to move in the kitchen, and his wife, with her pudgy red cheeks and dirty fingers, which she kept dipping into the pots to sample the slop that always tasted the same anyway—of rancid fat and cheap root vegetables.

For the first time in my life I felt like I couldn't relate to Nara. When I thought back on how me and Erka had gone and picked out new tablecloths only for Nara to curse in disgust as she scrubbed them; how we bought a vase to put on the counter and filled it with fresh flowers every day only so Nara could break it, instead of changing the flowers, so she wouldn't have to squint through their scruffy twigs all day, as she put it. When I thought back on all of that, my eyes swelled up with tears. And Erka said such nice things about her.

Suddenly Nara exploded. Them and their do-goody goodness, taking pity on the poor girl from the country. I couldn't take it, don't you understand? The word *understand* she screamed.

She'd never given me such a nasty look in her life. She'd never been so distant.

I pulled the blanket up to my eyes, feeling the wound that Nara's words had opened between us like the chop of an ax, and with each moment of silence it was yawning into a chasm that neither of us would ever be able to cross. I knew all those words and what they meant, but I couldn't see why she was talking that way. What had anyone done to her? But I held my tongue. After all, I was the older one, how could I not understand the little sister I loved? Today I know that nothing that horrible happened.

Back then all I knew was that to tell her how all those things had been new and interesting to me—how to work had been my dream come true and how, with Biamkhu, I had known true happiness—would've been no use.

To say that being a cook in a good *guanz* is better than lying with men for money wouldn't've gotten me anywhere. In a couple of months, I was over all of that know-it-all talk. We started to get along again. And little did we know that it was men we had to thank for it.

But one thing I admired about my sister even then. Even though she probably felt just as rotten inside as I did, she was the hottest thing ever to grind her heels into the Ulaanbaatar grit. And she showed that same undaunted spirit later on as well. In spite of all the rash and angry words that spilled from them, her lips stood out red and full on her alabaster face, her eyebrows plucked into graceful, provocative arches. Her neck was powdered too, but not like the cheap girls that knocked on men's car windows at night and pressed their breasts against the glass. They looked like Chinese opera masks, white faces plunked down on top of their dirty brown necks. Lipstick smeared all over the place, the smell of their unwashed bodies wafting through their T-shirts. Nara knew what she was doing. When she blinked those long, blackened lashes of hers, it was like the world had died and been born again. Her eyes weren't the dark needles of coal that all the rest of us had, but the creamy seeds of the cedar. She wore her hair long, and it tumbled down her back in waves like dunes of desert sand. The fish merchant from Verkhoyansk had done his part.

But a pretty face does not a woman make. That was according to Grandma, but also according to the men who came for Nara. She told me. She said slender legs, wide hips, and breasts firm as the bags packed with berries we used to gather at the foot of the Red Mountains every fall—that's why men lined up to see her more than anyone else. What did I know. What did I care.

I remembered all those obnoxious boys who used to make fun of Nara's hair when we were back in school. And the fat, mean Buryat teachers who taught them to do it.

Now the guys that belonged to women like them were wrapped around a single lock of Nara's lush blonde mane. They kept coming back, and they paid for it too.

I was tired, starving, and achy, but nothing really serious. I stayed in bed a couple days and that was it. Nara took care of me the way Soldoo had taken care of her Little One. When it was time to eat and Nara didn't have anyone in at the moment, she would prop my head up with pillows and feed me the fattiest mouthfuls of *khuurag* so I would get straightened out quick. No one's going to want you like this. Look how skinny you are, she'd say, wrapping her fingers around my arm. See? Nara's wrists were as big around as my ankles and it wasn't as if she was fat. Gradually it dawned on me that Nara took it for granted that I was going to stay there and spend my nights in a cramped little room, hopping in and out of bed with men. Mainly, I didn't want the two of us to lock horns again, so I let her go on thinking that for as long as I could.

Nara didn't get mad when I left. She had company at the time, so she couldn't even see me out. While the man was getting undressed, she just quick poked her head out the window and cheerfully waved good-bye. For a long time after that, my head was full of Nara no matter where I was—working at the candy stand, cooking in the school cafeteria, stamping letters at the post office, babysitting the Russian lady's blond little Nikolai, tearing tickets in a nylon jacket and cutoff gloves for the bus from Bömbögör to Bökhiin Örgöö and back.

I slept where I could for a couple of *tugriks*, which turned out to be almost everywhere. I discovered all of these things bit by bit. Bit by bit, more and more things became clear. Maybe I began to understand a little what Nara had said; maybe not. But no one ever laid eyes on me in Erka's *guanz* again. I couldn't do something my sister thought was stupid, with someone my sister talked about the way she talked about Purev. There was no way. But to do something that I considered revolting, that I could do.

A few months later I found myself wandering in the direction of the inviting neon lights: Divaajin. It was late morning, the door was locked, and the shade was down on Nara's upstairs window. I knocked. There was a sound of shuffling footsteps slowly growing louder. Her foreign features were caked in makeup. Peering out through the crack in the door was a familiar and yet foreign face, the face of my aunt Shartsetseg.

I'd suspected all along that she was up to something fishy. I'd wondered where Mergen got the money for his daily vodka sprees and why she never took me to the meat plant where Purev said she worked. I didn't wonder long, though. There wasn't time. The next day, after a good night's sleep, my aunt put me to work.

She showed me everything. The whole place, all the girls, the women from the tap downstairs, and the room I was assigned. Dark and stinking of men. A bed with a shabby, faded sheet, a lamp with a red-and-yellow shade.

Don't shout, be nice, always get the money up front. Those were Shartsetseg's rules.

The only ones she had.

I learned that early on, after the first couple of days. It was my fourth shift. I was worn out and achy all over. Nara said it takes a body a few days to get used to. First it's painful, then it's disgusting, and after a week or two, give or take, you learn to be two places at once. You're there and you're not. Nara said she'd often borrow one of Anra's horses and go for a ride in her favorite hills. She also went to see Khuchtei, a quiet, tongue-tied orphan boy she'd brought to the *ger* the summer before the headmaster put a stop to it, and when it lasted longer she would picture everyone from our *ger*, one by one, and wonder how they were doing.

I think Jargal also wound his way into her family scenes. I respect Aunt Hiroko, but there was something in Nara's eyes that never went away. Something of those wilted wedding flowers she used to wind around the *ger* poles.

The last one I had on that fourth day was a shriveled little man. He didn't have any special requests, so I just lay there listening as the City awoke outside my window, the cars zooming past one by one as the traffic grew thicker and thicker, and the cries of the sleepy vendors drifted through the streets.

The guy was on top of me doing his thing, when the next thing I knew he was on his feet and halfway out the door. Wait, wait, I said. That seemed to startle him, and he grabbed for the handle and the door slammed shut with a crash. I flew out after him, and I was running down the stairs when I saw Yellow Flower holding him by the corner of his coat while he twisted and groaned in protest. Finally he broke free, leaving Shartsetseg grasping at empty air. Outside, Dorji and Batmunkh, the two guys we kept around to handle weasels like this one, gave him a good going-over. The next day in front of the door you could still see the red drops that ran off of him as he scurried away.

My aunt chewed me out pretty good.

There was no one else waiting on me, so she took me into her little room under the stairs and gave me the lecture. When she was done, she repeated her three rules and hustled me out the door, saying to go wash up and get some sleep. She wiped the smeared lipstick off my face with a swipe of her hand and waited for me to get lost. But I didn't.

I just stood there, rooted to the spot. My feet were frozen like a weak horse's hoofs in the frost, and I gaped at her the way country kids do when a stranger comes to their *ger*. Yellow Flower, my aunt, who had cooked us *buuz* when Magi died and Papa was sucking vodka straight out of the bottle because his hands were shaking so badly he could barely untie a quiet horse.

The aunt who had laughed with us and knew thousands of spooky tales, and when Nara found a wounded bird she had helped us make a little pen and let us pinch off bits of our supper meat to feed it. If my mother had seen, she would've tossed it out in back of the *ger* and me and Nara with it. Yellow Flower. If not for her, I wouldn't be a brothel girl but a teacher in the *somon* school, with a husband, a *ger*, and kids by now, and a set of shallow bowls and embroidered bedspreads of my own. If not for her, I'd be spending my days doing arithmetic with first graders and drawing letters in blue-lined notebooks. Or I would've put up a third *ger*, next to Oyuna and Naima's, and I'd be searching the hills for my flock by the sound of their bleating, and at night I'd stretch out on my very own bed without some filthy stranger running his paws all over me and interrupting my young dreams with abuse and false endearments.

If Shartsetseg hadn't invited me to the City, I would never have had the courage to go on my own, and in fact she was the one who gave me the idea. Every girl should love her first guy, and the whole starry universe should glisten in the sweat of their childlike bodies, and the moon should rock like a cradle in their awkward girlish and boyish gestures. I knew that now. There was no way to go back.

Mergen wasn't a bad man, I didn't have any regrets about that. The only thing he left behind was a bottomless black hole. Biamkhu was the first to tumble into it, then all the rest who let me sleep by their side during all those fruitless months of searching the City for work, till once again I knocked on the accursed door of this place and the powdered face of Shartsetseg peered out of the darkness. I doubt anyone else could've plucked me up from the Red Mountains and slapped me down on the asphalt rug of Ulaanbaatar's main square as graciously as my aunt.

I couldn't go back anymore. After months chasing my luck for the second time around, invoking the smooth-worn figures of the gods in moments of weakness and squeezing my knees together at night, so at least they couldn't touch me in my dreams, I couldn't just pack up my Russian lime makeup and crumbly pink lipstick, and step over the threshold of our eight-sided *ger* with an apologetic smile again. I'd tried my luck and no one could say that I went about it wrong. Maybe when I went back to the City and headed straight for the market. One phone call and I'd have had a place to sleep and something warm in my stomach in the morning, and no one would've asked for a thing in return. There were people I knew. I'd had friends from the start. Erka and Purev were tremendous to me from the moment we met. Nothing stood in the way of my having a *guanz* of my own. Just a little nudge from Burkhan and I could've had rosy red cheeks and a stack of pots and two braided girls working under me, just like Erka. But what did I do but walk out, call Nara from the little boy's phone, and go to see her. No one said that's how it had to be. There was a time when I wanted to run a lunchroom of my own, with sparkling brown linoleum and colorful posters on the walls. Hopping around twelve hours a day in the muggy steam, which condensed into tiny drops and slid down the walls, leaving a greasy trail on the tiles. There was a time. I left Erka standing with folded arms and never went back again. It was over. I didn't look back even once. Until now.

All the jobs I did lasted too short for me to learn them, and too long not to stop being fun. But the post office was the only one I left on my own. I couldn't keep up with the packages, and I still had to scrub down the hall every night and soap the counters once a week. The woman who was head of my department couldn't stand me. It was too much to handle, and the money wasn't keeping me there. I made twice as much at the market, and I didn't mind freezing all day in just a light jacket and boots with no fur. I got thrown out for stealing two pairs of gloves and a scarf from Naran, my employer. Naran gave a little sigh when he said he'd already found someone to replace me for the next day. We'd got along great till he nabbed me. He couldn't see why the money he paid me wasn't enough.

I kept the gloves and sold them to a lady at the hairdresser's. By then I wasn't working for Naran anymore.

They liked me at the hairdresser's, so they hired me to sweep hair. Sometimes it was sad.

Young girls' long, thick hair should be protected. Like the mountain chamois, or the monastery of Erdene Zuu. They don't know what's right or wrong, these silly little girls. Right away they go and get all crazy over something, then the next thing you know they're in tears.

Every other day some girl would come in saying she wanted it short, and before the coins had left her hand and they'd pulled the plastic sheet off of her, she'd start sobbing uncontrollably and have to be escorted out. That was also my job. Telling them it was all right and comforting them with lies. Some of the women would slip me a couple coins on the side. I didn't cut their hair, but I dried it for them afterwards, and I'd tell them all sorts of stories from home.

These women had never warmed a premature lamb under their *del,* and wouldn't've known an eight-year-old mare from a three-year-old gelding, so whatever popped into my head I could tell them and they were entertained.

That money was also the reason I got fired. They didn't want me doing well. They weren't about to do the country girl any favors. I wasn't ashamed in front of them. Not by then I wasn't, and maybe they didn't like the smell of that either.

There were other things that didn't work out. There's always a catch. In everything.

For example, brothel women. They get more money, but they have to put up with all sorts of stuff, and they can't tell anyone what they do if they want to get any respect.

Shartsetseg's been covering it up for years now. Hard to say if my mother has ever suspected. You can keep a secret forever, even from those closest to you.

We must've stood there an hour, my aunt and me, staring at each other in that little room under the stairs, clouds of dust sifting down from the cracks between the ceiling boards. I wondered what I was doing there, and she must've sensed that nothing could make me leave until I'd made up my mind to go. Her lips were locked tight, and her normally dainty nose reminded me of a beak. Underneath the makeup was the face of a hardened old woman. A woman whose womb was parched dry, incapable of life, which explained the bitterness in her eyes, the lack of compassion for the young girl standing here now, wasting her time for nothing.

That was what I thought, wasting her time, but actually, she just didn't how to begin.

I was bewitched by that face; my blood ran through it too, and I searched for myself in it. Someone waved teasingly at me from the other shore. My aunt thought I'd come for a story. For a piece of my mother that had been snatched up along the way and haunted me as a child.

I relived that moment when my mother hung by a slender thread, my heart pounded in alarm, and standing in front of our *ger* was a man who wasn't our father, and my mother wanted him. Only Yellow Flower knew about that. From my mother and from him, and she thought I was going to stand there under the stairs till she made up her mind to come clean. What she knew, she would tell, she finally said.

Mergen came from Inner Mongolia, the southern part of my country, carving deep into the territory of our age-old archenemies, the vast and fiendish Middle Kingdom. Inner Mongolia is a province of China, stolen from us by the sneaky Chinese, who pass it off as their own. The only Chinamen there, though, are the tens of thousands of bastards that our women who are enslaved there give birth to every year. Every Mongolian woman there is forced to marry a Chinaman, and their kids are officially Chinese.

There's fewer and fewer of us in Inner Mongolia every day, and not a thing we can do about it. There are too many Chinese settlers, and the days when the Mongols ruled from the saddle are long since buried under the Gobi's golden dunes.

People from Inner Mongolia aren't too popular around here. It goes without saying. In a way they're just like us, but the danger of fraternizing with a Chinese bastard, an impure *erliiz,* is so great that it's better to just avoid them. That's what everyone says. I remembered Davja, Liu Fu, and little Gerla, with her tiny Mandarin cheeks. I can do without the Chinese myself. They double-cross whoever they can, don't let in outsiders, and multiply like bedbugs. But Liu Fu wasn't a bad man, and they still ran him out of the country, and Davja's been on her own with Gerla now for years. Now she's all dried up and spent, but nobody wanted her even before. No man wants to be gossiped about. No man wants to make a laughingstock of himself by raising a daughter that advertises her origin like a red lantern over the door.

I was pretty lucky. Eventually I grew out of my Chinese features, and since Papa was an upright Mongol who swallowed his pride and who no one dared to challenge, nobody pushed any dog meat on me except for in my school years.

Mergen looked much more Chinese. His face was typical *erliiz,* plus he went bald early on. Which is always a guaranteed sign. Mama's and Papa's clans were both pure, from healthy, untainted stock on both sides, with an unconcealed attitude of contempt for the Chinese.

I already knew the story of how my parents had met from before. No secrets there. Grandma used to grumble about Mama's lowly origins, as though she suspected her of marrying my father so she could move up in the world and Papa just came with the package. But I trusted that Mama was sincere as far as that went, and even if I didn't, it was still better than the other way around.

For a young, rich girl to marry a poor man would be a disgrace. That would've been just Papa's luck.

But the story my aunt told was different.

According to her, Tuleg, my father, wore Alta, my mother, down. He wanted her badly and wouldn't take no for an answer. Mira, my grandma on my mother's side, who I didn't know nearly as well as Dolgorma, was unbending. Mama wasn't particularly opposed to the idea—Papa was a kind man and knew how to handle a herd—so they wed. Before a year had passed, Magi was born and Alta became a mother, and therefore honorable in every sense of the word.

She had nothing to complain about, Shartsetseg went on, and I could tell from the tone of her voice, she must've envied Mama even then.

One thing my parents were never was poor.

No matter how bad a year it was, they never had to go begging. Just the opposite, in fact, they gave loans to everyone else, and as a result they always had a pretty big say in the area. When Magi was maybe a year old, Papa went into business.

For the first and last time. Eventually he learned that money runs even faster than sheep and went back to his herds, but like so many others around that time he figured he'd give it a try. He imported radios and insulated wire from China, which at that time were just beginning to cost less than the Russian ones. He took long trips to Urumchi, and sometimes even as far as Peking, while Mama was left alone.

Mergen wasn't some traveling fishman, Shartsetseg said with a grin and a wink, who stopped by the *ger* for a bite to eat one sunny summer morning. He was the man who Tuleg was in business with.

It went pretty well to start with, and since Mergen was going to pass through on his next trip anyway, Chinese or no Chinese, Tuleg invited him to the *ger*. At first Alta was against him having any dealings with the Chinese at all, but it did bring in money, and Mergen was reliable and knew the territory, so it went on like that for some time.

The strangest part about it is that Tuleg was there the whole time and Mergen still got to Alta. He never came alone at first—that was out of the question—so Tuleg was always nearby. The two men would sit and talk business while Alta poured them milk tea and later, come evening, vodka.

My aunt shut her eyes for a moment and all of a sudden I pictured my mother, sitting in some hollow in a brier patch with her, pouring out her whole heart, all her secrets and forbidden thoughts, like me and Nara used to do. No, Mama couldn't have known. She would never have trusted a hussy for hire, an old, unscrupulous tramp, when it came to the sacred matters of love.

Every day of Shartsetseg's life, as far as I had seen, took everything human, everything fragile and defenseless that Mama must have felt for her Chinese Mongol lover, and drowned it in vice. Maybe my aunt was different back then. Like Nara before she met Jargal. Who knows which parts Mama actually told her and which parts Mergen only hinted at later on?

I wanted to ask, but I was afraid my aunt might shut down and I'd never get to hear the rest. So instead I left her alone a while, standing there with her eyes shut, maybe going over the day's receipts or regretting that she even brought it up in the first place. In a moment or two, she started back up.

This went on for several months, Mergen coming by with Papa every now and then. It was always the same. The two men would sit and talk long into the night. Mama never tried to interrupt, and besides, they wouldn't have let her. To give advice to any man, let alone in front of another one, was an act of disrespect, and Mama was always a stickler for manners.

Shartsetseg paused for a moment again, and I thought I saw a trace of contempt in the hard lines of her mouth.

The one thing a sorry woman like her had to be proud of. No one ordered her around.

Who would want to try?

Then Mama began to get careless, she said. It often begins that way. When she served them, her hands would tremble, making the bowls shake like a cold animal and the soup slosh over the edges.

The men were too busy talking to notice, till the day came when she spilled a bowl of boiling tea on Mergen. That was the first time he noticed her, according to Shartsetseg. Mergen told her himself, she smirked.

Papa yelled at her not to just stand there. Mama took the ladle and went out in front of the *ger,* where they kept a pail of cold water, and Mergen got up and went after her. That was their first time alone together.

When Mama told Shartsetseg about it, she said she never would've believed that a woman could go so soft over an ordinary man's hand. She took his hand in hers, dipped a cloth in the pail, and rubbed the back of his hand. Like this, said my aunt, making some crude circling motions. I could tell the way my mother did it must've been pretty different. Then she put the cloth back in the pail to soak and did it again. And again and again. She'd never seen such a beautiful hand on a man, she told my aunt.

Shartsetseg scoffed. A hand's a hand. But my mother went on and on about the veiny bluish bumps; about the knuckles, wrinkled in circles like the skull of a shrunken old man; about the hard, ridged nails and their big white half-moons; and I don't know what all besides. I only know what my aunt said. There was too much to remember it all. But from then on, Mama knew she couldn't keep fooling herself anymore. She was his.

Then Mergen slowly turned over his hand and the shine from his callused white palm was so bright it was like daybreak.

To me those hands were forever linked with the smell of tobacco and that one broad sweep of his that knocked me onto the couch. It still made me anxious sometimes even now. To someone those hands were beautiful. I shuddered. All I could remember was the trembling way they gripped my wrists, drunkenly damp and impatient. I couldn't get it out of my head the whole time my aunt was talking.

Mama ran her fingers over his palm and laid her hand in his. No, she just grazed it and jerked it back. Meanwhile the cloth slipped out of her hand and plopped onto the ground. As she bent over to pick it up, Papa came out of the *ger* and Mergen disappeared back inside. They left the next morning without a good-bye, and Mama was just counting the days, which dragged by slower than ever, and anyway it was more than clear that Papa would come home alone. That's how it was, and Mama thought of nothing else but the man whose name she didn't even rightly know, and his outstretched hand, which wove its way into all her fevered dreams.

After a week, Papa left, and another seven days later, seeing dust on the horizon, Mama assumed there must be some reason he'd had to come back sooner.

But it wasn't him. Papa was in over his head with work in China, and didn't return till after four long weeks of sweet celebration, which Mergen neatly arranged for by sending Papa off to the Xa-li-mu-xe River to clear up some business, while Dolgorma, who was still young at the time, was coincidentally away at a cousin's in Khovd for two months.

Shartsetseg said I was conceived during those weeks, which were the happiest weeks of my mother's life, and I owed my mother thanks, because some of her happiness from that time was tucked away inside me. When Mergen left, since my father could be coming home any day, Mama made him promise that they would do it again in the next three months. Mergen craved it as badly as she did, so less than two months later, Papa headed off again, almost as far as the last time, and the two of them were alone together again for days on end. It was also the first and last time that my mother asked Grandma Dolgorma to take her granddaughter away to visit her roots, and so Grandma set off west, cradling Magi in her arms, to see relatives my mother had never seen and had no desire to. Who knows why she really left, because Grandma—being sly as a snake, as Yellow Flower said—certainly wasn't naive enough to actually trust my mother. In short, Grandma's motives will forever be a mystery. Though she did manage to spice things up for Mama later on. Maybe that was why. I knew more than my aunt did about their feuds. My childhood had been full of them.

During those couple of weeks they carved out for themselves, Mergen and my mother managed the household in common. Mergen may've been *erliiz* by blood, but he knew livestock as well as any true Mongol.

Still, it was obvious it couldn't last for long.

No matter how trusting my father was, no man is going to leave his wife alone forever, and it got harder and harder for Mergen to convince him to take such long trips. Especially since he always had to find a way out himself. One day Papa told him no for the last time, and when Mergen tried to press him, he just dropped the whole thing once and for all and headed home.

The welcome he got was ice-cold. Mama wouldn't speak to him, let alone take his seed, but all the same her belly started rounding out again. Papa just assumed it was his and didn't give it a second thought, but talking to her was impossible, and slowly but surely Papa began to lose patience. Mama would go running out of the *ger* out of nowhere and slump down sobbing in front of the door. Papa knew pregnant women were sensitive, nothing wrong with that, but as Shartsetseg said, too much is too much.

One day he smacked my mother across the face, dragged her onto the bed, and said he wasn't letting her out of the *ger* until she could act like a proper woman again. Mama grit her teeth, turned her head to the wall, burrowed into the blankets, and stayed like that for three days. Finally Papa came and begged her to eat something, if not for her own sake at least for the baby. Mama agreed to get up, and everything went back to the way it was before. She spent hours staring off into nowhere, tears rolling down her cheeks, while one minute Papa comforted her and the next he just raged helplessly. One day Mama confessed the whole thing to him. All of it. Even the shining hands and how she sent Magi away with Dolgorma.

When she finished, she sat there, chin thrust forward defiantly, face apologetic yet proud, waiting for the first blow. She thought he was going to kill her. And he did punch her, according to Shartsetseg. She didn't even flinch. He slugged her across the face and walked out the door.

Mama heard him saddle his horse, then the fading thrum of hoofbeats, and then silence. That was just Papa's way. Instead of getting it over and done with and giving his wife a sound licking like most men would've done, he cleared out for a couple of days. Let her choose for herself.

It was up to her. She knew where to find Mergen. Magi wouldn't be any trouble, they'd already argued that out before, and Mama could always scrounge up some work. Mergen was a *naimaachin,* true, more a hustler than a man of the herd, but Mama was willing to live with that, according to my aunt.

And here's where I stop understanding, Yellow Flower said. I still don't believe the main reason was Mergen's, how shall we say, unclean origin? She smirked again. But that was how Alta explained it, and given how much she had told me already I didn't see why she would lie about that. Plus Mergen also nodded when I asked him about it later. He said that everyone would've condemned her.

That's what my aunt said. Me, I think she was just scared. It was just plain old ordinary fear of the unknown. She wasn't twenty anymore, so she gave herself the excuse that Papa was actually really nice and who knew how Magi would do with a new father. Plus Mergen *was* a Chinaman. I do agree with my aunt, though, that couldn't have been the main thing. Even if Mergen did nod when she asked if that was the reason. I don't trust him.

Mama was willing to pass me off as Papa's. She got down on her knees and swore to Grandma: May the midnight goblins carry me off, may I be gored by a raging bull, may the child be born without hands if it isn't mine and Tuleg's.

She stayed with my father. But Mergen kept coming to see her. Now and again.

Mama was furious at him for putting her in a dangerous spot, but still she always begged him to stay just one more night. In the morning she would run back and forth from the *ger* to his horse, throwing her arms around his shoulders and whispering sweetly in his ear. Mergen seemed to sense somehow when Papa wasn't home. People in love can do that sometimes, it's like they can smell it. Meanwhile the games that Mama was playing with Grandma grew more and more obvious every day.

Though the real decision was made when Papa rode off without a word of protest, it was as though every time Mergen left, Mama had to decide all over again. Still, Papa had won, once and for all, and he never left her alone again for any length of time. Not while she was young, at least. Papa returned home to a table spread from heaven, the *ger* so clean it sparkled, and Mama chirping away like a spring chick.

One day Mergen suggested the two of them spend a few days alone in the City. What better place to hole up? It wasn't a bad idea. But I was close to five by then, and I guess Mama just couldn't keep it up anymore. She was Papa's again, like it or not, and not even her heart could change that.

ZAYA

She packed up a few things, dropped the two of us off at school, but then went back, unsaddled the horse, drove to the *somon* and brought us home, and changed back into her house clothes. She never did make it to the City. But she'd already given Mergen my aunt's address, so he laid around Shartsetseg's place for days, sitting in the window with his cigarettes and booze, even when it was clearer than sunshine my mother wouldn't show up.

We got used to each other, Shartsetseg said, like she thought I'd be moved or something. At one point he was truly handsome, his features carved like a wooden *baatar*, his limbs like tree trunks, strong and hard.

"Why wouldn't I let him stay with me? I needed a man myself, and like I said, we didn't mind each other." That's how she put it, word for word, exactly just like that.

I was surprised she even felt the need to explain herself. I wouldn't have guessed it, coming from her.

But however you look at it, it was a pretty dirty trick.

No doubt she passed it off as sisterly solidarity that she'd taken on this huge burden, when all Mergen did was drink and squat around her apartment, taking money from her, and she didn't have the heart to kick the poor guy out. Not a word about how I had come and then she'd thrown me out.

Men are strange.

But I don't see things as harshly now.

I never used to understand how Mama could've loved such a stinking rotten drunk. And how he could've done such a thing to me. My aunt had told him who I was, he knew who he was dealing with, and it didn't stop him for a minute. It happened. I was young, it was a dark fall night, and Shartsetseg didn't give him much, apart from a little cash. He wasn't even that rough. I could've bitten and kicked him, and I didn't do any of that.

The room had gotten dark. My aunt brought out a long, thin candle, dribbled some wax on the bottom, and stuck it in a glass. She sank down into a soft, tattered armchair and I did the same across from her. A pouch of yellow knucklebones lay spilled out on the table between us, and I thought back to the ones that me and Nara used to have—I wonder what ever happened to them—and to Hiroko, who used to foretell the future using those very same bones. I bet my aunt knew all sorts of interesting things about her. But it looked like that was all I was going to get from her for now. Her thin legs, covered with purple blotches, jutted out from under her skirt. Wearily, she kicked off her slippers into the corner, laced her hands behind her head, took a few deep breaths, and slowly regained her usual air of self-assuredness, mouth pinched bitterly, with a look of amused detachment from everything that others wasted tears over. Finally, after a tiring night, it was time to get some sleep.

Nara had changed quite a bit in the months I'd spent trying out various jobs around the City.

The number of days we didn't share a laugh together grew, and there were times when one word was all it took and we'd both shrink into our shells. It was frightening how much she reminded me of Shartsetseg. Her smile had turned bitter, and suddenly it was like she had the answer to everything. Her tongue was like a razor.

She always dressed better than any of us. If Nara got a run in a stocking, she didn't bother to mend it; off it flew, into the corner, atop a growing heap of other practically new rejects. She only smoked select *tamkhi,* the long, skinny kind you couldn't get anywhere in Mongolia, and when Nara tossed her heavy locks, which she wound around a curling rod every afternoon, the air filled with a swooning scent so thick you thought you'd faint. When I suggested she might want to try something lighter and offered her my flask, she flew into a rage. That was the last time I tried to give her any tips. Even if her teeth were smudged with lipstick, or her tears made her mascara run, I kept it to myself.

Nara lived several lives at once, and each of them was so different it was like three women crashing together on a crowded street. Nara the lady for hire was a totally different person from Nara the wild thing, or the person I loved more than anyone else, the Nara of our childhood games. It was like she had lost herself somewhere. After all, a woman isn't some steppe lizard that changes colors out of nowhere. But that was what Nara was like. I think that Mama, Papa, Oyuna, and the Red Mountains were lost to her much sooner than they were to me. But she was still my one and only.

Yet I was forgetting too. What colors danced in the stallions' eyes when Papa brought in a new mare? Which camels did Papa have to beat to make them kneel for Mama? Even I couldn't say for sure anymore. But I knew they were all out there somewhere, I still had that inside me, and it never ceased being important to me, even after months of men banging almost everything out of my head except the desire to get out of here and my appetite for food, which was huge.

Ever since I started having these weird cravings I had a hunch, and when Nara saw the way I was stuffing myself, she asked me flat out. I was glad.

My first thought was I wouldn't be able to live on my own so I'd have to stay, at least for a while. Now it was for certain I'd never end up like Shartsetseg, and that lifted my spirits, so my last months here were happy ones, for the most part. There were plenty of men who wanted to do it with me when I was like that, so I wasn't as low on money as I thought I would be with my belly and all. My only worry was Nara.

The last thing that keeps women going is the hope that they'll get out of this place. The thought that they might meet a man who's worth walking out on the money for and freezing out at the market again, polishing other people's shoes, and maybe, if they're lucky, opening up a little shop of their own.

I also used to dream that a man would come along and take me out of here. That he'd tell me I was different, better, that he loved me and would take care of me. But even after I stopped believing that, since men like that didn't come here and I was just a whore to them, even after that, I knew I couldn't stay. Though if it hadn't been for the baby it could easily've turned out that way.

The days rolled by and it still wasn't clear what was going to become of me, where me and the baby would dig our nest.

Somehow I gathered up my courage and I went and knocked on Shartsetseg's door to ask if she knew of anyplace cheap in the city where I could stay. I wanted to ask, but I was too slow. To a trained eye my belly was already starting to show, and as soon as I walked in the door my aunt's eyes lit with a crafty gleam, and she launched right in that I didn't have to explain a thing, Hiroko had helped plenty of girls out of jams like this before, and if I wanted, someone could take me there first thing day after tomorrow. When it came to the misfortunes of others, my aunt was fast and reliable. She could fix anything. When Magi had her accident, my aunt showed up the very next day.

But as soon as I started to ask about housing and saying I didn't need Hiroko's help, she cooled off and snapped right back that I was on my own with that, she had too much work right now, but let her know if I changed my mind, she knew what she knew when it came to these things.

The next few days flew by like it was nothing, and one day I just keeled right over.

I had felt weak since morning and could barely stand on my feet. Nara took a few of my men and I went to go lie down.

I woke up feeling guilty, because this wasn't the first time Nara had had to cover for me and I didn't have any way to repay the favor. I staggered out of my room, orange spots of light dancing before my eyes, and slammed into the banister with my elbows. My head swung down, my eyes slid down to the ground floor, and there, floating in through the open door, was Papa.

Then bang, I hit my head and my arm, and my heart was flapping around my chest like a butterfly in a jar. I was helped to my feet by a woman who said there was no Tuleg here as far as she knew. I would rather've had an abortion than run into Papa here. It would've killed him. Nara said that was silly, what would he be doing here?

Shartsetseg said that she hadn't seen him either, but if I thought Papa was some young pup who'd never been to a whorehouse, I didn't know much about men.

When my belly got so big that Nara had to take one of my johns for me almost every three days, I finally made up my mind to leave and go back home to the mountains. Roaming the streets with a baby inside me wasn't exactly appealing. Who'd give a job to a pregnant woman? Besides, I had nowhere to stay.

As a going-away present, Nara gave me some baby booties she'd sewed herself in her spare time, and made me promise I'd bring the little one back to show her later on.

She tried to convince me if it was a girl I should call her Narankhuu, since she saw this movie on television where the main character was a beautiful girl who worked in the Erdenet zinc mines, and that was her name. But nobody could sway me, I had a girl's name all picked out. We both agreed on a boy's name. It isn't such a big deal with a boy.

Before I set out with my pack to try and catch a ride, I don't know what got into me, but I headed over to the old apartment in Sansaar.

The person who answered the door was a dumpy, shaggy-faced man in a moth-eaten T-shirt and sweatpants. His face was flat, all of his features wiped away by vodka, but still, there was a tiny glimmer of something in those elongated eyes of his, something from those long-ago days when he nearly wooed a woman away from a rich *nuudelchin*, then settled in at her sister's place and lived there for free for years, tossing butts out the window and lying on the couch until it rocked like a cradle.

At first he was surprised, then he slowly spread his arms. I took a step and he pulled me in tight. Feeling confused, I shrieked that he was going to crush the baby and shoved him away. Mergen grinned, his watery eyes sizing me up and down. He offered me a smoke and a drink. I turned down the vodka but agreed to come in for a while. The kitchen reeked, and there were two lines of ants trailing up and down the wall. I didn't remember it being that bad. The tabletop was rotted from the constant spilling of booze, and the shade on the lamp was battered. The window was open wide, matches and strips of newspaper lying on the ledge. Mergen had always liked watching the bustle on the street below. He knew almost everyone just by their hats. He looked pretty content, and when he filled his glass and lit a smoke he seemed to want for nothing.

He asked how I was, and I rattled off a sentence or two about everything that had happened in the years since I had seen him. That was over with quick. He knew from Shartsetseg what I was doing now, nothing to add there. He just said it was good I was having a baby, better not to put it off before I got too old. I asked if he had kids of his own back in his province, and he nodded and said actually it was about time he dropped in to see how they were. He was going away, he said. He said he didn't know if he would come back and asked where I thought I would go. I just shrugged. He said why didn't I stay there, he'd work it out with Yellow Flower. She only came by a couple times a week anyway, to tidy up and make some food, and the rest of the time she was over at Divaajin. When he saw how relieved I was, he said he'd go right over to see Shartsetseg and find someplace else to spend the night. In the end he didn't go anywhere, he just passed out on the sofa, and early the next morning my aunt shook me awake, like she did years ago, on the morning she threw me out. She didn't seem angry, though. She said the water wasn't running, so I should go wash up at a neighbor's in the next building, and don't mix up my things with hers. Then she tossed the keys on the bed and I fell back asleep.

Mergen stayed on for another few days. My aunt didn't show her face even once. The two of us spent the whole time smoking at the kitchen table, Mergen knocking back shot after shot. The baby was born with a big brown spot on its tummy. The doctor asked whether I drank or smoked, but I think what did it was the shock. Even if that wasn't Papa that time, the little one must've felt it.

When I told Mergen, he laughed and said whores were much cheaper in Inner Mongolia. Then he tore Damdinsüren's face from the paper, rubbed the tobacco to soften it up, and rolled himself a fat one.

We didn't mention Mama. But one day Mergen said women were all the same, and it hit me this wasn't the first time that this sort of thing had happened to him. The way he talked about Shartsetseg you would've thought she was his servant.

However much I didn't like that crooked, mocking grin of hers, she'd never pulled anything dirty on him.

There was plenty of vodka and taunting back and forth in those five days with Mergen in that baking-hot apartment, but I was sad to see him go.

I waited in vain for answers to the questions buzzing around my head. He didn't offer them. I was dying to know what had really gone on between him and my mother, whether he felt like the baby's grandpa, and who were the women who had the kids he was going back home to check up on. Downstairs in the doorway, he fished some money out of his jacket and stuck it in my pocket, and I flashed back to the johns at Divaajin, who sometimes after a good trick would slip a little extra down my shirt. He waved his arm and rode off in the first car that drove by. That was the last time I saw him.

On my way back up the stairs, I remembered the time he'd come up the stairs as drunk as I was now, and I had let him fall.

The next few days I spent washing out the stink and polishing off the two bottles hidden under the mattress of the couch that had made me a woman.

I'd been calling my baby Dolgorma from the moment I first felt it move. I wanted a boy as much as any woman did, but I was glad it turned out the way it did, because of that blessed name. Magi was somewhere out there floating around some other worlds, and Oyuna had the first boy, so the name was left for me.

I had some money saved up, and with the couple of thousand *tugriks* that Mergen had given me, it was just enough to eke out a living till I could look for a job again. So I sat in Mergen's chair at the window, rolling his crumbly, dried-out tobacco, watching the people and waiting for Dolgorma to announce herself. The kitchen window looked out onto a square slab of concrete in the middle of four apartment blocks. When the weather was warm, the *jijuurs* would all get together and talk shop about what needed fixing in whose building that day. Boys dribbled soccer balls, shooting through a metal hoop. Little kids tottered around the railing, scratching puppies and getting bonked in the head by a wayward ball every now and then. Women sat around in the corner, feeding their babies and chewing the fat with the women up on their balconies hanging the laundry out to dry. Girls sat perched on the railing, giggling away.

In one corner an old lady stood with a ladle and a pail of *koumiss,* cloudy gray with twigs and drowned flies bobbing around on the surface. Sometimes people stood in line for it, but that thin, watery liquid had nothing at all in common with the thick, rich-white brew I knew from Munkhtsetseg. Sometimes the bigger boys from our building would chase them all away with rocks and occupy the railing. They'd sit grinning into the sun, smugly swinging their legs, passing a cigarette back and forth, up and down the line.

Usually I would take some sewing to the window with me, so Dolgorma would have some nice things to start out with.

My second-floor neighbor Nairamdal took me to the hospital. By the time he stopped in again with a bag of my things the next day, Dolgorma was already here.

Totally healthy except for the spot.

She had a little blue fleck on her back, so even if I didn't know anything else about the father I was glad he was a Mongol, though it never really weighed on my mind, and it still doesn't to this day.

It went so fast that by the third day I was already back in front of the window again, with a view of everything important that went on in Sansaar, only now with a little white bundle that some of my neighbors came by to see.

When they didn't see any man around, the women shook their heads, but I did my best to be nice to them, and eventually the gossip stopped.

Life was good for us.

The only one who ever got new clothes in our *ger* was Magi. I went dragging around in her beat-up hand-me-down *del,* tripping over her boots, which were always two sizes too big and all worn down on the insides of the heels.

I was proud it was different for Dolgorma, and I did my best to make it as different as I could. Whatever she wanted, she got, but I also knew how to be hard too. Whenever she started to fuss and whine about something I told her she couldn't have, I knew how to straighten her out. If she had had a father, he would've thrashed her for being such a brat. Me, I just gave her a swat, and I always tried to explain everything.

She grew like cream on milk. Everything went like it should. The fluffy down she was born with soon grew out into a silky shock of jet-black hair, then her first little teeth came in, and before she was even one year old she stepped across an asphalt crack three fingers thick without batting an eye. I saw it. So did my neighbors out on the playground. She was tenacious as a tick, and on the day of her first birthday she said her first sentence. It was about me. She spread her little hands and fell into my arms, and I rewarded her with a caramel. Tears sprang to my eyes.

The bigger Dolgorma got, the more stubborn she was about getting her way. That should've been a warning to me. I should've taken a stand before it was too late. But what could I say to my precious gem when she stomped her foot like a cute little lamb? And money was one of the few things I always had enough of. Sometimes I would buy an outfit and also get a teeny one just like it made for her. Then the two of us would get dressed up and go out to the square and sit on the bench, and everybody's heads would turn and some of them were frowning. That girl had my devotion. Usually a child gets something from its mother, something from its father, something from its aunts, its uncles, its grandmas, and all the other generations up the line. But Dolgorma just had me and a little bit of Nara. I had to give her everything.

When Dolgorma was seven, after giving it a lot of thought, I decided to show her her next of kin.

You can't just leave your relatives out completely. It wasn't for me to deprive her of them, they were hers as much as mine. Besides, sooner or later Shartsetseg or Nara would've blabbed it to her, and she never would've forgiven me if she'd found out from somebody else. The only one I told her about was Grandma Dolgorma. That was it. She didn't ask too many questions. It probably never occurred to her that there was even anyone else.

My knees were shaking the whole way on the bus to the Red Mountains. I tried to tell her a little bit about Papa and Oyuna, but anyway she had already figured out some of it for herself. My daughter was amazed at the huge herds of animals, and made me explain why camels' hoofs were pincushion soft while cows' hoofs were like thunder, why there were so many horses and so few yaks, and which horse was the head of the herd.

When I was in school, we used to make fun of kids like her. As good a job as I'd done of raising my daughter, she hardly knew a thing about the world I came from.

All my family embraced her. Even Papa, who had let me walk away in tears the first time we had come. Like a deserter taking something that didn't belong to her, and for a long time he wouldn't even call my daughter by her name.

This time he was too old for that sort of thing anymore. He was just stunned at how big Dolgorma was, though he frowned and let her slide off his lap when she asked if she looked like him. But other than that, he wasn't cross with her at all. He even scolded Oyuna's kids when the three of them started telling lies and laughing at how eagerly my daughter fell for them, and he called Dolgorma to his side and gave them each a crack on the head to teach them a lesson.

Batjar, Zula, and Tsetsegma were the worst. They'd join together to rig the games, and every time Dolgorma lost she'd come running to me about it.

I had a talk with Oyuna, but she stood up for her kids, saying Dolgorma would just have to learn, so in a couple of days my little one started to tug at my sleeve that she wanted to go. I didn't let it discourage me. Family relationships take time, they can't be rushed. Like *koumiss* they need to ripen, and Dolgorma had to learn how to deal with it herself.

I was really curious about Oyuna. I had only known Batjar as a baby, and the girls I didn't know at all.

Naima had gotten old, his shoulders drooped, and he spent more time talking with animals than with people. The only sound that ever came from his spot in the *ger* was a loud smacking of lips or the quiet rustle of softened tobacco when he was rolling a smoke. Oyuna managed her wifely duties superbly, so there was no need for any husbandly reminders.

Oyuna was probably the one of us three that took after Mama the most. At least as far as the *ger* was concerned. I always had to lift all the lids to check which pot was water, which was milk, where the leftover meat was, and which pan was washed and empty. Even at home I did it, but Oyuna could go around blindfolded all day and still never spill a drop of soup and polish her chores off faster than me. And still keep an eye on Zula and Tsetsegma. Batjar went along with Naima in the mornings.

Oyuna was one of a kind and she knew it.

You just couldn't talk to her was all.

I tried not to laugh in front of her, after one day she let me have it, saying that she wouldn't stand for such insults, nobody was keeping me there, and if I thought she was jealous of me because I was a city girl now, then I'd better think again, because the only thing she felt for me was pity, pure and simple.

I let her scream herself out, and the next day it was fine again. But every day from then on, we talked just a little bit less. She had a good thing with Naima, though. Ariuna, Naima's mother, knew it right from the start. Nothing could come between those two. Oyuna yelled at times, and there were days when not a single word would pass Naima's lips, but then again there were times when she'd be at the stove and he'd slip his arms around her waist, and even though she'd harp at him for keeping her from her work, in the end she would bow her head to her chest and leave the spoon standing up in the noodles like an *urga*, or press her bottom against his legs and keep stirring like it was nothing, and a smile would play across her face like a child being tickled.

Mama was the same, except for paying more attention to Papa than she used to. It was just the two of them in their *ger* now, and whenever there was something major Oyuna came over to lend a hand. But even with her shaky health, Mama couldn't stand being helped, never mind her youngest daughter butting into her business. That was one thing she wouldn't allow to the end of her days.

Before me and Dolgorma left at the end of that first summer, we also got to see Ariuna and Tsobo, and Maidar and Munkhtsetseg, who all came by for a visit. Papa hadn't had company all year, so we went to drink in my parents' *ger*, and Mama proudly filled the bowls. Everyone asked about life in the City, and Tsobo said next year, definitely, they were going to join me there. Ariuna giggled into her hand. Naima kept to himself, tossing down bowl after bowl.

As we all drank a toast to their upcoming move, my brother-in-law turned to me and whispered in my ear that he wouldn't trade Oyuna for anything in the world.

Then he staggered outside and we heard the dogs fighting over his vomit.

In the years after that, I usually sent Dolgorma to the country by herself. She wasn't exactly thrilled, but when I was young I had all kinds of givens, and no one ever asked me how I felt. That's the way it has to be. What good was a vacation roasting in the streets? Better to be in the mountains, where she could be of help, than to twiddle her thumbs out in front of the building all summer long. She could think what she wanted, but one way or another I always got her to go.

Besides, I was glad to get rid of her for a month or two. When she was gone, Nara came to see me almost every day. We'd hole up in the kitchen together, the air so smoky you couldn't breathe, gabbing away about men, while a steady stream of flies marched up and down our naked thighs. Exactly what I wanted to spare my daughter. The gossip of old women.

I couldn't complain, I was satisfied like this, but Nara wasn't so lucky. She still looked all right, but only if you took into account that she was forty. As soon as we got out on the street and you saw her next to the young girls, you could tell she was no great shakes.

I myself had given up on trying to find someone. Nairamdal, from the second floor, who I used to leave Dolgorma with before she started going to *khuukhdiin tsetserleg*, had been coming by to see me for a couple years by then. We would have a cup of tea, and when my toilet overflowed I had someone to drop in on, and whenever he went off to visit relatives in the country he would leave his keys with me, and he'd always bring a couple bottles of *koumiss* back with him. It was enough to make me feel good, and that was all I needed.

But Nara didn't have even that, and she didn't have any Dolgorma, and she hadn't shown her face in the Red Mountains in so long, there was a moment of awkward silence there when anyone said her name.

Nara was hopeless with men. She'd drag them home with her first thing, then wonder why they ran off in the morning and never showed their face again. And if by some fluke they weren't put off, she'd burn them out so fast that they were gone within a month. Nara offered up everything at the slightest sign of interest. She'd hand over her heart to a man like a fistful of small change, and then if he still wasn't interested, she would try spreading her legs. Which would bury the whole thing completely. She never learned. Nara was a cheap slut and didn't know any other way. But she's still my dearest sister. Nothing can ever change that.

I kept telling her, You need to know what you're worth, but maybe she knew better than I did. Only that could explain why she came to me again and again, fancy cigarette trembling in her fingers, only to tell me the same story, word for word, every time. Whenever I tried to explain, she just blinked back at me with those long lashes of hers, her two eyes, drowning in tears, peering out at the world from underneath them in terror, and I knew the only thing that they could understand was my caresses. It never ended.

Usually Dolgorma came home early from vacation. She'd talk someone in the center into giving her a lift, and get back to the City as soon as she could. I was glad to have her learning new things in the country, and foolishly I told myself that maybe she'd find a man there and those skills would come in handy, but Dolgorma had a head like a rock.

Papa was right. A child's too much for a woman on her own, and I was tired of saying the same things over and over again. She never had to go far to find a harsh word, especially when it came to her grandma and Oyuna. If only she'd lived through half of what they had, if only she wasn't so stupid. But no, she knew it all. Sometimes I could've just hauled off and slugged her.

One time I almost did. I was drunk and it ended badly. I was a young hotblood too, but never as sassy as that. Mama would've slapped me across the face. I didn't slap my daughter.

I was drunk and babbling nonsense, instead of just locking the door and throwing the key out the window. Dolgorma was newly sixteen, and she walked out and slammed the door.

I believed the two of us could talk it through somehow. After all, the girl wasn't dumb. She was the best in her class at school, and she wasn't exactly a child anymore. She had to know that everything has mainly been for her sake, I never did anything wrong to her, I've always tried my best, and even Nairamdal said what a tremendous job I was doing with her, even other people say she looks fresh as a flower, and now this. But I can't blame myself, not after all these years. If she'd given me a chance at least, but no, she went and sorted it all out for herself, I could've promised the moon and the stars and it wouldn't have done any good, she wouldn't listen to me, that little girl thought that she had the right to judge me or something. That little girl who hadn't brought home a single *tugrik* her whole life, and now here she was all high and mighty, her and her dainty little hands that didn't have a clue what it's like when you're hanging on to your last resort and the weight of it is crushing your fingers, when it's a woman's last chance, and every decision she has to choose from is worse than the ones she had years before, when either one is the wrong one but there's nothing else to grab on to, that little girl didn't know any of that, and yet she had the gall to tell me what was right and what wasn't. How could she know that what she figured out in the blink of an eye, what fell into place like a jigsaw puzzle for her, took me years to put together, and even then, I still needed her to figure it out completely. I pondered it all for nights on end, I couldn't stop thinking about it, even before she knew that she would be born again from my womb, even back then I was already thinking about it, and later, when my belly had gotten big as a keg and I could only lie on my back, and that little girl was kicking me from inside, like she was trying to tell me, Hurry, don't wait another day, if you put it off again, it'll only get that much harder to bear. And then all of the years after that. The weight of my own final decision tossed and turned inside my guts, and that was the point. I couldn't swing back and forth anymore, I didn't like not being settled, and the only work I had was with men, and I won't say it was that bad, there are people who do things a lot worse and they don't let it bother them nearly as much. And for what? For a girl who thought that at age sixteen she could tell me what was what.

At first I told myself that it was just one of those hot-blooded things that blows over by morning and the next day she'd be back. But she didn't come back the third day, or the day after that either.

Nara said not to worry, but that only made me angry. I needed to hear something different, I wanted to hear that it wasn't my fault, but what kind of comfort would that be from a girl that worked in a brothel? What could she possibly say? There wasn't room in that head of hers for anything but men. She would've had a breakdown trying to talk about anything else.

I said we'd had a fight because Dolgorma said she would never go back to the Red Mountains again and no one could make her.

My sister's face exploded in laughter, trailing into a smoker's cough. This was right up her alley. For the next hour I was treated to an avalanche of unwanted advice: Try and understand the girl, and Picture yourself in Dolgorma's shoes.

I was furious. I didn't like lying to Nara like that.

My daughter was gone for almost a year. During that time I became an old woman. If before I had the feeling that I hardly turned anyone's head anymore, now I was sure any man would rather count the asphalt patches under his feet than cast even half a glance at my sagging, yellowy face.

I asked everyone I knew, and everyone I knew she knew, but they all just shook their heads and started in on their own stuff.

The City turned ashen gray, my world had been plundered, my heart trampled like the steppe by a stampeding herd of horses, and I sat out on the balcony in a thin cotton coat. The boys jostled and shoved below, a few new babies arrived on the block, and none of them had the slightest idea that every pale sunrise could be the last, because that's what I was wishing for, and also I prayed.

ZAYA

Every week I went to the temple and pasted up a new appeal on the rotating cylinder, since in the seven days in between, the writing smudged off on the hands of all the others who spun the mills, and they carried off my prayers on their palms into *gers* and high-rise apartments, where men with bottles lay in the hallway, while others, behind closed doors, wiped away their grandkids' snot, and my daughter was somewhere out there among them, but none of them would tell me where, even though I knew some of them after a couple of months.

We'd nod to one another, and I was glad there were also others in mourning, pasting up prayers like me. Women asking for their men back, for Burkhan to hold his hand over their sons, and they also prayed for money, and the mills spun under the hands of those fulfilling obligations too, since it's fitting that everyone pay their respects to the holy temple now and again. Winter was here, and when I came home I would warm my hands in hot water and right away start to feel better, because I'd never stopped believing in prayer, but as soon as I feel good I put all thought of Burkhan out of my mind.

But that unhappy year, my pleading thoughts belonged to him morning, noon, and night. I never felt good.

I'd often go downstairs to have a chat with Nairamdal. Those were the only times when things seemed all right. We didn't bring up Dolgorma. I knew what he thought. That young girls act up and misbehave, but they come around eventually. He gave my daughter a couple weeks at most, he swore. She was basically a good girl, we both knew that, he said, and sooner or later, at some point, she'd have to start missing her mother.

Nairamdal would take my hand and we'd sit in his apartment, holding hands, sipping tea, and watching TV a few nights a month. When Nairamdal held my hand in his, it made the sadness bearable. He could've been holding the hand of a younger woman. He was well preserved, and his place was nicely kept too, but he was holding mine and I could tell it wasn't out of pity.

After several months it hit me that it might always be this way. That the colors would never come back to the flowers, that even warm sunny days would be freezing, and I would curse the sun's rays for the rest of my life for touching her when I couldn't.

It never even occurred to me that something might've happened to her.

That couldn't happen to *me*. I'd had more than my fair share already. Is she in for it when she gets home. My mind swung back and forth.

After a while it passed. I mainly just wanted her back.

So ever since her fifth month gone, I pasted up prayers every day.

■ □ ■ □ ■

2. DOLGORMA

I HEARD THE STORY LOTS OF TIMES. MY MOTHER USED TO TELL ME it lots.

At night, when I couldn't fall asleep, she'd sit down by my little bed and press her head to mine. Her hands were always cool. She'd gently cover my mouth with her fingers to make me stop my fussing and say it was time for her to go but if I would just quit bugging her she'd tell me one more time.

There were lots of nights like that. It was the same almost every time. I never wanted her to go, it's always worse to sleep alone, and I knew mothers weren't supposed to leave their kids alone like that, and I knew she knew it too. That's just how it was with us. So at least I'd make her tell me the story before she went.

There's lots of things I don't believe that she just takes on faith. We've got a Burkhan in the living room on a decorative table by the TV like most other people do, but I know that that stuff doesn't have any real effect on my life. All that magic and spell stuff just doesn't exist. The shamans are all dead. But Great-Gramma is different. That's the story my mom would tell me at night before she left. But the main part isn't Great-Gramma. The main part is me, my name. If I didn't keep repeating it to myself over and over, how else would I get to sleep?

My great-gramma was known throughout the region. She could cure the deathly ill with a touch, and one look from her was enough to stop a bleeding wound. She was rewarded for her advice with the finest cashmere fabrics, and when people sent to her for help, they stood at the doorstep to welcome her and pay their respects, like old people bowing down to painted temple figures. When Great-Gramma got close, they say the heavens turned ruby red and her arrival was announced by thunderclaps and lightning bolts like gold jagged knives, like chain saws ripping through the sky and hurtling down to earth. If lightning struck the *ger,* that meant it was too late for even Great-Gramma to help. But it didn't happen too often, which was why everyone held her in such respect.

My great-gramma understood every sickness, of body and soul alike. She could ease the pain of backs bent by brimming buckets and heavy pots, as well as of those unlucky in love. She could heal serious grown-up illnesses but also the scraped knees of little kids who'd fallen off their horses.

When Great-Gramma stood, she could talk eye to eye with even the biggest horses. She was that tall.

As soon as my mom got to that part, I'd always ask why she didn't get Great-Gramma to teach her animal talk. She said it was too hard, and besides, Great-Gramma passed away before they got around to it.

There wasn't time. Too many sick. Always were, always will be. Like grains of rice in a lunch bowl, like fleas on a shaggy wolfskin, my mother used to say about things there were a lot of. Like bruises on the bodies of the Ulaanbaatar bums, like gobs of spit on a street corner of this lousy, filthy city, I say. I've never seen a wolf. For all I know they don't even have fleas. Not that it matters.

Great-Gramma was the kind of person you couldn't hide anything from. She could tell when someone was making things up, and anybody who lied to her would break out in red spots all over their body the next day, and scratch at them for nights on end, and no one could make it stop.

When Great-Gramma was alive, you could tell all the liars in the area by their fingers, from the blood under their nails.

Only Great-Gramma could help them. And after that they never said a crooked word again. Not in front of her, anyway.

Sometimes even my mother's *ger* would shudder in fear of her. My mom obeyed her every word and kept an eye on her herbs to make sure nobody tore them up, since when Great-Gramma gave an order, if you knew what was good for you, you did as you were told. She always knew what she was talking about, and when she spoke, it was like a butcher chopping meat. Where she hit, it stuck. What she said, went.

It was like that even with her death. She just got old and decided to quit. She sent everyone in the family away, and when they got back, she was lying out in front of the *ger,* all ready to go.

She had on a silver-stitched *del,* head turned to the east, and she sang up to her last breath. As her breath slowly grew shorter, her words turned softer and softer, mingling with the murmuring rain, splashing graciously down in cords to cast a shroud of dignity over Great-Gramma's final moments, as Mom put it. She refused to be taken inside the *ger.*

In the morning they found her cold body, wrapped in her rain-soaked *del,* far out on the steppe. On her face was a solemn smile. The colorful paints she had smeared on her forehead and cheeks had run together into a strange, blurry picture.

Everyone in the area gathered to try and decipher the colorful blotches, seeking to divine from them the fortune and ruin of years to come. Naturally the grown-ups on my mother's side had the biggest say: my grampa and gramma. Their children squeezed in next to them: Mom, Aunt Nara, and my late Aunt Magi, holding Aunt Oyuna, who wasn't even two yet. Some saw raging clouds in my great-gramma's face and prophesied dire events. To others the bright smears suggested fat herds of spotted cows, and they laid odds on a mild winter and a long summer of sunshine. There were also a good number who saw in them a huge settlement of yurts, like here in the City, and predicted the purchase price of meat would rise, or some important bigwig was going to visit the *somon,* or the *somon* center was going to suddenly expand and our region would take on unusual importance.

It wasn't Mom's place to say anything, so she just stood there quietly, between her gramma's knees. She said Great-Gramma's face kept changing colors, and growing and shrinking back again.

Until finally she couldn't hold back, and all of a sudden she screamed out, A mosquito! Look, a giant mosquito!

The others fell silent as all at once, before their eyes, the shapeless blotches joined into wings, with the dark twig of a mosquito body barely visible in between. My mom saw it first.

The next summer a plague struck the region. People were swollen and bloated, and going out of the *ger* at night was out of the question. Some children died of mosquito diseases, others couldn't see for the swelling, and the same for the grown-ups. No one in my mom's region had ever seen anything like it. Animals swishing their tails all day, cows butting heads.

The *aimak* was besieged by swarms of mosquitoes for a whole month. Lots of people died of fever and others had their clawed-open wounds infested with foul-smelling bugs. My mom had been right.

Grampa, my great-gramma's son and my mother's dad, decided it wasn't just a coincidence. Everyone agreed. It was a message from Great-Gramma. Delivered through Mom and her alone. It's true she didn't have any other special abilities, but if someone had taken her seriously, it wouldn't have had to turn out as badly as it did.

Finally it was decided. My mom's first girl would be named after Great-Gramma. Just to be safe. And to the great and everlasting glory of Dolgorma, the most excellent woman in the domain of Bashkgan *somon.*

Mom would always say that sentence exactly the same, and if she left out a word I would scream. I couldn't get to sleep without hearing that bit about the domain of Bashkgan *somon.* I didn't have any idea what it was, but it sounded grand. Little did I know it was the region I would be going to every summer for two months to stay with Grampa and Gramma.

I couldn't stand those vacations, but I liked hearing that story every chance I got.

It always made me feel like somehow I was important too. I could feel it. Even if my mother did go out almost every night, and when I woke up with freezing feet I couldn't snuggle up to her under the covers like other kids, and when I rubbed them with my hands I'd get this weird buzzing sound in my head and this black sludge would come oozing out of the hollows in the walls. The only thing that could comfort me was the peaceful hum of the cars driving back and forth past our building. There outside was the City I knew, full of friendly sounds and lights, and my mom was also somewhere out there, floating around. The apartment was full of spooky rustling noises, so when I started to fall back asleep—now with fear and without my mom—I'd imagine myself making Berke itch like crazy, like Great-Gramma knew how to do.

Berke was a girl in our school who was always telling lies—one day it was her family, the next her big brother who didn't exist—and I would get these fantasies where her whole body would sting so bad she couldn't even sit down. She'd have these gross red spots all over her body, including her face, and lying there between sleep and dream I would picture her hands covered in blood, like they'd been dunked in ketchup. The thought of it made me happy.

I felt strong, because Dolgorma was the most excellent woman in the domain of Bashkgan *somon* and I had the honor of having her name.

Life was good with Mom. We had a place in the City, and we never had to beg for meat and milk from our relatives in the country like most of the kids in school. In winter I went over to Inkhe's between lessons. She lived right next to school, and the thought of freezing all the way home and back again just to stick my feet under the hot water faucet for a measly twenty minutes didn't appeal to me. Being at their place made me see how good I had it with Mom.

My mom would buy only the best cow meat, plus canned peas and jarred vegetables, and big yellow bags of mayonnaise in threes, light, crumbly hazelnut wafers, and long, airy baguettes. None of those heavy, sour loaves like they had over at Inkhe's.

And even them they only had sometimes.

Whenever I was at Inkhe's we would go out on the balcony, where they had a frozen goat jammed in between the crates. Every day Inkhe's mom would slice off a hunk and throw it in a pot with two fistfuls of cheap noodles. That was it. Sometimes we'd also get a piece of candy with bits of paper stuck to it, but it had to be a pretty special occasion for that.

It might've seemed normal to Inkhe, but not to me.

My mom gave me some chocolate to bring them every now and then, so I wouldn't seem like a freeloader, but when I asked if I could take them some of our pear compote and spices, she said no. She said they might think that we were trying to tell them something. It's true it probably didn't occur to Inkhe to think they were poor. But I knew we were better off.

I dressed the way they did in the foreign, non-Mongolian films, and so did Mom. Her silky stockings and delicate blouses were the envy of every woman. And Aunt Nara was even better dressed than her. I don't think there was ever anyone closer to my mom.

Sometimes when I got home from school the two of them would be sitting in the kitchen together talking. I could smell the expensive tobacco from the foyer. Nara smoked these long, thin cigarettes that I never saw for sale at any stand around here. They didn't even make her fingers yellow, and as soon as I stepped in the door she'd call my name through the smoky haze, and I'd go racing in to sit on her lap. Nara had big breasts, bigger than my mom's even, and much whiter. She smelled of cigarettes, heavy perfume, and sometimes alcohol. She wore a brooch, two rings, and spiked high heels. She was a lady. Every time she tossed her curls, the room would fill with the scent of exotic flowers. The only thing harsh about my aunt was her voice. It reminded me of the women at the market, whose voices were rough from shouting.

Me and my mom didn't go to the market. I only ever went if I was shopping with a friend. All they have is the worst, cheapest stuff. The salesladies in the shops wear nice clothes, plus it's warm and you don't have to haggle. My mom always bought me whatever I wanted, and did the same for herself. Which is why it was strange when I'd sometimes find her huddled on the sofa, or locked in the bathroom, and her eyes would be red from crying when she finally came back out. I thought we had everything we wanted. But it also got to me sometimes. I huddled also.

I started to get the feeling pretty early on that there was something fishy going on with Mom. I already knew from the other kids in *khuukhdiin tsetserleg* that none of their moms worked at night. Not one. Only mine.

She'd always cut me off quick when I'd start asking questions. I was still too little to understand, she'd say.

When I got older she would snap back that it was none of my business, and why don't I take a look at how my other friends go around with hungry looks in their eyes, and how all their shoes are hand-me-downs from their older brothers and sisters.

My mother went out every night for years.

By now I was used to that muffled click of the door that meant the start of my night.

Mom groping around in the dark foyer for her shoes while I slowly sank into sleep, and her final good-bye was the clap of the door.

Sometimes she'd stay home at night and I couldn't get to sleep. Then she'd joke she'd better leave or I'd never get to bed, and I'd laugh and send her on her way.

That was when I was older.

But still, I never forgot it. I never did learn to be by myself.

My mom would tell me stories about her sisters when they were little sometimes. I had no clue what it was like to be stuck with a brat, she said. The smelly diapers, the constant chatter pounding in your temples like a thousand jackhammers going at once, the endless distance from the door to the window when your stupid little toddler is over there fooling around.

Bogi was always dragging her little brother around with her. She was a friend of mine, so I knew what it was like when a child keeps putting his hands everywhere and doesn't understand that a pot of hot water means death. Bogi's brother didn't learn till he tipped one over on himself and almost died. He wouldn't leave us alone so we locked him up in the kitchen, and when Bogi's mom got home she told me not to come over anymore since whenever I was over Bogi didn't watch her brother. Which was true, but I still wanted a sibling. Of my own. Just mine and Mom's. It wasn't till my mom said it takes two to make a baby that I started to wonder how I got here.

At Inkhe's I found out what men and women do at night. I would sleep over there whenever my mom went out of town or had some business to take care of.

Inkhe woke me up one night, took an old pot from under the bed, and put it against the wall. I couldn't see anything, but then Inkhe showed me some pictures that her older brother had under the bed, and it was clear. Unthinkable and disgraceful, but absolutely clear.

I kind of knew it already from the time I'd spent in the country, but not like that.

For me the blankets moving around on the grown-ups' beds at night was just one more of those weird, disgusting things that the countryside was full of.

The fact is it was a pretty long time before I had any idea that there was even anyone else in our family besides Mom and Nara.

I finally saw Bashkgan *somon*, wretched and dust-choked, spread out before us like a cigarette-burned tablecloth, just before my seventh birthday.

Gramma Alta, Grampa Tuleg, Aunt Oyuna, Uncle Naima, my three cousins. When I was little I used to laugh at their tiny gleaming figures, shrinking smaller and smaller as I watched them from the jeep on my way back home to the City after vacation. In the City you never see anyone look as tiny or far away as that; the buildings get in the way.

They were supposed to be my new kin. But somehow it didn't work out.

I had the same feeling every time we left Oyuna's *ger*, as they stood waiting faithfully for our jeep to sail over the next desert hump. They were never dear to me.

At least not the way my mom had hoped.

Grampa said he saw me once when I was just a baby. That was the first thing out of his mouth. He didn't look that surprised when I crept in the door, after my mother gave me a nudge and said I should go first.

Afterwards she asked me what else Grampa had said, and when I snapped back, Just that, and got all mad about why we hadn't come before, since everyone here seemed to know about me, she started unpacking our things, and my cousin Batjar came running in with his sisters, Tsetsegma and Zula, and we went to go see a dead snow leopard.

After that I didn't even ask her anymore. It was obvious. I figured out there were lots of touchy things in our family, and me and my mother were one.

Batjar, who was two years older than me, said my mom had stolen my name. Actually what he said was, She stole your name as shamelessly as the Altai horse thieves steal the finest of our herds. It was ridiculous. My mother wasn't some sneaky guy creeping around with an *urga* and ropes, and what did my name have to do with horses anyway?

I went straight to my mom and asked how anyone could steal a name, but instead of an explanation she told me the story she used to tell about Great-Gramma every night, and how she was the only one who noticed the mosquito and how Grampa decided that my name would be Dolgorma. As if the fact he was the only one who'd seen me as a baby somehow proved her version was true.

I liked Grampa. I didn't like Oyuna so much, since Batjar told me that he got the horse thing from her, and my mom didn't have very much do with her either. I couldn't see why she'd waited so long to bring me here, and when it came out that Tsetsegma, Batjar, and Zula had heard about her before, I think I cried. Still, after two days I was already starting to feel like I couldn't wait to get back.

That was my first time there with my mom. After that, I almost always went by myself.

Give her time, I overheard Gramma say to my mom, and from that moment on it was clear to me she'd never understand.

I was old enough to realize that the country wasn't like school, which you just have to get used to, since the parents go to jail if their kids don't go to school. It wasn't like it would've hurt anyone if I'd gone back to the City with my mother after the first two days. They hadn't missed me all those years, and I hadn't missed them either.

I tried to tell my mother, but Grampa heard and cut me off. Then he gave Mom a lecture. So this is how they raise children in the City, is it? he said, and I saw my mother weak for the first time in my life.

She was a totally different person when she was in the *ger*. It made me sick. As soon as Gramma handed me a stirpot or a *khutag* or a *tavag* of warm, smelly blood, I'd start looking for how I could dump it off on Zula or Tsetsegma. Mom helped Gramma with all her chores and did as she was told.

They all called me *zalkhuu*, but I was only lazy in the country. Nothing there belonged to me. As soon as I got old enough to understand, I just walked away. Left the meat half sliced, still unsalted, the decorated door closing behind me with a sharp, accusing squeak, for the whole rest of the day. I can't even describe the feeling of triumph when one of the *nokhois* would get its tail caught in the door. Gramma could yell all she wanted. It might've worked on Mom and Tsetsegma, but it didn't work on me. Gramma standing there, flailing her arms, brow all scrunched up, wrinkles flapping across her boxy feline face.

It was a joke.

It was only that first summer that I was afraid of her, and I never trusted her.

Her withered head bobbing around on that skinny little brown neck of hers, and those fidgety hands keeping a lid on each and every thing in the *ger,* even without any help. It was rare that she didn't have something in them.

The only time she ever had them folded in her lap was in the evening, waiting for the men to come home, the soup ready and happily bubbling away on the stove, finished with everything until tomorrow morning. In tiny, unattractive, knotted little fists. But even then, she would twist her fingers or rub her thighs to keep warm. She never left me alone, and I longed to be back in our apartment with corners. It doesn't work to hide behind the poles inside a *ger.*

Gramma never gave my mom a pass on anything. Russian, she would spit when my mother wore her nice clothes, and when she washed her face in the morning, my gramma would grumble that the water could've been used for milk tea that evening instead of her splashing it all over the place for nothing. Usually it was me who went to fetch the water, but the way Gramma railed on my mom you would've thought she was the one with calluses on her back from lugging buckets. Batjar was usually out with the livestock, but Tsetsegma and Zula feared Gramma like a steppe scorpion. That's how Aunt Oyuna put it.

Another thing I didn't understand about my relatives: at least once every vacation we had to go to the *ovoo.* Us kids carried the *khataks* and the cookies, and Grampa and Gramma would dress up in their finest. Then we would trudge for hours over the scorched-white landscape, dust stinging our eyes and mixing with the sweat that trickled down our faces, leaving behind a brown smear every time we wiped them. The horses would rasp with thirst, tripping and stumbling over their legs like horses of drunks. And all that just so we could circle around a stone mound, lay a couple melted pieces of candy on the rocks, and tie some blue and yellow scarfs on a bunch of shaky old tree stumps, so the camels and wandering horses had something nice to look at. Still, I always went. It wasn't like gutting goats or gathering *argal,* where everyone just shouted *zalkhuu* and wrinkled their brow at me. I had to go. Still, in spite of everything, it was nice to have some family besides my mom and Nara.

After a while, I could put up with just about anything.

Not like my mom, though.

She had it harder. She was more one of them than I was, and did all she could to make up for the fact that she lived in a different world and they had stayed where she left them. Every one of her smiling glances full of dread, every move of her hands that wasn't as skilled as Aunt Oyuna's, was begging for forgiveness.

What I didn't get at all, though, was Great-Gramma. I knew her story better than my own, yet I looked in vain for any sign of the respect with which my mom spoke of the most excellent woman in the domain of Bashkgan *somon* and which I could lay some claim to myself. It was like Gramma had never known her. My mother told me that Grampa honored her memory, but except for a box with a piece of Great-Gramma's *del* and her embroidered summer boots, which he wouldn't let us touch, it was like everything else had fallen down an elevator shaft.

Maybe that had something to do with his long trips into the horizon every evening, but how in the world would anyone know? Mom said when she was little, he used to take her and Nara. But he never invited any of us grandchildren. Or Gramma, or Oyuna.

I never got a good feeling from Oyuna. The only person in her *ger* I liked was her husband, Naima. Sometimes he'd take me out on his horse, hardly talking, pulling cigarette after cigarette from the pocket of his *del*. The only time he went to the *ger* was to sleep, and he never yelled at his kids the way Oyuna did. He only spoke when he had to, and nobody knew their way around the area like him.

He was the one who showed me the *risunki* for the first time, tucked away in a few spots in the mountains. Some drawings everyone knew, but some of them only he knew, till I coaxed him into showing me. He would toss me in the saddle, jump on behind me, and we'd go burning out of there without a word to anyone, away from the endless scrapping between Gramma and Oyuna.

Some of the stones just had zigzag lines and handprints, but other ones had people in the middle of concentric circles, little stick figures holding hands. From the animals, it was mostly cows and horses.

The biggest one he showed me was a drawing of a huge square with hundreds of circles of all different sizes inside it. Animals, Naima said. A herd.

He said people didn't used to know how to draw, so for goats they just used circles.

Zula, Tsetsegma, and Batjar turned their noses up at that kind of stuff. Tramping out to the rocks to look at some who knew how old they were circles wasn't their idea of fun. Idiots. What really bugged me was their games, though. My clothes would always get messed up and still I never won. I couldn't even sneak through the grass as quiet as Zula.

One day Naima rode into the center for some leather straps and came back with a can of white paint. He winked at me and I knew right away it had to be for us.

Later that day we rode out to the rocks. Naima took out a paintbrush, pried open the lid of the paint can with his knife, and together we walked to the circles. Then slowly, one by one, we carefully traced over all the *risunki*. He only let me do the straight lines, after one careless stroke of mine, on the first one I tried, turned a horse into a yak. We painted till it was so dark our eyes began to water, and then went home to eat. For the next few days, whenever Naima had time, we would ride out to the rocks with our paint and touch up anything that was getting too hard to see.

The *risunki* shone like new. Then we showed them to everyone else, and even Batjar, who hardly talked to me, admitted that it was better. That was the best vacation in Bashkgan I ever had. I wasn't ashamed anymore, I picked up some skills, and I was too young to notice the misery they were living in.

Gramma said I must be amazed by the country, seeing as it was my first time setting foot outside the City. But I wasn't amazed. I was disgusted.

In the City, for instance, we take our plastic bags of Sprite cans, vodka bottles, and leftovers and toss them out the window. But at Gramma's it was all just piled around the *ger* like a wall and I had to fight to keep from gagging every time I stepped over it. It wasn't even worth thinking about trying to wash yourself, and they almost never did laundry. Before, when I saw people from the steppe in the City, I thought they got that shiny bronze from being out all day in the wind and sun, galloping around the herd and rounding up strays. But it's just plain old soot and grease. It was the same scam with the knucklebones, when my cousins played to see whose turn it was to gather *argal.* Give me a break. I pulled the same trick on Zula. But when Gramma threw the bones to see whether it was a good day for milking or not, or if Grampa should buy a new door or wait until next year, it was a joke. The older I got, the more it seemed like everything in the country was a joke. And an obnoxious one too.

Mom had told me Grampa's sheep were the best-tasting in Mongolia west of the City. Supposedly, because of the herb pasture they fed on, their meat was so flavorful it didn't need any seasoning but salt. But I still ended up with nothing but fat in my bowl, which whenever I tried to swallow it got stuck in the back of my throat, and every time I burped afterwards it stank like goat's breath. It didn't even come close to the canned franks in Sansaar.

Plus, after a while, Tsetsegma and Zula weren't funny anymore but just plain obnoxious. I always had to fight to get any respect from them. Meanwhile, they spent all year at school and still didn't know what year our republic was founded or where to find the Volga or the U.S. on a map. Chingis's biography, though, that they knew front to back. It's all made up anyway.

When my mother sat in the kitchen at home, with Nara or whatever friend of hers happened to be over that day, I could hear the howling laughter all the way down the hall. They would cook and play the radio while I sat in the next room, head bent over my textbook in math or natural science, ears perked up like the dog on my favorite police show.

Sometimes, if the radio was playing something lively, I would hear the sound of feet stomping across the kitchen floor, or my mom bursting into laughter at some funny story of Nara's.

When we were at her family's, my mom turned sad and gloomy, walking around with downcast eyes, and whenever Gramma snapped at her, her chin would start to quiver. You would've thought she was the baby of the family, not Oyuna. I was embarrassed for her, and I hated my gramma for that.

I saw just how clueless Gramma really was one time when Mom and I brought her a flashlight from the City. She didn't even know how to turn it on. Then she was shining it at the sheep and laughing at the way it made their eyes glow red in the dark. Then she did it to Oyuna and Tsetsegma, and my mom just sat there quietly the whole time.

Gramma didn't know a thing about the world, and my mother nodded to whatever she said.

Whenever Gramma would give her some free time and Oyuna didn't need any help, she would go sit out on a flat rock near the ones with the *risunki*. The stones would be hot from the sun, and my mom would always warn me to watch out for the snakes that she said made their nests beneath them.

Sometimes I'd watch my mother walk. Her walk was different from everyone else in the *ger*'s, light and floating, like if she ever got tired of being around her family, she could lift off into the air and fly away south with the herons. She never sat down until first she had laid her shawl out and smoothed it with her hands. Then carefully she would seat herself, like she still had on her fancy stockings and didn't want to get a run. Whenever I saw her coming and I was already out there, I'd creep up on her from behind and try to surprise her.

I'd grab her hair from behind like she was an animal and I'd caught her, but I never knew for sure if she was glad to see me or if I should go and leave her alone. Sometimes, though, she'd tell me to come up and look with her, and help me swing up on the rock. But as soon as I sat next to her, I'd start squirming around all over the place, trying to catch the bugs on my knees and asking her all sorts of stuff.

It never was my thing. I still don't see what was so great about it.

For my mother, those sandy gray open spaces were like staring into a mirror. Every little bump and dip meant something to her. To me, the steppe was just one huge slab of scaly dry dead skin. There was nowhere I could rest my thoughts; they were all in the City, on the other side of the mountains. Then my mom would slap my face and I would start to whimper, since there really was nothing to look at but a bunch of baked earth with some pale clumps of grass.

I wandered back toward my gramma's *ger*, the sharp grass cutting my soles as the evening wind kicked up a dark cloud of dust.

The *ger* crouched in the distance like a big lump of dirt, and I knew that inside waiting for me was a bowl of noodles, a dirty pot, and my cousins' two smirking faces, since they always came up with some excuse to take me down a notch.

My mom, up on the boulder, didn't budge an inch.

As I drove off with Grampa at the end of the eighth month, I looked out the jeep at the women, all lined up in front of the *ger*, and made the most contemptuous face I could think of. Naima was the only one I gave a smile to, beaming through the window as I made a little circle with my thumb and index finger and pressed it to the glass. We were conspirators.

Maybe I did go a little too far. But by the time it dawned on me, it was too late. My mother's secret was out. I was sixteen, Batjar was in the army, and I hadn't seen either of my other two cousins in years. Grampa was dead and gone. Why is it the good ones are always first to go? Gramma's hard heart beat for another couple years still, but she didn't outlive her siblings. She just couldn't give up the fat, and Naima's jeep was too slow to get her to the center in time for the doctor to do anything.

Maybe my relatives weren't as bad as I thought. After all, I took it much worse than them. When it dawned on me what my mother did for a living, I left. She just ceased to exist for me. When it dawned on me where the money had come from to pay for all those clothes of ours and our nicely furnished Sansaar apartment, the sticky, sweaty bills my mom had used to pay for it all, I walked out and slammed the door.

My mom sat in the kitchen screaming that I didn't know a thing about life, that she'd sweated and slaved and degraded herself for nobody's sake but mine, but that starting tomorrow things would be different, she could easily do something else, she gave me her word. My mom was drunk and slurring her words, and when I got out in the hallway I heard the stool tip over, and judging from the string of swear words coming out of her mouth she must've cut herself pretty bad. She used words that even the drunks at the cheapest dives in town didn't know.

I headed straight to Ochir's.

I never could've walked out like that if it hadn't been for him.

There wasn't anything I was good at, and I wasn't cut out for life on the streets. Being all scummy and dirty, washing shop windows for food, sleeping out in the gutter and mixing with people who'd cut loose from the country and headed off to the City, or who'd fled from beatings at home and were drowning their sorrows in shots—I couldn't do it. I'd been wanting to move in with Ochir for a long time anyway. I just couldn't find an excuse till the blowout with my mom.

He said at least my mom didn't teach me her trade. He took my bags, tossed them in the closet, and I had myself a new home.

Ochir had a pretty big place, all the way on the top floor. The wind up there howled something fierce, and when a *shoroo* hit, the whole place would sway back and forth, and gales of wind would come wailing through the cracks around the window frames. But still, we had the whole balcony covered in wire mesh. Ochir said you never knew, some tricky bastard might find a way to get even this high up, and I didn't exactly like the idea of some stranger's face peeking in the balcony window myself.

Ochir was over thirty. He was honest enough to tell me the whole story the very first night I showed up with my things. His wife and kids had left him. Over money, he said. But as he ran through the list of things his wife demanded, and only the best would do, of course, I couldn't see how he'd lasted so many years with her. And he still even paid her alimony.

We talked through all that the first night I was there.

As we lay in his wedding bed, holding hands together under the big flowery quilt, I could feel how huge my heart was, throbbing like a living, breathing thing, and Ochir filtered through it like the scent of a thyme sachet. He was like a father to me, his chest so broad I could barely wrap my arms around him, and yet at the same time he was small, curled up in the palm of my hand that night. And I felt the strength a woman has when her fingers entwine with a man's, smoothing all his knotted scars with nothing but their shared silence, and all his wounds are swallowed in those few still hours of night.

Ochir owned his own business. He had a driver who worked for him, and occasionally someone else, and he drove around Mongolia showing foreign tourists the sights. First he'd run them through the City, then he'd take them on a tour—Erdene Zuu monastery, Tsogt Taij's palace, a few other spots—and he raked it in pretty good. Sometimes, if they were interested, he'd take them out to Uvs Nuur and Khövsgöl, which had much bigger fish than the ones they could catch at home, and the *juulchin*s always got a thrill from riding between the camels' humps.

Ochir took me along, of course. I knew some foreign words from school and caught on pretty quick.

I guided them through Gandan, saying whatever Ochir told me

to, and if they asked me something I didn't know, I'd wrinkle my brow and say it was secret, or everyone had their own opinion, and that did the trick. Ochir made all the decisions and handled all the arrangements, so it wasn't like it was that challenging, considering the money I made. Which also meant I had lots of time to myself, so I'd walk around the stores and do a little cleaning, and cook nice things for Ochir that I'd learned to make from my mom. There was nothing kept in shadow. Nothing for me to worry about.

The days flowed slowly by, like the Tuul through Ulaanbaatar, black nights and white days skipping past like the squares on the chessboard me and Ochir would sometimes pull out at night, and I took it for granted that we'd be together like that to the end of Ochir's days.

But it ended as fast as it began. I came home one night to an old lady I'd never seen before standing in the kitchen, with two kids sitting on a stack of bags in the foyer. Ochir stood in the kitchen with his back to me, like he hadn't heard me come in. He didn't even turn around till the woman made a disgusted gesture and squeezed past me to the kids.

Any grown-up woman would've gotten the message right away, but I stood there half an hour, gaping openmouthed while he stammered through his excuses. I didn't even put down my bag of groceries. Ochir said I could go ahead and take the groceries too, and out of the corner of my eye I glimpsed my two bags, sitting against the wall like a pair of fat baggy monsters, all packed up and ready to go.

In five minutes, I was out the door. I plopped down on a bench outside and bellowed like an ox, bawling like a stupid beat-up little kid, which I was. I took off my shoes, stretched myself out, and threw something on to stay warm. I'd been gone too long to go to my mom's apartment this late. Luckily it was a mild night and there wasn't any wind. I couldn't stand it. Every time I woke up, I'd sit up and tilt back my head. The light was still on in their window as the stars began to fade.

3. ALTA

IF ANYONE WERE TO ASK ME WHEN WAS THE HAPPIEST TIME OF MY life, I would say when the children were little and Mergen disappeared from my life. Still, there were plenty of times I regretted my decision. To live with a man, to know what his every slightest gesture means, to one nod bring food, to another go and quiet the kids, to mend his slippers and stay by his sickbed till pale morning comes, to know every little wrinkle and to watch, day by day, as they spread across his face like fans, knowing all along that my legs want to break into angry flight, that my eyelids twitch with forbidden dreams and the touches of my husband are like the passing years for me, painful and unavoidable, to bear that man children was the saddest thing in my life. And yet it may've been my great fortune.

Mergen waited days and nights at Shartsetseg's for me. My head was ready to burst. I saddled up the horse, readied some food for the journey, then the animal raked its hoof and my arms lost all their strength. My legs went weak and back it all went: saddle up on the shelf, *khuushuur* out of the sack. Four times in a row like that.

As dusk fell and the horse began to get restless from the endless preparations, I said to myself, Alta, morning is wiser than evening.

My determination was unbreakable.

I fell asleep pressing my lips to a small framed picture that he had given me once when, fingers locked in his, I had begged him not to leave me. In it, Mergen stood holding a rifle, chest puffed out like a khan warlord. Just before the flash went off he'd downed four wolves, he said. But they aren't in the picture. All night long that little wood frame wouldn't let me be, pressing red squares into my back while I tossed and turned in bed. Toward morning I wasn't so sure anymore.

I woke up feeling like my body was made of wood. My arms wouldn't move, not even my toes. I couldn't even stand, let alone saddle the horse again. I spent the day lying in bed like a shapeless piece of scrap meat, and the next morning woke with a fever. Even if I had wanted to, there was no way I could go. I was relieved.

Several weeks later, Tuleg returned. I no longer had to lower my eyes, I was pure again. I felt a great happiness. I never did anything like that to Tuleg again. But never again did his palms remind me of carved temple bowls, and never again did his kisses feel like anything more than the pecks of a bird taking what was his. I tried that much more to make up for it.

Our *ger* was run meticulously, not a single grain of spilled rice, no pieces of sheep hoof lying around, the way it sometimes is. Tuleg carried on again for a couple weeks after Oyuna was born, just like in the old days.

He'd never gone so crazy over anything except Magi.

When he sat Oyuna on his shoulders and let her pull his hair and snatched at her fingers until she squealed, I wouldn't have given even a broken snowshoe for Mergen.

Mergen walked out of my life quietly, and I'll carry the shame of that inside of me forever.

Every now and then I coax Shartsetseg into telling me about him, but she doesn't even like to let on much about herself these days. Anyway, I'm sure he's still there in the window. I just want to hear someone say his name. To hear aloud the name of the man who in breathless memories wraps me in his firm embrace and then slowly fades away, like everything else from the past.

My parents were washed away years ago. It's hard to hold in your head the color of someone's eyes, the shape of their lips, the tremble of their voice. And so they're gone. The pictures of them are lost.

I still hear Mama's voice sometimes, there's nothing left of Papa.

People used to say I had his courage, but all of them are gone now too.

If my belly didn't hurt so damn much, I wouldn't remember them either.

It was different with Dolgorma for me than it was for Tuleg. For him she was a somebody. Me, I could do without her; she was always too much of a know-it-all, and we'd stand in the *ger* with our backs to each other for days on end at a time. But her word carried weight, and she knew how to speak with such wisdom you could've kissed the hem of her *del.* I experienced it more than once. But the rest of the time, she was a cranky, spiteful old crone. As long as we each minded our work, we got along all right, because not standing still, that was her kind of thing, but as soon as it came to deciding something, then she would start screaming and pounce on my words, she always knew everything best.

If Dolgorma had been my mother, she would've caught it but good. No loudmouthed words ever fell in our family, though when Papa was riled up and had a couple swigs to boot, some blows were known to fall. We always had a bottle at home. It was often all we had. We ran around like ragamuffins, Gerla, Shartsetseg, Onon, and I.

Ogoi and Mira, my parents, never should have had us. People like them should be locked up, each in their own *ger,* so they can't crawl under a blanket together and make babies there.

Our parents had a few scrawny goats, some rawboned horses, and a couple of camels whose humps were so empty they sagged like an old woman's breasts. And then there were us children. Just part of the gang like all the rest. Every night Mama would count to make sure that nobody was missing, and Gerla and Shartsetseg and I were always glad when Papa was gone. He had his good moments too, but they were as rare as black sheep. I wasn't around for any of them.

The livestock grew; we grew. Mama cooked and screamed and hollered; Papa screamed and hollered. Sometimes he beat Mama's brains in and drank.

Gerla left as soon as her breasts grew in and she was old enough to have a man.

She went off with a Mongol whose name I forget. I waited for her to come back for me, but I never saw her again. She did the best she could. I remember the way she used to bounce me on her knee, and how one time she hit Papa for not being nice to Mama. The rest of us were whispering and playing under a blanket. Whenever our parents locked horns, we would crawl beneath a sheepskin. We'd be all covered in sweat from the wool, and after a while Onon would start to whine that he wanted out. I waited until there was nothing to hear. But until then, I kept him between my knees and no matter how much he moaned and groaned I wouldn't let him go.

Dolgorma used to accuse me of marrying Tuleg only because he was better off than my parents. But if it was just for money, I never would have married him. It was true he stood to get lots of livestock from his parents, but the main thing was the constant noise was driving me out of my mind.

How could we have ever been rich, when Mama had to buy new dishes every two months and Onon was always coming to me with slivers in his soles? I didn't want to be saddled with him, but Mama considered him one of the lambs, just another young thing to take care of, and that wasn't enough for Onon. He was a Mongol, not a camel.

It was tiring having him tagging around behind me all day long, but you can't keep constantly chasing away your own brother.

Papa said he would make Mama kids for as long as it took her to give him a son. Luckily, it wasn't that long, but except for being so excited he opened three bottles instead of one the day Onon was born, Papa completely ignored him. Soon I was sleeping in bed with Onon instead of Mama. I almost smothered him more than once. But when I tried to put him in Mama's bed, he threw his arms around my neck and hid his eyes in his hands. Even a horse-drawn carriage couldn't have pulled him off.

Onon stayed with me and Tuleg the first few couple of months. It might've worked, but Onon wouldn't give us a moment alone, so Tuleg turned him out. A filling station in the next *somon* over was looking to hire a man, and Tuleg knew someone there so he set it up for him. Three weeks later, Onon came to tell us good-bye, saying he was off with the Russians to somewhere near Krasnoyarsk. He brought us a stack of full gas cans.

He sent some postcards to Shartsetseg from a couple of cities in Russia, and two letters for me. One said he was doing well, and the other told about a big city on the shores of a cold sea and how he'd be back within a year and would be bringing a woman with him. It would be nice to see her someday.

We scurried away from our *ger* like cockroaches, all of us. We were each quick to find our own way, and now Shartsetseg's all I have left. She was always the cleverest of us. When Gerla and I would try to catch weevils and they kept slipping out of our fists, she would come flying in with a bowl and, bang, trap the bug underneath. When a she-camel went astray and we walked all over and still couldn't find her, she would strangle its baby's neck with a rope till the braying brought her back.

I even forgave my sister for Mergen in the end. I can recite her Ulaanbaatar address forwards and backwards. I could be on my last legs and I'd still be able to rattle it off. I know where I can find her—and Mergen along with her, planted in her kitchen. That's nice for me, and I thank her for that. The only way I'd be angry was if they had children together, but Shartsetseg is too old now to be able to cope with that.

With Zaya, it's much worse. May the steppe open beneath my feet and drown my blasphemous thoughts in its bowels for all eternity, but it's true. If anyone should've been riding that horse it was Zaya, not Magi.

I never said a word to her, and it's years now since it happened, but I can never fully forgive her. Mergen be dragged into the filthy clutches of Uregma, but Zaya's a sensible woman, and on top of that my daughter. If I had known I was dragging my belly around so that cunning she-lion could go and cheat with a man on her very own mother, I'd have stoned her right out of my womb. The image of my parents may have faded from my mind, but the memory of that will be before my eyes forever. The next time I'm born, those bad dreams will be born into my head with me, they'll creep in there, whoever I am. You don't forget a child. Or the pain of her betrayal.

With children it's never sure how they'll turn out. When there's more of them it's safer. Only one child is left to me, but of the sort that precious few are lucky enough to have. Oyuna alone hasn't left me, and I could go to my grave tomorrow knowing that a good piece of me would remain. The blessings of my old age. My dears. Oyuna and Tuleg.

I wouldn't have left another man for Tuleg. But he got me out of a *ger* where the pots flew back and forth like rocks between rowdy children, and stayed by me even after I almost slammed the door on him. Now we're old and need each other. Who would run to Oyuna for help if the other wasn't there? We talk about our ailments, and I gather the herbs prescribed by Dolgorma's ancient recipes. Tuleg hasn't got anything left to sink his teeth into since we gave most of our livestock to Naima, so he's taken up cooking in his old age.

We eat our meals together, then I wash the dishes, and we sit quietly by the stove. Neither of us sleeps very well. In bed, we just warm our flanks and stare into the dark. Tuleg's started to snore something fierce, and even when I doze off first his raspy breathing wakes me. So I slap his cheeks a couple times, he mumbles, and it's quiet again.

Sometimes our grandchildren come to visit. I always have a box of candies ready, so as soon as they arrive I pour them out a few. I also crumble up some *aaruul* and put it on a plate for them. Tsetsegma talks the most. Zula nods along. Batjar munches on *aaruul* and mostly keeps to himself.

Old folks are a nuisance. Just a burden to be rid of. Everyone agrees on that. When I was little and my grandmother was still alive, my parents would make us go see her. She didn't live far, so we went fairly often. Gerla and I would always take a deep breath of fresh air before we stepped inside her *ger* and hold it as long as we could. Nobody makes Tsetsegma, Batjar, and Zula visit me. So I hardly see them. It's only a little ways, but you'd think I was on the edge of the earth. I asked Oyuna one day if I stank and she lost her tongue. So much good advice I give them. I guess it's not enough.

I know quite a bit and I don't want to take it with me when I go. This gallbladder just won't let me be, and Oyuna says she hasn't got time. So who am I supposed to talk to?

With Shartsetseg you could talk about almost anything. When I was young and still had all of my children here with me, she used to come and help out. Now she would probably give up the ghost after traveling all that way. It's been a few years since the last time she came, I hardly see her at all anymore, but her words stick in my mind like snow on the mountains in June. She tried to get me to go with her back then. This isn't living, she said. One time when she came she brought pictures of the City, and when I saw all those people in all different clothes, the soaring concrete walls, dotted with windows reflecting the blue of the sky like a river, I wavered. But Magi was on the way by then, and the last thing Tuleg wanted to hear about was moving.

Shartsetseg made it somewhere in life. She was head of a meat plant, and with one month's pay she could buy herself a TV set, or a bed and a radio, if that's what she preferred. She said Tuleg's horses were handsomely built, and according to her the meat of our cows was the juiciest she'd ever tasted. We gave her some to take back to the plant with her, but it didn't work out. Supposedly they had their own suppliers, so they were all set for meat.

When the talk turned to Mergen, Shartsetseg would just sigh and bury her eyes in the ground. It must've been hard with him. From what I remember, a bottle was never too far from his lips, and he wasn't in a hurry to bring home any money either, according to her. Shartsetseg's eyes are like needles. When she frets like that, they get misty, and she says that this isn't living. Like the time when she tried to sway me.

I told her flat out that she didn't have to let Mergen stay with her on my account, but she wouldn't hear it.

If I hadn't pushed her, what happened between Mergen and Zaya would still be a secret to me. I don't want to spoil your beautiful *khuurag,* she blurted out at supper one night after she arrived. It took until morning of the next day before I had heard the whole thing. In the time it took her to tell it, the sky blackened and brightened again. The words slid out in time with her palms. Over my shoulders back and forth, like Hiroko when she soothed Nara.

When Hiroko bent her face to another and traced her healing patterns on a person's back with her hands, the sickness was half gone already. Seriously. Her hands were big and her arms as hairy as a man's. She was at least a head taller than everyone else, and when she spoke it was like a cow lowing over a skillet. Her breasts were small and her chest as broad as two men's put together. I was about twelve the first time I saw her. This enormous woman burst into the *ger* and my mother turned white as chalk.

Onon kicked me under the table and flashed his teeth. If she'd said she was our mother's sister, that we would've believed, but when we found out she was *our* sister it was more than we could swallow. She walked up to our table, dipped a finger in the soup, licked it, and looked at Mama. Like she had wires attached to her limbs that ended in Hiroko's fists, Mama rose without a word and followed her out the door, as Hiroko slowly backed out, facing us the whole time.

Like a little girl who'd been caught in a trap, was how Shartsetseg said our mother looked, leaning toward me over her bowl and speaking to me in a whisper.

There weren't many things that could get a rise out of Papa. Not even this. He pushed away his empty bowl, picked up a bottle, and went about feeding the stove between gulps. It was late fall, our mother was outside in only a light house *del,* and a chill seeped in through the felt walls of our *ger.*

I was almost asleep by the time the door creaked open again and Mama tiptoed into bed. Onon gave me a poke in the side and murmured that he was afraid. I turned onto my other side and fell fast asleep.

When Hiroko came the second time, I was out in front of the *ger* peeling potatoes with Mama. Gerla had been gone for several months by then, and Shartsetseg was off somewhere running around with Onon. The potatoes we had for lunch that day were boiled to a mush.

Time shrank down to the length of my mother's bare sentences, and I was uneasy about how quickly this strange woman had become my sister. Mama nudged me forward and said to introduce myself. Then the two of them talked about money while I ran to take the potatoes off, and when I got back, my mother was crouched on the floor again and Hiroko was slipping some sort of package into her *del.* At least three of me could've fit inside that crimson *del* of hers. Her head was bald and her monk's slippers were tattered and gray with dust. When Shartsetseg got back, she also had to say hello. But before she had a chance to meet Onon, Hiroko had to be on her way, and Mama told us he was still too little to have a new sister, so it would be better if we didn't tell him for now.

The third time I saw Hiroko was at the monastery. My mother brought me there with her and then left us alone.

The fourth time, Hiroko told me what my mother had lacked the courage to say. Or maybe that was their agreement. Either way it's too late to ask my mother now, and I won't get to Hiroko either if my gallbladder keeps acting up like this.

Hiroko never called our mother anything but Mira.

When Mira was very young, just a long-legged girl in braids still, Khaira, her mother, noticed one day that Mira had gotten fatter. This puzzled her, because Mira ate the same food as everyone else. Mira, her parents' oldest daughter, was pregnant by a boy from the *somon* school, and didn't even know it until everyone in the *ger* was talking about her belly and Khaira took her aside and explained it all to her. By then it was too late to do anything about it, and so one hot morning in the eighth month, Hiroko was born. Mira was sent to her relatives, and Hiroko was raised by Khaira along with the rest of her children. Mira was forbidden to visit, so she didn't see anyone from her *ger* at all for years. Eventually she got pregnant again, but the relatives collared my father, and so they were wed and had Gerla, and then me and my other siblings in the *ger* they built for themselves.

Until one day Hiroko learned that the woman who sent her out to gather *argal* every evening and taught her to tie the knots on the *ger* wasn't her mother. She stepped up to her, scratched her across the face, and went off in search of her real mother.

Hiroko said the first time she came was before the time my mother turned white and Onon was so afraid. Onon was still crawling back then, and when Hiroko and my mother began to talk he started crying. Nobody else was there that day, so that was her longest visit. Mama told her to scuttle off quick before Papa came home from the herd, and it took a lot of convincing for Mama to give her a quick little hug.

The rest I knew. Hiroko didn't want to hide her visits anymore, and so finally we met. Papa couldn't even see his fingers through the vodka haze, and most of the time he was gone anyway, so it didn't make any difference. Just one thing still wasn't clear to me: How had she found my mother?

When we saw each other the fourth time and she finally told me the story, I blurted my question out right away. She didn't even know what Mama looked like, after all. And none of our relatives had any clue where Mama and Papa grazed their flocks.

Hiroko just smiled, hitched an eyebrow, and took me by the shoulders with those oversized hands of hers.

I felt like a grain of rice that might soar up into the clouds at the slightest careless move, and at the thought of that headlong plunge my head began to spin. Don't be afraid, she said, as I twisted my shoulders to make her let go. I may not have liked her strong, hairy arms, but what she said, absolutely. It isn't bad coming into a big sister like her.

From then on I went to see her several times a year when she was at the monastery, and after as well, when she moved to the City. Until I met Tuleg, I'd never known a firm, dependable embrace except for hers. To this day I still don't understand how she found Mama.

When I wriggled free and asked her again, she put her hands on her hips like a wrestler at Naadam, as if to say, Wouldn't you like to know? A quiet smile played around the corners of her mouth, but I had the feeling that, inside, she was snorting away with laughter. What a silly, silly girl you are, and still so very young.

Hiroko visited Mama more than any of the rest of us. We were glad to be gone from home. Just because someone is old doesn't mean they deserve respect—that was Shartsetseg's favorite. I don't like that kind of talk, but the result was the same in the end. My children barely even knew their grandmother Mira.

I was ashamed of her and my father in front of Tuleg. Mama's teeth were falling out, so no one could understand her but us, and I was afraid when my husband bent down to try to catch her words, she would spray him with spit and I'd be disgraced.

Young or old, Papa went on drowning his innards in booze, though in the end he got so weak my mother had to hold the bottle for him. At least he stopped making a ruckus. And my mother stopped walking around with bruises all over her body, and for the first time in my life I was able to sit down and talk with him. A couple of times we talked about what it was like when he was young and cars were metal bears and villagers were afraid of them, and what a beauty Mama had been when she still had hair and teeth. Then Papa passed away, and Mama shortly after him.

After Hiroko finished her stay at the monastery, she moved into a *ger* in the Ulaanbaatar yurt district, whose white felt domes spray out from the center in every direction like drops of milk.

The true City, where the buildings stand side by side like fingers on a hand and there are more people on one street than if all the people in all the *gers* I've ever been in were dumped out at once, I never did make it in to see the inside of that City.

Hiroko had a cozy *ger* on the very edge of the outskirts. In her yard she had ten goats, no sheep or cows, and two skinny horses. My older sister had authority. She may have shed her monk's *del* when she left the monastery, but she still had powerful contacts. She didn't act half as proud as old Dolgorma, so people didn't fear her, and her broad shoulders served to comfort many an unfortunate with nobody else to cry to. And if a woman who lived alone with her children needed help with a man's work, she was there for them as well.

She could carry a bull on her back, put up a *ger* all by herself, and her healing hands and curative spells were there for all in need. In return, people brought her vodka, sweets, the finest cuts of young ram, wolfskins, cashmere, and other things. Hiroko lived a good life in her little six-sided *ger*.

What she loved most of all, though, was little children and animals. She rarely turned down a woman's request to watch her little ones. She often carried four or five on her back at once, whinnying like a mare, to the pounding of little fists on her fence from all the others who wanted a turn. She always made sure her pockets were full of candies, and whenever a child came sobbing from home, she brewed a soothing cup of tea and let him spend the night.

Apart from little children, the creature closest to Hiroko's heart was Seruul, a silver-gray horse she had snatched from under a *nuudelchin's* knife before he could finish him off. Seruul was born with crooked legs and could barely carry a child. Underneath a grown-up he would wobble until he collapsed in a heap, and if Hiroko, as big as she was, had ever tried to mount that horse, it would have been the end of him. I remember Seruul from when Hiroko lived in the City. Right up to his last days he looked like a young colt. A scrawny, fearful little horse. There was something of the eternal child in Hiroko as well.

She never did become a woman. She had the thick, bony legs of a not yet fully grown girl, and she never had any interest in men. My sister was also one of the few who cut her hair in a short fringe, so she looked like a man from behind.

All kinds of homeless people passed through Hiroko's *ger*, staying two or three nights and then, warmed and fed, moving on again. Some returned and others didn't, and my sister's reputation grew. In a few years her healing skills were known throughout the district, and as her reputation spread, so did the rumors. The fact that she'd never been seen with a man was more than enough to start people talking. Some of her regular visitors I'll never forget. The boy with rubber hands, who could write with one foot while he scratched his back with the other. His story was he was an *erliiz* who ran away from the Russian circus, the bastard son of some ballerina, supposedly. He stopped in at the end of winter every year to fix himself up after months out in the freezing cold, living on water and gristly scraps that he wrestled away from the dogs. Or the gangly, green-eyed man who walked the district *ger* to *ger*, helping out with whatever he could in exchange for a bite to eat. Nobody knew their way around the Ulaanbaatar yurts like he did. He knew everyone, and would always bring Hiroko up to date on all the latest gossip that people had made up about her over the past year. During his five or six days there, he would gather so much *argal* that Hiroko wouldn't have to worry for months. She also liked him because he always sensed when his time was up, and quietly he'd pack his things and leave without a fuss.

Nara butted heads with her over that right from the start. After that unfortunate business with Jargal when nobody knew what to do, I decided a couple of months at Hiroko's might snap her out of it. Hiroko said she wasn't opposed, and so she came out to see us and the three of us rode back to her place together.

With Nara resisting along the way we kept her in between us, since there was no way to know when she might turn tail and go galloping back to her loved one. A couple of times she tried it, but then Hiroko had a word with her, and the rest of the way she followed our lead in silence. The two of them seemed to get along, but only until we got to the City and Nara found out how my sister ran things.

We left her in peace for a couple of days, just keeping an eye out that she didn't make a dash for it, and Hiroko outdid herself with all the smiles, pleasant nods, and kindness she could muster. But the quarrels weren't long in coming. Nara began to take liberties, and whatever she said it was hostile. To me Hiroko was a kindhearted soul, ready to part with her last possession to help her fellow man;

to Nara she was an old, selfish, inconsiderate witch. I respected the way my sister cared for the children who came to her with their troubles, rather than bringing them home to their parents. Nara took it badly when some poor soul left after a couple of days and Hiroko was glad to see the gate click shut behind him. This isn't some shelter I'm running, she'd say, and Nara got so angry she was ready to explode.

I must say, Hiroko coddled that horse like a baby, and anyone unknowing enough to speak to Seruul crossly, or smack him on the neck, the way you usually do with a rowdy horse, fell promptly into disfavor. I was there once when a starving man had no sooner dipped his spoon in the soup than Hiroko chased him out because he'd given Seruul a kick for rummaging through his knapsack. It's also true that anyone who overstayed his welcome heard things never spoken where Seruul's long ears could hear. Hiroko knew how to yell too, though usually all it took was a few frowning looks for the poor stiff to realize that if he ever wanted to come back again he'd better pack up in a hurry.

Hiroko had her moods when it was better to avoid her. She could flit around for days on end at others' beck and call, but then her mood would darken, she didn't want to see a soul, and if anybody knocked on the gate she would yell there was nobody home. Then Nara would go and let them in, and the shouting would start all over again.

Nara should have been grateful that Hiroko had taken her in, but instead of that she lectured her and let children in to sleep in the *ger,* which got on my sister's nerves. It dragged on like that till the day I left, because waiting for me back home were not only Tuleg, Oyuna, and Zaya, but the livestock and a *ger* that was going to the dogs.

The moment a woman goes away the man stops taking care of himself, and the thought of the chaos awaiting me made my hair stand up on end.

I had to leave Nara to her fate, so the rest I know only from Hiroko. I never really spoke again with Nara after that. I only saw her once more in fact. At Oyuna's wedding. Oyuna had her mind made up that she couldn't get married without her, and so I went and brought her back for a few quick days of food and cheer, and haven't heard of her since. She isn't at Hiroko's anymore, and the only other person that I know in the City is Shartsetseg, and she doesn't know anything either.

When I asked her about Nara once, years ago, she laughed and said if I thought the City was really that small, then I'd better not ask what she thought of me. I know, the birdbrained country girl, but I didn't mind it coming from her. I even laughed at myself, which not every woman can do. It's good for you sometimes.

If only this aching belly of mine would leave me in peace. Hiroko took a look at it once, tapped around my belly button and all along the sides, listened to it rumble. She said it was hard and made a funny noise. Then she rubbed my calves and said to soak a scarf in herbal soup and wear it around my neck for three days.

It doesn't seem to have helped much.

Old Dolgorma, when it got really bad, would level with the sick, rather than making a nuisance for them and her by giving them a treatment that wouldn't do any good anyway. My sister gave everyone something. Plenty of people who came to her ended up dying anyway, but others recovered, and those were the ones that she talked about.

Hiroko told me that, after I left, things got unbearable between her and Nara. She thought she could draw her unhappy niece out of her tears, and prepared all sorts of herbs to that end, but Nara was like a demon. My sister got rid of the barking dog and built a pen to hold the goats so they wouldn't go bleating all over the place. She cleaned and swept the *ger* and laid in sacks of flour and snow-white rice, all so Nara wouldn't have any worries and needn't trouble with anything. And instead of being grateful, Nara started telling my sister how to run her life and treating things that weren't hers as if they were her own. For a woman who'd stood on her own two feet since she was just a child and had gone through her whole life without any help, it was insulting. Nara was barely twenty, and had always had me and Tuleg behind her.

That's how it should be for every young girl, I didn't deserve any special thanks for what I'd done, I know, and it occurred to me that what happened with Jargal may have been my fault as well—no well-brought-up woman would kiss a man's hand, after all—but still, Nara should have realized she had it easy compared to my sister, and that it isn't a young girl's place to give advice to her elders. Hiroko would never have made the allowances that she did if Nara wasn't her niece. Hiroko stuck it out with her for several months, and still it was Nara who walked out and slammed the gate in the end.

Hiroko said Nara was playing games with us. And that it had never taken her so long to see through such a sham. The first time Hiroko saw her in the Red Mountains, she was just as horrified as all of us who were living with her.

But why, though? Why would the girl lead us on like that?

The happiness that beamed from her face when Jargal agreed to marry her was real. I know how my daughter looks when she's in seventh heaven, and her sorrows aren't false either.

But Hiroko wouldn't budge. She said Nara was just looking for a way to get to the City, and I got angry, since there was no way on earth that she could've known she was going to end up at Hiroko's. It was only after my daughter dropped off the face of the earth that Hiroko told me all this.

I came to visit her and arrived to find the boy with the rubber hands in her *khashaa*, along with the man who knew everyone, gorging on chunks of boiled meat my sister had cooked for them. Meanwhile she sat off in the corner, nuzzling with Seruul. As soon as she saw me she frowned.

She isn't here, she blurted with a mischievous grin on her face, as if Nara had pulled some incredible prank and the whole thing was just hilarious. Meanwhile I had come hundreds of miles just to see if my daughter's face had finally started to blossom, only to find her nowhere in sight and my sister sitting next to a horse, acting like it was nothing.

The two of us parted that day on bad terms for the first and last time, tempers on edge, each one convinced that the other was to blame. I held Hiroko responsible for Nara. She said it wasn't her fault I had done such a bad job of raising her. I dumped my gifts on the table, downed two cups of cold tea, and walked back out to try and find someone heading toward our *somon*.

I never would have believed that my granddaughter would be the one to tell me about my daughter. Dolgorma had to be born for me to find out anything definite about Nara. When Dolgorma spent her vacations with us, she would join in on whatever conversation we were having. Nobody asked her too many questions about the City or what her mother was up to, since it was clear from the start that she didn't have any more idea than we did.

Naturally, she couldn't get a word in edgewise with us, so most of the time she would listen and just slip something in every now and then—for instance, if we were talking about something having to do with the City and she wanted to shine for us.

One night we'd sorted everything through and were quietly sitting around the stove, our faces shining with fat and the glow of the fire, when someone—Oyuna, I think—started in on Nara again, and Dolgorma jumped clear out of her seat. Here she was, not even ten, and raving about silky hair the color of pine, lashes so long they made a breeze, the sweet-smelling haze of cigarette smoke, and blouses that made her hair stand on end when she rubbed her face against them.

Some of us forgot to close our mouths and others' jaws dropped in shock the way old people's do. It had been ages since the *ger* had been that tense, and it would be ages before it was that tense again— like a beast ready to pounce, like a tarbagan ready to flee. Dolgorma talked of Nara at length and with great admiration, but nowhere in her description of the perfumed woman about town did I recognize my daughter. The more fervently she gushed, the more heavy the air in the *ger* became, the words pressing down on me from every side.

We weren't worth a word to that little miss la-di-da for years, not a single sign that she was alive, and here this child worshiped her. I breathed easier knowing that she was all right, but I was through with her as a daughter.

Mama used to tell me about her brother the family disowned. He had renounced her father. In front of the soldiers. In order to survive. My grandmother warned him never to come in her sight again. Nara hadn't done anything bad, she just dropped us from her mind, and I wish her all the best, but I don't want to see her again.

The next time Zaya came, I waited for a moment when everyone else was gone and asked her what she knew. As her mother and also as the mother of her sister. I had barely begun when she suddenly blurted, Kids, they always exaggerate. We chatted until Naima appeared with a fistful of tarbagans. Then Oyuna came in to skin them, so we had to cut it short.

All I know about Nara now is she works in some classy establishment, brings in decent money, and she thinks of me often, supposedly, but because of how she ran away she's afraid to come and visit. She hasn't got a husband or children, but she and Zaya get together every now and then. At least they still have each other. They've always stuck together for as long as I can remember.

Zaya comes to see us from the City once in a while, and we have Dolgorma with us on vacations. I'm always delighted when she arrives, since every summer could be my last. Lately my gallbladder's acting up more and more. Tuleg won't let me eat anything fatty. But if I can't have any pleasure in life, I'd rather drop dead. And gladly. Why torture myself for the doctors' sake? I eat what I feel like. Nobody can tell me what to do.

Dolgorma stayed with us when she came on vacation this year. That way she didn't have to squeeze in at Oyuna's. None of Oyuna's children are ready to go it on their own, so there's no room to move in her *ger*. Dolgorma had it good with us. I was there just for her. All that Tuleg needs these days is peace and quiet and plenty of milk tea and tobacco, and with me he has all that in spades. But you couldn't have a proper conversation with him anymore, and a young person's voice is priceless, in my opinion. Not to mention I'm bad on my feet. A few years back my soles swelled up, and ever since then they're like pillows. My walk is wobbly and unsteady, so Dolgorma was a big help her last summer here. I just told her where and what and didn't have to budge. Feet up, some simple sewing in my lap—that's for me. I can still cook and clean, but on limber legs it takes half as long, so I try as much as possible to leave it to the young. As soon as I got accustomed to her clumsy little city hands and stopped trying to rush her, she dropped the idle comments and things seemed to be all right. She even agreed not to bring any new contraptions into the *ger*.

Zaya brought me a lamp from the City the other day, and that was plenty. Making day out of darkness when I wake at midnight feeling faint and need to go out for a gulp of fresh air, all right. But I'd rather trip on the doorstep and fall flat on my face in the grass than have anyone laugh at me. There needs to be respect, and these new gadgets rob me of it. I told Dolgorma first thing. I tossed an old *del* on her bed, and a pair of boots with yak laces—I wouldn't have her traipsing around in city clothes on my watch—and shot her back a withering look when she rolled her eyes at me. The main thing was to keep the girl occupied so she didn't have time for shenanigans. I'd show her to disrespect the gray-haired.

I wanted it to be nice for us, so before she came I cooked up a big pot of goat soup and heated up as many *buuz* as a young body could possibly need. I put something nice on for Tuleg and bought a pouch of tobacco from Dorj, so he could enjoy himself and not annoy Dolgorma with all his petty grumbling. And in return all I got was ingratitude. I made a genuine effort, and mending family ties is what old women are here for. It's not as if I have that many grandchildren, after all. But her whole two months here, she went around with her teeth clenched, scowling like an angry child.

I talked about how easily hurt a girl is when she's foolish and young. I talked about Zaya, who dressed her like a khan princess yet couldn't snare a decent man. I talked about short skirts that reap only colds; the decent life of a righteous woman, the only one that bears fruit, juicy and full of pips; children who know their father. I talked about prayer and clasped hands, which help when all else has failed. I talked about happiness, and Dolgorma wanted to hear none of it. It was like she had pine plugs in her ears. The girl was incorrigible. No upbringing whatsoever. But I didn't give up. I took my mother's headdress out of its box and talked about women who remain forsaken in old age because they don't know how to arrange things. I talked about winter nights that lure a woman underneath the blankets like a devil-may-care young man, and how you should always keep to your feet, and how if you want to make a baby you have to press up close against a man and reach between his thighs. I even told her that. It's not as if I were some prudish old hen; what I know, I say. I wanted to be a hollow tree that she could tell her secrets to, I wanted someone to listen to all my good advice. But no. Dolgorma went on rolling her eyes up and down the walls of the *ger*, and Tuleg went on rolling his smokes and lining them up in a row. One next to the other, so tomorrow he could rest. And with that line of thin white tubes, like the sun-bleached ties of the Baikal–Amur railway, my fervor grew as well. There wasn't much left to tell before I'd told her everything. Including that I only know the Baikal–Amur railway line from pictures and I'm glad of it. But when I turned to look at her again, Dolgorma was asleep.

I won't be discouraged. My words speak of summers spent among goats, of winter nights without *argal*, of dozens of mended *dels* and thousands of righteous suet soups. What about her?

Next summer I'll tell her it all again.

It doesn't do any more good with Tsetsegma or Zula either. Batjar can shake his head, he's a man, but it isn't for girls to be wagging their heads. With Oyuna there were no troubles at all. Every mother's daughters drink from a different crock of milk, and that's all there is to it. When they were little they used to trail around behind me like ants after sugar. They'd come to me for candies. My pockets were always full of them. Now when they come see me, which isn't very often, I pour the candies in a dish so they drum down like hail on tin, and still the girls don't want them. I don't know what to tempt them with. It worries me that they're still here, that some men haven't come and swept them away. At their age I was already rocking Magi in the cradle, and here they are still hanging around Oyuna's neck. I only hope they don't disgrace us.

Oyuna and Naima are pureblooded, both. Neither of them is an *erliiz*. Ariuna was never the run-around type—Tsobo guarded her closely—and Oyuna is Tuleg's without a doubt. A spotless lineage.

When they were little, Zula and Tsetsegma were as cute and cuddly as they come. But as they got older they went downhill. They're no beauties, I'll tell you that. Zula's the older one by two years and her nose is like a radish. *Buuz* for a nose, as Tuleg says, and an ear like dried fruit. The first thing Oyuna said as soon as Zula was born was she was going to comb her hair over it, but even hair can't hide an ear rolled like that. Her skin is as porous as dough that's been left out for too long, and her other ear droops like a Burkhan's. Her hips are big, though, and so are her breasts. Actually I'm surprised that nobody's scooped her up by now.

Men are hard to please.

Tsetsegma is her sister's spitting image. Her ears are normal, but her arms and legs are as flimsy as a barren goat's. She's got a bleating voice and an immodest heart. *Khon, khon*, I used to hear the little ones shout at her when I picked her up from school.

I had to say something. If only they weren't so stubborn. They only had to reach out and take what was theirs and they would've been out of the *ger* by now. There was nothing wrong with those men. Either one. Choilin was a bit of a clod, I admit, but he was ready to give Tsetsegma the world on a plate. His family had a house in the *somon* center, and his father I had known since he was just a little boy. Girls would've fought to the death over him. Davaanyam worked in the cashmere plant, and cashmere never goes out of demand, so a girl could be sure they would never go without. But Zula and Tsetsegma weren't sweet on the idea. They were all in the same class together in school, and after they finished, Choilin and Davaanyam used to come out and see us sometimes. Good, decent men. That was several years back.

They arrived together, all dressed up in their finery like *noyons* for the *kuriltai,* and Tsetsegma and Zula didn't even make tea for them. They fled like little girls. So we sat there in Oyuna's *ger* and waited until evening. Oyuna fussed over them all afternoon, sending Batjar out to look for the girls, telling our guests they had gone picking berries, and blathering on about nothing. By the time the orb sank behind the mountains, Davaanyam and Choilin knew our whole family history going five generations back.

On their way home they met the girls. My eyesight may be bad, but even from here I could see their outlines. Like figures made of sticks. Choilin held out his hands to Tsetsegma. I held my breath. She snatched her sister by the hand and they broke into a run. They breathlessly came to a stop at the *ger* and exploded in thunderous laughter. The two fine-dressed men urged their horses on, and a moment later they were gone.

May horse teeth grow into your heads, I told the two of them afterwards. You're digging yourselves a pit so deep, no one will ever be able to pull you out. Old maids! I shouted at them as they walked away from me.

Oyuna has too little say in her *ger.* And the same goes for Naima. I was there one time when Naima asked his son a question, and Batjar just went right on buttoning up his *del* like his father was a mangy dog. But on one thing at least Oyuna is firm. She refuses to let her girls go to the City. They could stand on their heads for all she cared, she still wouldn't give in. But how're we supposed to meet anyone, when the only men we ever run into are Papa and Batjar coming home from the herd at night, they moan.

You spurned the good fortune that fell at your feet, that's what I say. Just grab the *del* of the first man who comes galloping past and pray. When it comes to men, in the long run they're all pretty much the same.

A couple of days ago, Oyuna said she saw Choilin at the *somon* store. Standing in line with a woman holding a baby rolled in a blanket. Oyuna said Tsetsegma was *tsaraitai* next to her, a beautiful belle in a khan queen's crown. Her eyes will be moist when she sees them together.

Batjar already has some experience under his belt. Oyuna found a blue-black wisp of hair tied in ribbon inside his *del*. She was all upset about it but didn't want to pry, so I went to have a talk with him. He grinned as I spoke and then patted me on the shoulder. It was a talisman made out of yak hair, he said.

I get the same feeling from Zaya sometimes. I wonder if she isn't hiding something. She doesn't like to talk about the City, and when she does, the words don't seem to chime, like beads knocking around in a box. Like she's reciting a line about some totally different person.

The main thing is she's happy. I never hear her complain, and she is a grown woman, after all, let her keep to herself if she doesn't want to brag. Nara knows everything, I'm sure. I was never fond of my mother's questions either. I told it all to Yellow Flower. That's the way it goes.

One of these days I'd like to see Shartsetseg again. Yellow Flower is living proof that not everyone in the City has to fall into disgrace. She's still the same. As long as I've known her, and that's more than sixty winters. She's always been a help to me. Just the fact of her listening was a relief every time. For instance, that time when the girls were little, before Magi had her accident, and I noticed that Oyuna had these little black-and-blue lines running around her ankles. She confided in me that Zaya and Nara would tie her up for fun sometimes. I flogged them both like horses, but the lines came back again, and she told me some other things too. They were resourceful, those two.

I don't love all my children the same and I feel guilty for it. Oyuna was always the dearest to me, and little children can sense these things like animals sense human fear. I know that, but how can I command my heart? Now they've got their own lives, but it used to keep me awake at night. Shartsetseg told me that that's how it is for lots of women, just remember what it was like with Hiroko and our mother. And suddenly I had a memory of Mama in front of the *ger*, standing there, legs spread, refusing to let Hiroko in, and all of us children also wanted her to go. I'm much better than that. All my children are welcome in my home, and everyone always got an equal share of everything. No one got bigger portions, no one was allowed to do anything mean to anyone else, and I never said to any of them, You I love, you I don't.

At first I didn't approve of it when my sister invited Zaya to stay with her in the City. It didn't fit with my ideas. I didn't want my girls to scatter to the winds like me and my sisters and brother did. But Yellow Flower said Zaya would think that I didn't want the best for her, so against my wishes I let her go. Mainly so she could see that I wanted to humor her.

Oyuna blamed me for it later, but that's something I can never explain to her.

The time Yellow Flower helped me the most was when Magi left us. Tuleg had eyes only for vodka, so I had to manage everything on my own. My sister offered to come without my even asking. The girls were all crazy about her. Her word was sacred. Even my nighttime stories paled compared to hers, like a wolf dog next to a Bankhar, like a skullcap in the hot summer. The girls only wanted to listen to her. And Zaya most of all.

At the time I still hoped that Shartsetseg would have at least one child. She wasn't exactly young anymore, but still, it wasn't impossible. When I saw how good she was with the little ones, I prayed. There's no disaster greater for a woman. No punishment on earth more cruel. And Shartsetseg didn't deserve it.

It happened to Nara too.

A woman without a child is like a tree without fruit. Solitary and strong, perhaps, but serving no purpose. The steppe is full of trees like that. Sprouting up from the cracks in the rocks, twisting with the wind, yet all year long not a single bee alights on them. They terrify me, those trees. Women without children terrify me.

I know a few. One of them is Anra, Nara's friend from when she taught in the *somon* school. Ulantsetseg, her mother, who cruel people know as Uregma, took her around to all the doctors. They saw every shaman in the region and nothing came of it. Anra's husband is a good man, but sooner or later, unless he's a fool, he's going to find someone else.

Everyone wants a child.

Anra is over forty now. Other women are bouncing grandkids on their knees and she's still waiting for a child of her own. When I ran into her in the *somon* center a couple years back, it was all she could talk about. Nothing has changed. Oyuna dropped by with some *koumiss* for her and told me about it afterwards. How can I tell her she's waited too long and now it's too late?

The women in the *somon* center have started avoiding her.

Who wants to go on having the same pointless conversation over and over again? I hear she's got a whole set of outfits stored away in her closet. And she's still sewing more. Altering the old ones and buying new material. That won't bring her a child, and it doesn't help anyone. People are going to think what they want. They already do. A woman in the shop told me that Anra was cracked in the head. She was dragging around two whiny tots with a third perched on the back of her neck. While Anra sits at home sewing booties and pondering the prettiest name, Ulantsetseg is wasting away and won't even say hello anymore. She gave life to a girl who'll never have anyone gurgle into her ear, a girl who needn't even have been here.

Now Borji, she took a different path. As soon as she saw that Burkhan wasn't going to grant her a child, she went and took in an orphan. Little Arinkhuu had parents, but he didn't even exist for them. They sent him away to boarding school and he never went home again. Then she took in another two boys: one of them a redhead—goodness knows where his father was from—and the other a sheer delight. Bright and eager as a wolf cub. Borji's a good mother, and at least this way the boys will grow up to be something.

Anra doesn't want someone else's, so let her cry her eyes out.

I talked about children with Hiroko too. She always liked to hold me, and when we snuggled under a blanket together I almost felt like a child again, and I poured out my heart to her every time. So that came out too. I didn't get it. Hiroko didn't feel bad about it at all. She said she had plenty of fun with other people's children and didn't need her own. And I don't want them either, she whispered in my ear, and I could feel her cheeks burning.

My big sister is the most unusual woman I know.

Then she gave me a kiss on the forehead. What more could she want? she said.

It's true, children can be a pretty big pain in the neck, and if Hiroko had to take care of her own, she wouldn't have had the time to help others the way she did. Being that I was blessed by Burkhan with a fertile womb, I could never have put someone else's children before my own. Maybe that and the fact that normal women didn't feel that way was the reason why I had so much respect for Hiroko.

If not for Oyuna, I wouldn't be doing too well myself. I gave life to four women and only have one grandson to show for it. Sometimes I dream that he'll bring home a woman and some new ones will come along to join us in our *gers*. Wouldn't that be something. Tuleg and I came here with our bare hands, and that's how we always pictured it. A big family is stronger than bast.

When Tuleg first planted his *urga* here and I was expecting Magi, he said the yurts of our children's children would stretch to the horizon.

I felt like I couldn't breathe from the hot wave that surged up from my belly into my throat. That was one of the times we pledged that, for better or for worse, we would always be together.

Tuleg wanted a lot of children from the start, but after I met Mergen, I only laid with Tuleg when it couldn't be avoided. I knew he would be nicer then, and that was good for everyone. Especially for the children.

With Mergen it was different. With Mergen I came to know what it is when a woman's drunk with rapture and each kiss tastes better than the one that came before. When a man's hands burn, sending a mix of pain and pleasure shooting down her spine. When I want a child from a man not because I want to nurse an infant at my breast, but because I long to hold his largeness inside of me forever.

I never knew that with Tuleg. Which was why Mergen made me a child right away the very first night and with Tuleg we always had to wait.

I'd also like to live long enough to see some great-grandchildren. In these parts women my age often have two or three by now. I don't want to die without at least once having heard the cry of a newborn in my clan. There had to be something behind that talisman of Batjar's. But in any case, it wasn't the mother of his children. If it was serious, he would've brought her around to show us instead of treating me like a fool. Let him sow his oats while he can. Just as long as he doesn't make some gullible girl unhappy.

Lately I've just about given up hope of ever having great-grandchildren. This doggone gallbladder won't shut up. Maybe Hiroko could give me some advice, but it's such an awfully long way to go. If I can just make it long enough to see Dolgorma next year. Girls change so fast at her age. Next summer she'll be sixteen, or is it seventeen, I've lost track. In short, a full-grown woman, through and through, and beautiful to boot.

If only she would take some lessons from my experience. But I still believe it hasn't been entirely in vain.

Whether she wants to hear it or not, it's stored away inside her head in case she needs it later on. She'll think back on her grandmother many times in years to come. And see that things are just as I said. Because that's how it really is.

4. OYUNA

ZAYA AND NARA WENT AROUND WITH THEIR NOSES UP IN THE AIR from the day they were born, and it shows in the way they turned out. Everyone knows the youngest have to fight for their fair share, and you better believe it wasn't any different for me. Nobody gave me anything for free. Not a lot of people know that. What can I say, I make do for myself, and I thank the mountain *Tengers* for seeing fit to make me beat a path through the thorns, so at the end of it they could grace me with a husband and three children.

What more can you expect from life? And being a proper woman, in return I owe thousands of genuflections and whispered prayers. For the rest of my life I'll be going to the *ovoo* to give thanks, and I could scrape my knees to the bone and sell all our goats to buy silk *khataks* and it still wouldn't be enough, because I've always had luck on my side. I took the same knocks as my sisters, but I knew how to grab onto luck and not let it get away. Hold on and don't let go, that's the way to do it. That's what I keep telling my kids, over and over, as much as I can. As their mother, they'll always matter to me, and when it comes to them I will never hold my tongue. Let them hear about life from a woman with experience.

They say that their world's different and shove the teapot into my hand. All of them are polite—*Tenger* forbid that they not be, I taught my kids their manners—and so they sit smiling patiently, thinking Mama will shut her trap and spill the tea with her shaky hands. But I slam the pot down on the table. Nobody does that to me. I say what I think. No matter what. It's for their own good. Later on they'll realize it and do the same with their own kids. The old have to teach the young, that's their sacred right. What else have they got left?

I may be worn out, but when Zula holds my arm I can go wherever I set my mind to, and I still have a voice like a bell. I've called my husband and children in at night so many times, the echo in our mountains knows my name. Even the branches sigh at my command, and if someone takes too long coming home, they always call for me. My voice can reach as high as the clouds and clear a hole in a flock of birds flying in formation like a stone ripples the water, and a boy or girl lost in the mist can use it to find their way back. Even when I was little I had a powerful voice. Our mother had lots of work, and if I didn't scream, Nara and Zaya would leave me hanging up in my leather crib all day. Mama fed me faithfully, that she took care of, but not much more. The rest was up to my sisters, and they wriggled out of their duties all the time.

Magi was pretty conscientious. I remember she'd always feel inside my boots so I wouldn't be tramping around in the wet, and after meals she'd always ask if I had had enough. The other two, never.

But evil deeds don't go away, misfortune dogs the wicked, and all wrongs do return. In this life or another, but they never leave the earth. I remember everything from my childhood.

Not Zaya, I guess. Whenever I drag something up from the past, she rolls her eyes insultedly and pouts like she's been wronged.

If only she could've seen the pained look of disgust on her face when Mama stuffed me into her arms—not that I wanted to be there, but someone had to watch me—she wouldn't toss her braid with that wounded look only she can do. By then I knew for certain that as soon as she got hold of me she'd turn around and lock me up or put me up somewhere high where I couldn't get down from. I knew it. But Zaya has no memory.

I still can't help but see in that bent, ugly woman the little girl who laughed at me from her hiding place behind the rocks while I broke down in tears. So many times on our walks in the mountains I thought I might never see Mama again.

Mama liked me best.

After my face got mangled by that wild dog, no one could take

Mama away from me ever again. She was mine and the whole family knew it.

It didn't do Zaya any good to be the best in school. I was the center of the family after Magi died, and that was why she left.

She thought nobody knew she was good so she had to prove what she was worth, but I was small and weak and that's why Mama paid more attention to me. Every mother loves all her children the same. But after a certain point, Zaya was the oldest, and above all an *erliiz,* so she shouldn't have been surprised. Mothers belong to their little ones; the older ones have to fend for themselves. I was afraid of Zaya, so I made things up about her. Mama would pick me up and fold me in her arms and I would breathe into her hair, hearing Zaya's heated protests while I drowned my eyes in Mama's *del* to avoid my sister's glaring looks.

The next day, in back of the *ger,* she rolled up my *del.* Nara kept a lookout to make sure no one was coming, and the sound of my sobbing was lost amid the chorus of bubbling pots and the general commotion of Mama's work around the *ger.* Nara always did whatever Zaya told her to. When Zaya was away, Nara taught me how to recognize flowers and hunt for edible roots, but whenever they were together she changed. I knew she was scared of Zaya too, which only made her terrorize me even more when Zaya was there, thinking up the most difficult tasks to try to show off for her.

One day they sent me out looking for wild mountain goat *argal,* but I came back with our own, from Papa's herd, and they got blamed for it. Lying and making things up made all sorts of things easier. That was all I learned from my sister.

But my heart wasn't spiteful by nature, not like the sneering worm-eaten lump of flesh buried inside our Zaya, and eventually I grew out of those childish lies and deceptions.

Whenever Papa called us together to tell us something, I listened.

When Mama took my hand and taught me the motions of milking, or slid a knife into my palm and made me scrape the membranes, I didn't balk.

I knew how things worked from early on, and from early on it was clear to me that that was how it had to be and any other way could only bring unhappiness. By age fourteen I knew all these things. But I was the youngest, so there was nobody for me to teach them to.

Which is why I have to do it now, before anyone can shut me up, because when Batjar makes a step with his hands and I climb up on a horse, I can still keep up with the young ones, and as long as I'm still able to work, nobody can interrupt me by clearing their throat, or snub my advice, even if I was the youngest.

My two sisters have been nothing but stuck-up brats their whole life, mixed-up little girls who never learned to stick to their own. And now one of them sits around the *ger* here all day long, her face gray and sunken, crying her wordless cries to the distant ends of the steppe, and still she thinks she's got some kind of rights here, that I lived life with my eyes closed and her trifling worries are somehow unique.

When it came to me, there was never any doubt.

I sprang from two Mongol clans, proud and pure. I've never had to bow my head, and the few times someone cast a crooked glance at me, it was always a mistake. It was my sisters their eyes sought, and my pupils fended them off like a shield, because when they looked in my eyes they found no hidden fear or guilt.

Every child's a soft little bud. The bad and impure bear the same fragile, bluish buds as the good, and every little bud beats with the same skittish, birdlike pulse. I never said Zaya was a dirty rotten *erliiz,* no matter what people think, and some of them are respected and otherwise honorable people. I never said any such thing. But Zaya lived like an *erliiz,* she didn't lead a decent life, and I was never anything but silly little Oyuna to her, even when I had a man of my own while she kept disappearing over the mountains time and time again, only to return to us with tears in her eyes, bearing gifts.

I didn't dally when I was through with school. I didn't even want to stay in the *somon* center, never mind head to the City. My parents were eternally grateful for that. I've always thought of others for as long as I can remember.

I wasn't nursed from my mother's breast to leave her behind in a cloud of dust just as soon as I could stand on my own. How many hairs on her and my father's heads had grayed because of me? That's the kind of thing you pay a person back for.

I pulled my weight, and Mama passed on to me all that my grandma Mira gave her, and every spell my grandma Dolgorma ever muttered. She guarded these things closely, and most of them were laid in the ground to rest with her, but the only one who knows what Mama got from her is me. Zaya's got her daughter's little head all turned around with all that talk about her namesake. Grandma Dolgorma knew some things that no one else did, but still it was just a sliver of what her own mother had taught her.

In the old days, everyone used to know more. Nowadays people think that if they understand the world, as they say, they can leave their ancestors' knowledge to the beasts of prey together with the bodies of their parents. Nobody wants to hear about those things anymore. If I want good, I also have to take the bad. Only a young twig bends.

Tsetsegma gets upset when I warn her to marry while she's still young or she'll be rummaging through the leftovers in a couple years from now.

Would that the dreaded Almas would snatch Batjar up in its paws when he joins in with Tsetsegma bleating about how they don't care what the custom is, there isn't time for us to drive around the *ovoo* three times, the shop in the *somon* center is only open till five and we can stop on the way back.

What does that have to do with the fact that we're bound by sacred duty?

They sit stubbornly holding their tongues and I'm the batty old bird.

Every time my children make me out to be crazy, I shudder and say to myself: Zaya hasn't raised even her one child with as much integrity as I have my three, and Nara's womb has yet to bear fruit even once. I can be glad.

Zaya always did bite off more than she could chew. When we had *buuz* on New Year's, she would load her bowl so full that they slipped over the edge like fish. If they fell on the table, she usually managed to scoop them up and toss them down her throat before anybody noticed, but if they splatted on the ground, Papa would lift his eyes and give her a good hard knock on the back. She almost never finished her food.

She never knew what was too much.

I don't doubt that she got some pretty hard knocks in the City as well. But those blows were dealt by other, harder fists, and she won't tell me about them.

It's already bad enough that she's got a child without a man.

Besides, who would go taking their scars to a place where they can't expect any pity? We know each other too well for that. I try to be nice. When Zaya just loafs around the *ger*, as if she didn't notice all the pots full of dried-on leftovers, I keep it to myself. When she sleeps in late, as if the sun that slices through my eyelids like a knife was the moon of deepest winter, I draw her blanket up to her neck and go about my business. I never snap at her, and whatever she thinks she sees in my eyes, it's a far cry from the scorn that her daughter accuses me of. Sitting around the *ger* all day, staring glassy-eyed at the mountains or wordlessly working her mouth is no way for a proper woman to spend her old age.

I never told her she was a leech. I never told her her daughter was a *zalkhuu*, inconsiderate girl who didn't have any direction. I never told her how obvious it was that what she lacked was a man like my Naima. Zaya thought she could slap together a Burkhan from the Ulaanbaatar mud with her bare hands. That someone would lay down his bags to throw open his arms and wrap them around a girl who'd left her home on the steppe in the hope that, of all the thousands and thousands of people in the City, happiness would find her, by her slanted eyes or whatever, who knows?

The number of wet, slimy lambs that had passed through my fingers over the springs. The dozens of winters and first fall snows that had passed in the Red Mountains, until once again the tufts of grass turned from pale to green, like a man's first timid beard, and that whole time she was gone.

While Zaya was still doing the petty jobs of a country girl in the City, I became a wife and a woman to be reckoned with. Mama kept me on a short string and didn't give me a moment's rest.

A woman's fingers need to keep moving morning, noon, and night, flashing with dishes, stroking children's cheeks, kneading dough, or giving relief to a man's callused palms. I tell my girls that every day. Papa used to say that Mama's hands never lingered. And that the first thing he noticed about her was those fluttering wings of hers. This is the woman I want, he said, and Mama wanted a good man to say the same of me.

Even in my youth there were times I was ground down at the end of the day, my legs swollen with weariness, my fingers too weak even

OYUNA

151

▼

to lift a puppy by the skin. Mama and Papa were still heavy sleepers in those days, and as soon as they laid down they were out. There was nobody else in the *ger* and I was full of rage. I thought of the sky over the City, which even at night, I was told, was pale and streaked with colors, the stars lost from sight in the buildings' yellow glow and turning out along with the streetlamps.

I hated that black maw in the roof of our *ger*, like the jaws of a hostile beast, and the stars in it were nothing compared to the lights in the streets, just these tiny golden drops.

It brought me to tears to be without my sisters, but their faces were tear-drenched too, in my mind.

Coming to a bad end in the City is easy. Papa was sure of it. Mama said it wouldn't be long before somebody would come along and sweep me off my feet.

I knew that he was worth it. Worth all my mother's preaching and my dreams about the glittering lives of Zaya and Nara, not one stray glimmer of which found its way across the mountains to us. I wasn't even seriously thinking about the City. My dreams just took their color from it. In my dreams the City's buildings were sprinkled across the steppe like yurts, far removed from one another and just as small and soft. And then they went away.

Naima came along and I became self-sufficient and whole, because a woman without a man is like a crescent moon, and Naima dissolved the dark part and I was round and bright as a hunter's moon. Just when I had gotten used to my new duties as a wife, Batjar was born, and Naima became the kind of son to Papa that anyone would envy.

I didn't know how it was supposed to work, and even now I don't really know. I only know my Naima. That's the way it should be, my mother always told me, that's what decent men are looking for. A woman should wait. For her own good. One day it'll come, and from then on she'll have everything taken care of. Men don't trust experienced women. That's the way it is.

Any girl who doesn't save herself for the father of her children will end up being sorry for it. My mother told me that, and I've been pounding it into my daughter's heads since they were in *khuukh-diin tsetserleg*. A woman has to have things figured out—those were Grandma Mira's words, and my mother took them to heart.

I didn't figure out anything. Papa said I was born decent. He was a little bit drunk. It was at my wedding.

He was sitting at a table drinking with Naima when all of a sudden he ordered me to show Naima my legs and roll my *del* up to my elbows. Naima nodded appreciatively, and Papa said that as far as in between my legs, that was understood. No wear and tear down there. Naima roared in satisfaction, and I scurried back to the women to help hand out the *koumiss*.

My husband's always been good to me. I do spout off at times, but when a woman spends her whole evening heating and reheating the soup, and her man comes strolling in without so much as a nod hello, it just comes tumbling out. Usually I don't even mean to. But Naima has a big heart and I always apologized afterwards. We rarely got in each other's hair. Only over the children sometimes. He was easy on them, but when a child interrupts a grown-up, a jab in the ribs is fully deserved. Even Zaya's Dolgorma shouldn't have gotten off without punishment, but Naima had a soft spot for her, and I also wasn't as strict with her as I was with my own. If Zaya wanted a little miss priss, then that was up to her. If she had been one of mine, though, I'd have rattled her pretty head so hard she might even have remembered her father.

Zaya thought I had it in for her daughter. But I accept everyone with an open heart; it's the only way I know. It didn't even take me that long to get used to her name. And if Zaya was upset that I told my son the truth about Dolgorma and her name, she had only herself to blame. I respect things as they are. I don't dress up the past for myself, and I refuse to do it for anyone else. The girl should know her name is stolen, she's old enough, why all the fuss? Zaya's been coddling her for far too long already. I can't even express how lazy she was. I had to tell Tsetsegma and Zula everything twice too, but they never would've dared to disobey the way Dolgorma did. Let alone in someone else's *ger*. Who taught her to act like that? I'd like to meet the man who made that little girl. A snake like that is too much for a woman on her own. I don't even see why she bothered to keep her. What kind of upbringing is a child like that supposed to get?

Such a shame. Her whole life, people are going to ask about her father and stare back at her in shock. If Tsetsegma ever came to me with something like that, I would flog that bloody clot out of her, no matter what it took.

I was even too generous letting her spend her vacations with us all those years.

She turned her nose up at the food, then ate enough for three, and never did a lick of work. I often even had to wash her plate when she was done.

Zaya dumped her off here like it was understood. But a relationship between sisters isn't something to take for granted, and she's never lifted a finger for me. Then all of a sudden, years later, she turns up here with a child and gets all bent out of shape that nobody's throwing their arms around her and her daughter gets called *zalkhuu*.

Some fine lady our Zaya turned out to be. And clumsy as a born city girl. What those lily-white hands have been up to, I'd rather not even know. Not that she wanted to tell me. Every time it came up she'd start to squirm, and when she did say anything, her face would blush so red that I didn't believe it anyway. I often thought the worst, but a sister is a sister, and the pretty gifts she gave us always made us shut our mouths.

One day the two of us went to check up on a sick mare. There was something going around, and all the mares were losing their milk and their coats were getting dull and balling up in clumps with scaly white skin in between. So Zaya said we should go have a look and see what we could figure out. Dolgorma was bigger by then and whipped around like a tail behind Naima, and I didn't cringe to look at her the way I used to do.

Zaya said she was glad she had such a good girl, she was sure we'd learn to love her in time, and every kind word we could offer, every bit of praise, would be repaid with the greatest goodwill on her part, and one look should be enough to see how much it meant to her, to see it wasn't easy. Dolgorma wasn't a country girl yet, but she'd get there. She swore it. If we could only wait a little longer, just a tiny bit of patience, Zaya wheezed. She was panting like an overheated dog. We were going up a hill, which she wasn't used to anymore.

I wanted to talk about the sick mares, since Dolgorma was back there somewhere, running around fit as a fiddle, and my hand stung from the staff I'd brought to keep from stumbling on the rocks, and I felt the twang of every pebble like I was a weak old lady.

I've always been unsettled by other people's emotions, so I started in about milk and Zaya bobbed her head, and when I said the mares would be over their sickness in two weeks, she nodded and said, That's right, Oyuna, in two weeks it'll be all over.

I didn't like seeing anyone's misty eyes. I feared them like a *mangas* fears black crows.

I only know how to mother my children, I've never known how to take anyone else's head in my hands, and Zaya kept moving closer, until I could hear the rustle of our *dels* against each other, and then we came to a stop, because even I was losing my breath, and Zaya drooped her head on my shoulder and left it there. I held the weight without a flinch. I can get through anything if I tell myself I can. I stood there, cold as a rock, streams of stinging sweat running down my back. When a woman presses up against another woman like that, it means she lacks a man to lift her spirits. I haven't clung to another woman since the day I let go of my mother's skirt, and I get anxious too sometimes.

A woman has to tend to her own happiness, to nestle it in silky cloths and warm it in her palms, and Zaya lashed its soles until it ran away for good.

But I kept my thoughts to myself and just held her head on my shoulder, and then we went on our way. I've been anxious plenty of times, and nobody's ever heard a single complaint out of me. Not a one.

When Naima came to stay and the two of us started going into the *somon* center together to do the shopping, and talking until sunset about cows, medicinal herbs, and his family, I was already starting to picture my frilly bridal gown and figuring out what embroidery would look best on the sleeves. I would just keep nodding my head while Naima went on talking, buying myself a little more time to think about my shoes and hat—I wanted my hat to be big, but not like the ones in Mama's day, which were like walking around with a kettle on your head. Naima told me about his brothers and his dog, which he'd found as a whiny little pup. Not a word about marriage, but I wasn't fooled. No decent man would tell a girl so much about himself and drag her along on errands he could easily do on his own unless he intended to marry her, and Naima was as decent a man as they come. He did what Papa told him to, and always stepped up to do the heavy work, even when nobody asked. He never told me as much about himself again as he did during those months before the wedding. No one really cares about all that stuff once you're married. There isn't time. Plus a man doesn't need to woo his wife, she's his forevermore, so they talk about the herd and they scream over the kids. I hardly even remember the words that Naima used to woo me with. You need to talk when you're going to get married, you need to sit on the rocks and tell each other about your families, but that's not what's most important. I was in a rush to have a *ger* of my own and a baby, one with Naima's dark eyes, a boy, so I would have respect. But it wasn't that simple. Naima said there was someone back home. Tsobo and Ariuna had arranged for him to marry a woman he'd always had a crush on, and now she was waiting for him and he'd given her his word.

Even then I didn't roll out any phony tears. I said it was time to get back to the *ger*. And I have to say, he'd felled me like an ox.

The rocks were beginning to cast long shadows and Mama was waiting with *khuushuur*.

My voice just faltered a little bit on the "*ger*." A whimper caught in my throat and then died away in the crash as I flung myself onto my mare. Naima climbed on his spotted horse without a word and trotted along behind me. Like nothing at all had happened.

I kept it quiet from Mama, and after we ate I could feel her contented gaze on my back when I waved to her and went outside to take a walk with Naima. He talked about his brothers some more, and the young he'd helped into the world. I moved a little away from him, playing with the pebbles, and when he stopped I couldn't think of anything to say, and there were angry drops of sweat glistening on his forehead.

I went on smiling, and when he tore his *del* on a bush I told him to give it to me and I mended it like before.

He wouldn't look me in the eye anymore, and when I served him soup and our glances met, he would helplessly throw up his hands. But it wasn't him who was powerless. No matter how pained he looked, I didn't feel sorry for him. I just wished the worst on his bride, and if he was going to leave me I also wished it on him. The wind didn't dry my tears; there were none.

I know how to grit my teeth.

It went on like that for some time, and then one day Naima and me were alone again when suddenly he blurted out that if he was annoying me I should just say so and he would go away and never look back. He took my hand, but I jerked it back and urged my horse along. He called my name after me, it echoed through the rocks. He rode me down, I dismounted, and he slung me to the ground. I just closed my eyes as he clenched his hands around my arms like a scorpion, then let go and walked away. The next morning he left.

He apologized to my father that he had some things to straighten out at home, and five days later he returned and knelt before my parents.

Things go bad between people every once in a while.

I never thought I was the only one with troubles.

Everybody knows that, but I had chosen a man who could hide me under his broad back whenever I came to him. When I wanted a warm, dark place to hide because Mama was cranky and the kids wouldn't give me a moment's peace, he gave it to me. Not once did he balk. Later, as I got older, I stopped going to him to be touched. Sometimes he would hold me close and I'd breathe in his hair, but less and less over the years. We were content and the children grew like weeds.

Zaya thinks I've found my little happiness here in our *ger,* while she wanted more and got slapped across the fingers for it.

Plenty of times I caught her watching me and Naima, amazed at how everything in our *ger* seemed to run on its own. When the kids stopped screaming and we all sat down together, bowls of *khuurag* wedged between our thighs, I noticed that look more than once. Zula calling out to her, Zaya hearing nothing, spoon suspended in midair, slowly dripping grease. Like a statue, my husband would laugh. Then I'd hoot at her and Zaya would shake herself off like a wet dog.

She could stay here. No one was chasing her away.

I was still a child when Zaya showed the Red Mountains her back, and things weren't exactly warm between us. I didn't feel any sorrow, but Mama must've been upset. Her oldest daughter, and as soon as she throws off her schoolbag she's gone. No gratitude, no word of thanks or talk of return.

Mama must've known she wasn't going there to learn something new, but was looking for a way to cut loose, to break away from the family. For me to do something like that would be like having my guts ripped out alive, but for her it was a dream. That was all she said. A dream.

And poof, it was gone.

I've been trying to pound the right dreams into my little girls' heads for ages now. Batjar's dreams are simple. In fact he could be the richest man in the province in a decade or two. He's certainly hard enough on himself, and a good-looking wife, well, the two go hand in hand. But a young girl's dreams are deceptive. Every pretty thing goes strutting around with her nose in the air, thinking I don't know what all is coming her way, but all she'll ever catch with bait like that is one good man. If she decides that she wants more, then she ruins her reputation. If she decides that she wants better, then all the boys are spoken for, her youth is gone, and even a moneyless drunkard looks good.

Or she can run around for the rest of her life.

Khurda used to be like that, she ran around with everyone. Now she's got a second child with the factory secretary and they seem to be content. But most aren't so lucky. Zaya should never've left.

Mama should've talked Shartsetseg out of it.

But when Papa didn't back her up and Shartsetseg stomped her feet a little, Mama gave in every time. And besides, what kind of father would put up a fight for an *erliiz*?

Zaya definitely uses it as an excuse. If only she wasn't a half-breed, she thinks, then everything would be different. She's felt sorry for herself for as long as I can remember. I never had anyone offer me dog meat or tell me to go back south over the Great Wall where I belonged. But then again no one ever left Zaya outside, pounding on the door, when it was so cold your breath tinkled like ice and even in the warmest boots your toes turned white. If Papa hadn't come home early from the herd that day, I might not even be here. I couldn't have been more than three, cheeks glassy with frozen tears, *del* covered with tiny little icicles of spit. Kicking the doorstep, beating the door. My little sheepskin-mittened fists drumming weakly against the wood. I was at the end of my strength and Zaya was inside giggling.

She and Nara wanted to be alone, but that was too long for me to be outside. Wicked goats.

My whole childhood I was terrified of my sisters. They may have suffered years of taunting at school, but they could dish it out as well as they took it when someone got on their wrong side. They were big and strong compared to me. The only thing that I could do was cry for Mama, and Zaya and Nara were smart enough to take me far away, so my screams couldn't carry across the imposing steppe.

I wasn't there, but Sanja, my friend from *khuukhdiin tsetserleg,* heard it from her older sister, who saw it with her own eyes. There was a boy who was writing nasty notes to Zaya, and when the teacher split my sisters apart he refused to share his textbook with Nara, and they gave him such a beating that every single night for weeks he woke up soaked in sweat. That's what she said. The two of them waited for him after school, yanked away the bag with all his pencils, papers, and notebooks in it, and dumped them into the dirt. Every time he reached down to pick them up, they kicked him. He only got away, fingers covered in blood, because some grown-ups came along and my sisters made a run for it. When they got older, they weren't brave enough to pick on boys anymore, but they still weren't as weak as me, who couldn't even tell Mama what they were really doing to me.

I was glad when Zaya left.

My family's all I've got. It's also all I've ever wanted, and I'm raising my daughters to be the same.

I think about Mama and Papa every single day. Whether I've got a lot to cook or I'm dashing around the livestock, I always find the time. All that's left of Papa is a couple saddles, his boots, and a few things for the horses. Mama gave me advice that in turn I teach to my kids. There's a warped photo of each of them on our table. Years ago I was tidying up when I took the table outside, and just then it started to rain.

It was summer. The last time Dolgorma came. She got here just in time to see Papa.

He and Mama let her stay with them. I couldn't be with them all the time, our *ger* was full. And at least the girl would learn to deal with old people then. I needed help, especially with Mama. I could tell she wasn't long for this world, and whichever way you looked at it, Dolgorma was her granddaughter, so why not?

Zaya and Nara weren't around for Mama's or Papa's last days. Dolgorma left a few weeks before.

Papa didn't move from the doorstep, and Mama didn't go out at all. Papa never was one to make a big commotion, and he stayed true to that to the end.

Mama did it for him.

From all the way in our *ger* we could hear it, for hour after hour. Only one thing could make Mama carry on like that. I went over to find the whole *ger* topsy-turvy, the cracker box spilled out, dogs roaming back and forth across the threshold. There were things pulled off the shelves, hanging out like tongues, and one of the *ger* beams was scraped from Mama running around, banging into things. I slapped a poultice on her bump and slid a chair beneath her bottom, so she would settle down.

Papa lay stretched out quietly like he was sound asleep, and I could see why Mama wanted to leave him that way. She said he didn't even sigh, and she always leapt to her feet at the slightest purr from him. His face wore a peaceful smile. I strained my back when we carried him out. He was heavy as a loaded keg.

Dolgorma stopped coming after that. Mama could hiss like a snake sometimes. I know she only wanted the best for everyone, but she didn't know when to stop and she could bring a girl to tears. She accused Tsetsegma and Zula of not coming to see her because she was old and they were young and didn't want to look at her.

It's true that after Papa's death she went downhill in a hurry. She wouldn't let anyone touch that skinny little braid of hers to the very end. Her teeth were rotten, her legs wouldn't obey her, and she shivered with cold even when the rest of us were pouring sweat. But one thing she always had strength to do was sink a claw into your heart and give a vicious tug. She had all the best intentions, or at least that's what I thought for a long time. Instead of a slap on the wrist, she just favored a crack of the whip.

Even my mother's only a woman, and even cruel women are somebody's mother.

Alta, our mother's name, will probably never carry as much weight as *Dolgorma.* Even if Zaya did exaggerate her story and the mark of a liar will never be branded off of her.

Dolgorma wasn't with her when she came a couple months ago to stay with us for good. She's a grown-up woman, Zaya said, not just some little tail that's stuck to my behind. One look from her and I buttoned my lip.

I can tell when it's not worth my while. I didn't have the guts to stand up to Mama either, to all of her whys and what fors. I just didn't ask. Especially when it came to anything touchy. And yet it's hard to think of anything more shameless a woman could do to her husband than let him go chasing around a bunch of bastards all his life. Mama took that to the grave with her.

I didn't think dying was like that.

Papa went off without a good-bye and Mama's gallbladder gave out. She died curled up in the back seat of Naima's jeep. I was up front with him and didn't even get to squeeze her hand. Life flew from her like an arrow from a bow. Swift and silent. Where did it land? Into whose womb did it plunge? Which *ger* is the baby that was once my children's grandmother toddling around now?

Zaya's a strange one. Whenever the talk turned to Mama and the fact that she was gone now, Zaya would look away. But she had no reason to hide her eyes. Mama had been torn apart by wild animals ages ago, and there wasn't even a trace of tears in Zaya's eyes. She didn't even wring her hands. *Erliizes* are ashamed of their mothers. They must be, at least a little. How else could you explain it?

Zaya dove right in hunting for Mama's earrings and her blackened silver ring. I said her finger had been too swollen for me to pull it off, but what I wanted to say was I never even got a chance to hold her fingers, or kiss her knuckles while they were still warm.

That damn back seat.

Naima headed straight over the rocks, and Mama bumped up and down the whole way, bouncing around like a madwoman even after there wasn't any life left in her body. She took with her all the words she meant to say but didn't know how. I didn't give Zaya the silver ring or the earrings. I've got two girls and each of them should have something of hers. Anyway, Zaya dug up plenty from Mama's boxes.

I showed her her place. She unpacked her things and laid them on the shelf. Grumbling. She had come to me, and I could've thrown her out. I may be eight years younger than her, but no one could've held it against me if I had.

OYUNA

161

▼

When Mama died, the only sound was the roar of the engine and the clatter of the boxes Naima forgot to take out of the trunk. I'd pictured my parents' deaths being different. Like it was with Grandma Dolgorma. The dignity, the sorrow, washing over us like black water for weeks. I was little then, clinking my spoon against my mother's shins beneath the table, but I felt it too. There was a draft under the table and one of the legs was creaky. Mama daubed at her tears with her sleeve. The *ger* was filled with solemn emotion. With Mama and Papa there was nothing at all like that. We got over it in a hurry.

I'll never forget that first supper when Zaya came to stay. Noisily praising the burnt *khuurag* and pinching my daughters' arms. They looked at each other and rolled their eyes.

She said Tsetsegma was a dead ringer for Naima, and did I wash my face in hot goat's milk to make it shine like that? And the men must be falling all over themselves to get to Zula. The only one she left alone was Naima.

We all kept our eyes on our plates, a regular clinking the only sound to break the stony silence. Zula may not've gained much in beauty, but she didn't deserve that. Zaya and me had never really liked each other much.

When Zaya used to come with her daughter, she watched her like a hawk. Dolgorma would complain about my girls all the time, and my sister believed every word. As soon as she saw Zaya coming, Dolgorma would throw herself down on the ground and start squealing like she'd been beaten up. Usually it was a lie.

Zaya would go on a rampage, lighting into Zula, and we would end up arguing while the girls went back to chasing each other around the clumps of *argal*.

Whether she liked it or not, to Tsetsegma and Zula, Zaya would always be their aunt from the City. She brought them nice gifts, but she rarely held them on her lap, and when they asked her to play games with them she either said no or got them wrong. They didn't have much fun with her. Or with Dolgorma.

The ties are severed between us. But I can easily string the memories together into a chain of words, reciting every incident, one by one, in order. My words can be referred to. How the mad dog bit me, how I got frostbite four times because of her, how I wandered lost through the mist until I heard my mother calling, how all my food got eaten up and my sister's face was grinning out of the shadows at me like a goblin. The things my sister's done to me sit in my head like a thick sludge. I leave it be. Old things just make me mad. My sister's got her reasons why she favored Nara all her life and didn't give a snot about me.

But I can tell stories and she can't.

Wrongs, those are my stories, but I never did anything bad to her. Zaya's got nothing on me. The ring and the earrings were mine. I was the one who took care of Mama, I lived with her all my life, so they belonged to me. She may think I'm greedy, but we aren't even of the same blood, and we were dead to each other for years. All I ask is no mercy lies. She doesn't have anywhere else to go. And so she's squatting here.

That quiet huddled presence of hers enrages me, and from now on our *ger* will be full of it forever. Naima said that Zaya won't ever go back to the City.

When it comes to people, Naima doesn't make mistakes.

■ □ ■ □ ■

5. NARA

SOMETIMES IT SEEMS LIKE I'M THE ONLY LIVING THING ON EARTH. When I'm stuck inside for a long time and the days are so gray that you almost can't even tell them apart from the nights. They just sort of glimmer like scales on a long, dark snake. It's getting like that more and more. I sit in the apartment that Zaya passed on to me, and everything here reminds me of her. The linoleum, scuffed white around the kitchen unit. The lamp, battered from one of our fights. The radio she always said she'd take to have repaired; now it's too crackly even to listen to anymore. I pace from the kitchen to the bedroom and back again. I can't remember. What was I going to do?

The kitchen floor is covered with crumbs that crunch beneath my feet, and I keep bumping my head on the flypaper covered with dead bugs. I should change it. I can watch the flies for hours. Flapping their wings and frantically rubbing their little legs till they croak. For two days now I've been drying beef for *khuurag* on the stove. I bought some mayonnaise, and a piece of nougat for dessert, but every time I lift the lid to spoon it out I feel sick. I haven't been able to eat a thing for three days now. I wonder what from?

This place is too noisy. I've already said so to Zaya. Ever since the Baldans next door came up with the bright idea that four brats wasn't enough and got themselves twins and a new dog to go with them, it's been unbearable. These walls are so thin they're like wrapping paper, and the pattern on the walls in the bedroom even looks like it. I can't stand those giant orange flowers. Lolling out their florid petals like brazen whores and creeping into my dreams. I put a poster of race-horses up over the bed so I could look at something green before I go to sleep. But sleep still won't come.

How many times will I walk into the kitchen only to walk right back into that flowery torture chamber? Thirty?

Soon now the horizon will turn pink around the edges, the corner of the room will turn from black to gray, and suddenly the streets will explode with buzzing cars. No more quiet again. Any minute now one of the Baldan kids will burst out in tears; either that or the dog will start to bark.

This apartment is cursed. Too many memories to hide from.

Zaya told me the story about the silver-plated *tavag*. It was the first job Yellow Flower gave her when she got here. Polish that plate till it shone.

Those are the glasses Mergen read with. When he tore up the paper to roll his smokes, he'd tear around the articles that he wanted to save for later. Those raggedy scraps of news piled up on the shelf for years. It was the only printed matter there was when Zaya lived here.

I wrap potato peels and used tea leaves in them. I'm down to the last few pages.

One day, in a burst of enthusiasm, my sister bought all these potted plants. Smooth-leaved, thick-skinned, knobby-stalked and prickly-needled. That was the main thing she stressed when she left. Water the plants.

But every plant likes something different, so at least half of them are always sick. If I water a little, the prickly ones are happy but the smooth ones wilt and break. If I water a lot, the smooth ones are fine, but the rest turn brown and the water in their cups smells like a sewer.

The window ledge is covered with dirt from the last time I repot-ted them. Mrs. Baldan borrowed my broom. That dog of theirs will never learn to go outside. I told her he wasn't the indoor type, but she's like a little girl. A peasant, set in her ways. She tapes newspaper up in the windows instead of buying fabric, and her kids climb the pipes in the hall for hours at a stretch, scrambling up and down and spitting cedar seeds on the floor.

Anyway, the apartment's nothing fancy. When Yellow Flower came, there was just one lonely woman holed up in here. Her sons and daughters were all married off, you could barely see through the dirt on the windows, and the whole place reeked of stale cooking fat and old lady. Shartsetseg always held her nose when she came to that part, her lips twitching with laughter. She got it cheap. All it took was a little looking after for the lady and a bucket of hot water and some soap for the apartment. It was obvious the old bag didn't have long to last, Yellow Flower would grin. She had a nose for that kind of thing.

Six months later, the old cow was belly up and Shartsetseg had the kind of place that people who move here from the country wait years for, making the rounds of the offices, handing out vodka left and right, pulling chocolates out of their *del* sleeves, and even then it's not for sure.

By the time I got here, it was overgrown with filth again. If before it had reeked of old age, at that point Mergen had been pickling in it for years. Like a cucumber in a jar, drenched in the sour stench of old alcohol, which had eaten into the rugs, the sofa cover, all of the cloths on top of the chests, even the foam seat cushions sewn into nylon covers, which Shartsetseg had used to try to cozy up the place. Mergen had grown into all of it.

A dusty display case used to house a set of fancy shot glasses from Moscow. When Mergen went away, it was like with the glasses. An empty space was left behind. Zaya swapped them for vodka one day. Mergen stuck them in her hand, and a few minutes later my sister was back with a first-class bottle of Kublai.

Lots of things got lost that way. Mergen didn't hold a job. But the shot glasses had been his. On front they had an oval with a tiny little Red Square inside. Originally there were six. Now all that was left was six dark circles traced into the dust.

Zaya told me that story. In those days I wasn't familiar with the situation here.

I saw Mergen only once, but I heard him lots of times.

At Divaajin there was a slut in the room next to mine who Mergen would drop in on sometimes. She was Chinese. Liu Li or something like that. The only hooker I ever knew who wore glasses. Without them she was lost. Sometimes she'd set them down by the sink so she could splash her face and the next thing she knew they were gone.

Without them on, her slanted eyes looked sunken, drowned in deep shadow.

She'd stretch her hand out in front of her and shuffle cautiously back to her room. She knew she'd get them back. She didn't yell. We would be dying with laughter. She looked so sweet like that.

Mergen and her would speak Chinese. She said it was sort of a story: Woman. Mergen. Bad woman. Good Mergen. Then: Mergen bad. Punish woman. She grinned and showed me her bruises. Liu Li's Mongolian was just enough to be a whore.

I knew Shartsetseg had a man, and I realized pretty quick that it was the same Mergen who was doing Liu Li, but I couldn't get over the fact that Mama and her sister were somehow involved in the whole dirty thing.

When Zaya told me about her and Mergen, I couldn't think of a single word that would do her any good. Those three fates are intertwined. All I could say was my father was a drifter too, and as far as betraying Mama goes, the man's the one that calls the shots when it comes to these things. The woman doesn't decide.

It wasn't like it was her idea, so forget it. That's what I could've said.

But instead I said, What's the difference, we only live in this form once, and dragged her into the bar for a shot.

We sat there all night. All of us that worked there got our drinks half price. I hadn't been hammered like that in a long time. One hand holding Zaya's, the other switching back and forth between hoisting shots and clawing at the flea bites on my thighs.

I'd wanted her to be with me at Divaajin all along. The first time she came I thought Burkhan himself had led her here to me. And once she came the second time, I knew she'd never leave. My heart lit up like the Ulaan sky during New Year's fireworks. I did everything to get Zaya to stay. I sent my steadies her way, saying I didn't have time, so she'd have a lot of money from the start, and since she wasn't used to it yet, whenever she needed a break I'd just take them back again. Eventually we each had our own regular johns, and that's what Zaya lived off, even after she had Dolgorma.

Dolgorma was our payback from the black *mangas*. Sort of a bonus.

I ran straight to Shartsetseg, so she could tell Zaya about Hiroko.

I couldn't tell my sister to rob our modest clan of a new generation. I didn't want any talk of knives coming from my mouth. I didn't want to be the bad guy. So I put it off on my aunt.

It must've been obvious, anyway, even without my telling her. Zaya was stuffing herself like crazy, and what madam would want to lose one of her biggest earners?

I went twice to the Japanese witch. Twice I went to Hiroko with a favor to ask and my pockets full of money. The first time was shortly after I started at Divaajin. I was young and doe-eyed still and it had me shaken up. Throwing up. My stomach was churning like a bucket full of fish, and the thought of being saddled with some little bastard monster I would actually have to love made me want to heave even more. A life sprung from that little white glob that some faceless man shot into me? No thanks. I'd sooner kill the thing. And the sooner the better. That was my thinking.

But I didn't go right away, and that was fateful.

When I finally told Shartsetseg where I was going and why, she sang back that I would be fine, there was nothing to worry about. I wanted to handle it on my own, but I was too scared, so in the end I wound up in that notorious part of town where the yurts blend into the steppe like interlacing fingers. White, green, white, green. Hiroko's *khashaa*.

As soon as she laid eyes on me, she shouted to me from the gate. I wasn't put off by her ironic congratulations. I just wanted to get it over with as fast as I could. She could talk her head off for all I cared. Just as long as I got rid of the thing.

I went back to her one more time after that. It was quick. I didn't even spend the night.

But that first time, my belly was puffed out like a bloated cow. The kid hung in there tooth and nail. I jumped up and down, guzzled potions, pounded my belly with rocks, stuck a spoon between my legs. No dice. That child was condemned to feel Hiroko's big hairy paws.

It was tiny, but it survived. I wasn't going to any hospital.

We kept him warm in a box. There wasn't anyone else around, and I lost the urge to take his life. It was hanging by a thread as it was, and a couple times he was so cold and blue I didn't think he'd make it. I was hoping he wouldn't give up, but I didn't feel like his mother.

We took turns with him day and night, so he wasn't alone for even a minute. We called him all sorts of things. Hiroko would call him one name a while, then I'd come up with a new one. But he wouldn't grow into any of them. He was nobody's.

In the end, that redheaded baby boy still wound up in our *somon*. The Red Mountains never give up their sons. But I'm not the one he calls Mama. The woman's name is Borji, she wasn't able to have her own, and the whole thing went off in silence.

Those weeks with the baby are hidden away deep inside me. When I gave him my finger, he held it. When I gave him my breast, he drank. When he cried, I did everything I could to make him stop. Then the woman from the *somon,* his new mother, was coming, so I left. That night the box was empty, and the next day I went back to Divaajin. It was so fast I don't think I'd even recognize him now. All I have left of him is the sound of his cries in my ears. But for a while I kept waking up at night to check if someone was watching the box. When there wasn't one I was relieved.

It's not like I'm some evil witch, an Uregma of the unborn, but I've learned to look at life from above, like an Aeroflot pilot flying over our capital. My mother would say like an eagle over the steppe swarming with mice. Like a girl at her embroidered sleeves, as people in the country say. It's the only way to tell right from wrong. I'm not the most sensitive woman, but my heart isn't made of stone either.

I only know things are right or wrong, regardless of a woman's tears.

I know Zaya had them when her belly got big and she had no place to go. She would've had them even if she'd had the baby scraped from her womb, there isn't a doubt in my mind. But it still would've been the right thing.

That's something Oyuna may never understand. She went and married the first sucker who looked her way, and if her insides hadn't gone bad so soon and her monthly blood hadn't dried up, she would've had one baby after the other. Her mother's most dutiful daughter. Neat and clean as a fresh-swept *ger,* straight as a stack of *argal.* Our little Oyuna. Their Oyuna. Alta and Tuleg's. Tuleg, a man who sowed two, raised four, and reaped only one. A man who everyone whispered about.

I saw the looks he got from other men, other fathers, when Mama and him would come to bring me and Zaya home from school. They took him for an idiot.

One girl a Mandarin, the other a Natasha whose skin burned red in the sun.

You had to hand it to Mama for finding a stepfather for her *erliiz* kids. Not just any man would've dragged that log with her.

Papa was still as a riverbank, as main street in the morning before the City awakes. But also tough when he needed to be. He would never've given Dolgorma's name to the child of one of his *erliiz* daughters. Zaya insisted that Papa had always liked Magi and Oyuna best. Magi all right, but Oyuna? What kind of man would trust his wife when she'd already stepped out on him twice? To the end of his days he would look into the eyes of his youngest and never be sure: Mine? Bastard? Mine? Bastard? Turning the question over and over again in his mind.

Zaya was mostly hung up on where she was going to live. She didn't want to raise a baby in a brothel. What'll I do, she said, check up on it in between tricks? Plus she didn't want it picking up any questionable manners, in case it was a girl, and there wasn't a bed in Divaajin that wasn't infested with fleas and its face would get bitten all over. This was what my sister was agonizing about. This was what would decide whether she'd bring forth a new life or nip it in the bud. Meanwhile she was ignoring the most important thing of all. Who she was herself.

As if she'd forgotten where we come from, as if she'd left the word *erliiz* behind on the steppe. But that we can never escape. The blood of our fathers will always flow through us, just as my hands will always be stained with the blood of my murdered child.

Bastard blood. I wish I could squeeze it out of my veins like lemon juice. That's how sour it is.

The blood of a Russian fish *naimaachin* will circle through me as long as I live. I could drill a hole in my head and still I'd know. So how could she ignore it? How could she stay on that merry-go-round? And she seemed to take it so lightly. Not a single word about it. Like it never even crossed her mind.

Years ago Zaya confided in me that the family back home didn't like Dolgorma.

And she wonders why.

I'm not going to tell her.

I'm not going to tell her that Dolgorma has no father and she'll spend her whole life dragging around the boulder of being an *erliiz*. As the younger one, it's not my place to preach. But that little bud should've gone right in the ground. Not for Zaya's sake, but for the sake of that kid she tossed in here like a fresh piece of meat. Sink or swim, sweetie pie.

Me, I cut that off quick. Add another Divaajin kid to the ones running around Ulaanbaatar? Not me. I got clear on that years ago. When my womb still bled and every sperm that got in there wanted to sprout.

It happened to almost all of us. I went to Hiroko, Liu Li to her great-aunt. Inkhe kept hers and left. Tula too. I'll never forget when Zaya left. I had a man in my room at the time, so I just leaned out the window. She stood out in front, hair blowing loose in the wind, with the look of a woman who feels a life inside her and is determined to do whatever it takes to protect and defend that life. Maybe she was thinking, My poor, miserable sister, walled in alive in that sweatbox. She waved to me and I waved back.

Both of us smiling and both of us feeling sorry for each other. That's how it felt at the time.

When Mergen cleared out, Dolgorma was born, and Nairamdal wasn't floating around, I spent most of my free time with Zaya. The two of us chewed over everything, sifting through all the Divaajin dirt. Laughing out loud at the new girls who got their heads chewed off by our aunt, and keeping our mouths shut about the ones who packed up and left. There weren't many volunteers; most of them had done something to step on Shartsetseg's toes. But there were a few. Nobody talked about them, but they had the admiration of us all.

One day the two of us were sitting around at Zaya's, drinking coffee and munching on pretzel sticks as usual, when I announced that in my opinion she screwed it up with Dolgorma. Zaya said she appreciated that I'd left it up to her and didn't get involved and waited till now to speak up. I promised that if anything happened to her I would take the girl in myself. I thought she might be offended, but it didn't look that way. And we drank on it.

NARA

Often the girls that left Divaajin ended up coming back. After their son or daughter grew up a bit, or their man kicked them out, and they realized there wasn't any better-paid work for a woman out there, they were back. We put all our hopes in them and they went and betrayed us like that. None of us wanted so much as to look them in the eye. They were shy as fawns. But at the same time we were always delighted to see them slouching back. Just one more reason for us to stay put.

It's been more than twenty smoggy Ulaan winters now, but when my mother went away and left me alone with Hiroko, things happened that still haunt me at night—nights flashing with the orange of my bedroom walls, nights so bad I'd trade them for the worst of my tricks with the Divaajin johns. The johns came and went, but I had Hiroko breathing down my neck nonstop for years. Compared to that witch's *khashaa,* knocked together from splintery boards, the brutalest prison on earth was a vacation *dacha.*

I'll never tell anyone else again what happened with me and Jargal, they wouldn't understand anyway. I did it once and that's enough to last me the rest of my life.

It all started when Mama left and went back to the Red Mountains. Up until then, it was all just mumbo jumbo, which maybe worked for Mama's gallbladder and the toothaches people came in with, but definitely not on my Jargal.

The moment my mother was gone, Hiroko put me to work.

I had to do all these crazy exercises using my arms and legs while she smoked up the *ger* with fragrant mixtures and chanted *om* and all that. Then, after two days of practically choking to death on the smoke, I had to wash up, change into clean clothes, and tell her the entire story with Jargal, day by day, minute by minute, breath by breath.

I told her everything.

I'll never do that again.

Then I had to strip. She ran her hands all over my body. My right half was Jargal, the left half was me.

She talked to them like they were people. First she whipped the right with a switch and smeared the left with ointments, then the other way around. My head was spinning in circles. It went on like that for weeks. She would call to me like I was him, and when I resisted she would just smoke up the *ger* even more. I sobbed and sobbed. Jargal's name just kept swirling around and around, and I had to do what she told me.

Mama had ordered me to obey Hiroko's every word. I was just a silly steppe girl and didn't know how to say no to an older woman. And what's more, for a long time I believed that it wasn't all just for nothing. In the end it turned out I was right. But in a totally different way than any of us except Hiroko imagined.

I didn't like the looks of it from the moment we arrived.

Hiroko could be amazingly generous, but at the same time cold and uncompromising. One minute she'd be waiting on some poor slob hand and foot, and the next she'd be shoving him out the door. She was rich, that's why they came to her; it wasn't that anyone liked her. Even the kids were drawn to her more for the candies than for that goatish laugh of hers, tumbling out of her monstrous mouth.

When I take care of someone, I do it right. That's why I took those orphans from school home with me on vacation when I was a teacher. That's why I gave my redhaired baby to Borji. I'd rather not even bother taking care of somebody halfway, loving somebody by halves.

That's why it ended so badly with Jargal. He didn't get it. I gave myself to him totally and completely.

Hiroko never knew how to do that.

Let some stray waif spend the night, watch somebody's kids, oh sure. But mainly give the boot to anyone that stuck around longer than it pleased the good witch. I fought about it with her, thinking maybe it would sink in. It wouldn't've taken much and she would've been the most popular person around. But it only provoked her when I gave her advice.

After several months of her curious cure I got over my rebelliousness. She could sweep the sidewalks with those poor slobs, just as long as she left me alone. I wasn't some dizzy young thing who'd lost her first love and thought the whole world had collapsed. Jargal wore the palms of Burkhan over his head, golden fingers flapped around his ears. I'd seen it. He was the one. But enough about that. I swore to myself, not another word about him.

Basically all that Hiroko's treatment did was make me sick. I was skinnier even than when I had been with Jargal, and tired out.

I spent a long time shut up in Hiroko's *ger*. More and more of every day was taken up by her touches. I was glad not to have to twist my arms and legs around anymore, but I didn't like this much either.

Finally, when Hiroko undid her *del* and I saw her saggy breasts coming toward me, nipples all swollen and brown, I said to myself, Enough.

Zaya said Mama had told her how she came to see me and all she found was Hiroko sitting out in the *khashaa* with Seruul and a couple of bums. Apparently Mama got upset and had words with the witch. How she wasn't supposed to let me out of her sight, and how if Mama had had any inkling, she would've stayed with me, *ger* or no, and watched over me like a *darga* over his charge.

Another one of those people who didn't have a clue. I always thought Mama and Hiroko knew everything about each other. But that's one thing Mama won't ever be able to see. She'd have to have different eyes to realize it isn't just men who lust after shapely thighs and buxom breasts.

I guess she thought all those cures of hers would wear me down or whatever. That after that I'd just sit there and take it. It almost worked too, but I still had the strength to keep up my pride.

My body belongs to whoever'll pay, but touching like that's something different. Hiroko thought she could teach me, but I don't have huge hands and arms as shaggy as a sofa cover. I would never cut my silky long hair, and I don't peek at women's calves, so early one morning I grabbed my bag with all my odds and ends, scooped some rice out of the sacks, took some dried meat off the shelf, and creaked through the gate of Hiroko's yard as quietly as I could.

That was years ago. Hiroko's been dead for a couple of winters now, so I'm not likely to ever find out the truth about her and Shartsetseg.

It was silly to think that running away from a witch would be that easy. I took a few steps, swallowed a few gulps of freedom, and the next thing I knew I was collared. She wrapped her arm around my throat like a cop nabbing an Ulaan thief for smashing in a display window. I couldn't even squeak. My arms and legs were paralyzed. I was so weak, she practically had to carry me back to the *ger*. This must be one of those witch's tricks, I thought as I dropped into bed and my eyelids sank like ten-ton weights.

I don't know how long I slept. Hours. Maybe weeks.

It was the first time I'd seen her since I was little. I groped my way blindly out of the *ger* and standing there was a black figure outlined against the sharp morning light. Hiroko introduced us, but I already knew who she was. The wrinkles that had only been hinted at before had deepened into furrows, her mouth grown thin, her lips pinched into two pale lines, but it was still her. Yellow Flower. She greeted me by name, and Hiroko did all the talking from there.

She said nobody was keeping me there, if I wanted to I could go. She smiled and so did Shartsetseg. But they had an offer, she said, that would be rude of me to refuse. She winked at Yellow Flower, who then reeled off a list of the perks of working at the meat plant.

We shook on it and Hiroko kissed me good-bye.

It made sense to have some money with me the next time I went home. Still, I didn't much feel like going.

Zaya was already gone by then, and seeing Oyuna at her wedding had been enough to last me for years. Mama no doubt was hovering over the stove all day, as always, with everything in the *ger* wrapped around her little finger. Actually, who I really wanted to see the most was Papa. Given that I wasn't his, though, I doubt if the feeling was mutual.

Zaya didn't believe me that Hiroko and Shartsetseg knew each other. Or, put it this way, that they were such pals. She couldn't get it through her head. Maybe Hiroko honestly thought she was sending me to chop heads off of rams. Anyone with any clue about Shartsetseg at all said that she worked in the meat industry.

There's definitely no denying that Yellow Flower had her good points. For a woman she was quite capable, and the brothel ran like clockwork thanks to her iron fist. And it wasn't as if she had to let Zaya have her apartment. Sure, Mergen okayed it, but what woman listens to a man who hasn't brought home a drop of cash in all the years she's known him?

Whenever one of the whores got in trouble, Shartsetseg would help her out. Plus she knew how to keep a secret and everybody there knew it. When Liu Li was expecting, she went straight to Shartsetseg. I didn't find out till a couple days later, when Liu Li came back from her great-aunt's without it and clued me in over drinks. If she had told any of us instead of going to my aunt, in a couple of hours every girl in the place would've known what was up. This way she got to have peace of mind, plus some comforting words besides.

The first place I worked was the kitchen at Erka's *guanz*. She was a woman who Shartsetseg knew, and Zaya had given our family a good name while she was there. Shartsetseg knows everyone. Her paws are all over the City. I don't believe in luck.

Yellow Flower told me I needed to lose my dialect, and shoved me into the greasy embrace of Erka's beefy arms. When she showed up again a few weeks later, I sank to my knees and begged her to take me away from there. Anywhere. I didn't want to sweat my soul out over a bunch of pots. And besides, I didn't speak dialect. My language was pure and still is. Just another one of my aunt's sneaky tricks.

If she was trying to get me to fall at her feet, it worked. I've never wanted out of anywhere more than I wanted out of that *guanz*. At least at Divaajin a woman's got money.

My first day there, some cranky lady showed me how to wipe off the tables and sweep away the broken glass so nobody would notice. After three weeks they let me serve drinks, and two months later I got a little room of my own upstairs. Whether Shartsetseg planned it that way or not, I have no idea. What I do know is she noticed men were stuffing bills down my shirt, and asked me if I wanted a room of my own like the rest of the girls.

I quickly forgot all about the Red Mountains. This line of work gets engraved on your face. I saw it day by day. I kept telling myself I would go. Every New Year's Eve I made the same resolution. That's what we do. That's the game of make-believe that worthless women play.

It wasn't as if anyone was keeping me there after all. I had more money than all my friends from the *somon* center would ever see in their lives. I was in love with short lace skirts, canned German franks, and kissproof Korean lipstick. I had a whole case. I adored money. Only one thing mattered more. Through all those years, more than twice as many as all the fingers on both my hands, lighting my way like the yellow beacon of the Ulaanbaatar TV tower, was the shining face of my dear one. My fondest dream has always been that Jargal will come back.

When Anra announced a few years ago she was going to have a baby, nobody believed her. More than twenty years she'd been waiting. Zaya told me. Uregma Ulantsetseg invited all their closest friends over for *buuz*. Oyuna went, and sure enough there was Anra, parading her belly with pride. Her little one must be at least five by now.

Things happen that no one would ever believe, and I'm a patient person.

All credit to Hiroko in that respect. When they robbed her of her mother, who they sent to live with relatives, stripping Grandma Mira of her firstborn child, no one would've believed that Hiroko could track her down. Separated by hundreds of miles of sandy dunes and grassy plains, without a single trail. And still they found each other. After weeks of trudging, Hiroko just showed up on the doorstep of a stranger's *ger*, gathered her courage, and said, Here I am. She said a girl didn't need a magic looking glass or a flying horse to be able to find her mother fussing over a stove on the other side of Mongolia. Hiroko's *ger* was stacked with all sorts of fortune-telling devices and magic contraptions. Bundles of jagged animal bones, colored teeth, wood twisted like human arms. But she just waved her hand.

That's all for show, she said. She took a pair of cow thighs and banged them against each other, once and then again. It was a joke.

Whatever it was, it wasn't that.

Shartsetseg knew when Hiroko died. She came to me and said, The witch's days are over. She handed me a list of arrangements to make and vanished off the face of the earth for the next four days.

This was sometime around when Zaya had to leave because of her belly. A month later she came back to show her little girl around and I started going to visit. We took turns washing diapers, passing the baby back and forth. She couldn't stand to be alone even for a minute. One night, when Dolgorma was about six months old, it was getting dark and I was ready to go. Zaya said she would walk with me. She poured out a little nip, dipped a shred of T-shirt in, and gave it to the baby to suck. She whimpered for a while, but by the time we put our coats on she was already asleep.

Whenever the Baldan twins next door start screaming, I get half a mind to barge in there and give that woman a piece of my mind. Common courtesy doesn't mean a thing to her.

I'm used to it by now, though. Especially from Divaajin. Every time new girls arrived and suddenly I was the old one. I'd help them get their start, then sit and watch while my usual johns went sneaking off to their rooms. In the space of a year or two, despite being all arms and legs they lured away most of my men. Trading my soft, cushy bottom for the hard rump of a filly. Men have no taste.

Zaya kept a handful of steadies almost to the end, and by lowering her price a little, she hung on to a couple of her thriftier johns for years. She didn't completely give it up, in fact, till her daughter ran away.

By then nobody wanted her anyway. Her face was sunken in, and her body had taken on the dumpy, shapeless form of an old woman. Some people used to say she was prettier than me. She was burying herself alive. I didn't tell her that, but you could see it, week by week. Wilting like a smooth-leaved plant when I gave it too much water. Overweight from sitting too much, eyes inflamed from lack of sleep. To me it was obvious that her girl would come back and she would've been better off sparing herself the misery. And I was right. It took more than a year, but like I say, everyone gets lonely for their mother once in a while. Even me. Not that anyone back home was sighing over me. But Dolgorma was well aware that Zaya lived only for her and that her every waking minute was spent waiting for the rattle of keys in the door, the step across the threshold that would bring her daughter back. She wouldn't even come out with me anymore, and every day she'd remake Dolgorma's bed, and every week she'd change the sheets, so everything would be ready in case her little missy returned.

Zaya lied to me. She said they'd had a fight. What she didn't say was Dolgorma had finally found out the truth after all those years of lies. What she didn't say was her little girl was no longer a stranger to the word *whore*. I told her from the start she was going about it wrong. It was bound to end up like this. Shame and lies go hand in hand. The chickens had come home to roost. Zaya never knew how to just enjoy the good in life and forget about the rest. There's two sides to everything.

So the proper Ulaan woman is back to being broke.
She could've left. She didn't want to.
So why all the tears and remorse?
Still, be that as it may, I don't have anyone else like Zaya. A woman I've got no secrets from.
She's been earning her keep in Oyuna's *ger* for going on a year now, so I don't really know how she is anymore. What is there there for her anyway? The Red Mountains are a shield keeping time at bay.

So now I just pace the apartment, touching the things she left behind and thinking of her face, of her cheeks, once as chubby as the cheeks on a Cantonese baby and all that was left of them now was a few loose flaps of skin. I walk from the kitchen into the bedroom and then right back out, as the sharp light of morning strikes the leering orange blossoms and they suddenly fill the room. I take the old flypaper down and hang up a new yellow strip. The color's the same as the pages in the notebooks of my kids at school: Narana, Khuurai, Batamjav, Davdan, Nogoontsetseg.

Names belonging to men and women I no longer know. Some of them probably even have kids who are bigger than they were when they were my students. I wouldn't want to see the faces those names belong to now.

I wouldn't want to go back. No one expects me to, either, and that's relieving.

Hiroko handled it skillfully. Like she knew that whatever went on in her *khashaa,* it would be safe with Shartsetseg. Tucked away in a strongbox, with the key around her neck, and woe to anyone who tried to get their hands on it.

On the other hand, it's good to protect the people close to you from bad things.

Mama lived over the mountains and never caught on to any of it, so she had a City all her own, where all those gigantic cooling towers and apartment blocks and rickety trolleybuses and curbside vendors were little. Like peppercorns in the palm of your hand. In her city, none of her daughters were selling themselves, and none of her sisters were hatching plots. Even that damned apartment that we all kept trading back and forth didn't exist in her city, and that's how it should be with parents. Nothing but good thoughts.

NARA

179
▾

I go on like I know so much about young people and old people, but it's all just an act. I wasn't around when Mama and Papa got old, and I don't have any kids. Well, actually, yes and no. She may be all grown up now, but a promise is a promise. And I gave Zaya my word. If anything should happen to her and Dolgorma's left alone, then I'll take care of her. We told each other that, sealed the promise with lots of shots, and hugged so many times I'd have to chop off my head to forget. But she's gone still just the same.

I never lied to Dolgorma's face, which is why she accepts me and Zaya's days are numbered. Who knows what she does all day, but we split the rent and everything else, so she isn't just knocking around the streets. I'll never shake the feeling that Dolgorma shouldn't have been born. Zaya wanted a child and that was it, end of story. Now the girl's on her own. I'm only her aunt, not to mention an *erliiz,* I can't be any more than that and I don't want to, either. And I doubt Dolgorma found her father like Hiroko found Mira.

But she's looking. Every youngster needs one. And they won't listen to reason. Ochir's married with two kids, and this one's still tagging around after him. She showed me his picture once. A man, I said, uh-huh. She frowned and slipped it back in her pocket. He isn't even good-looking, not to mention he's taken, and anyway he's too old for her. She's just going to get the brush-off again. As if she didn't know.

Anra's celebrated child, the answer to all her prayers, was stillborn. Anra was old. Even older than Soldoo was when she gave life to the Little One briefly, until Burkhan took her back again after just a couple years. Miracles don't happen that often, and all the ones in our family got scooped up by Grandma Dolgorma and the Japanese witch. By the time me and Zaya came along, there weren't any left.

Zaya's earning her keep at our little sister Oyuna's, and I'm worried she's digging her grave there. But my tongue isn't nearly nimble enough to convince her she should leave. On the other hand, she seemed happy enough the last time she came to see me.

She had on a scruffy *del* like some peasant woman who'd never been out of her *aimak,* and a thin, gray ponytail, braided into a rye spike like Mama used to do. I wouldn't even have noticed her in the hubbub of the bus station. She said she'd taken up knitting and had clothed everyone in Oyuna's *ger*. She took my measurements, saying she'd bring me a beige cashmere next time. No doubt she'll bring two and push one of them on Dolgorma. I wish she'd give it a rest. It's finished between the two of them, and now every time Zaya comes I have to give her a report. I just say she's fine. The truth is I don't know, so I just hope I'm not totally lying. We don't tell each other much.

Dolgorma doesn't know that I'm still waiting too.

I pace the apartment like a conductor tearing tickets up and down the trolleybus, touching things as I go. I can sense he's somewhere nearby. My hands have been tingling, which is always a sign of something.

Now I know. I was going to put something nice on. To welcome him.

I don't know when it'll be. But I've got patience to spare.

From time to time I go and help out at the store across the street. When I wrap meat behind the counter, I always stand on a crate so I can see over the heads of the women shopping outside.

If I'm home, he can't escape me. I keep a watch out the window, and besides, I can pick his footsteps out of a crowd of a thousand people. My ears are perked.

Jargal'll show up sooner or later.

■ □ ■ □ ■

6. ZAYA

IT WASN'T ANY BIG DECISION. ALL MY THINGS FIT IN ONE BIG BAG.
I stuffed my money in my boots and filled all of my *del*'s inside pockets. My savings weren't great. The whole year Dolgorma was away
I didn't work, and lining the kitchen all around with vodka bottles
costs something too.

Slowly I got used to the thought that my wait might be without
end. Month after month I offered my prayers, and my days took on
a steady routine.

When it was warm, I'd take the folding chair from the entryway
out on the balcony and watch as the sun's rays crept along the railing
from one side of the banister to the other. When it got chilly, I'd sit in
Mergen's seat in the kitchen, pouring myself mug after mug of tea till
the pot was empty. In an afternoon I'd drink three or four pots.

Every other day I went shopping for groceries, and every day I
went to Gandan with my prayers.

Nara dropped by every once in a while, though not as much as she
used to. Shartsetseg had gotten old and just sat in her cubbyhole under the stairs, leaving more and more things to my sister. Nara didn't
have any more men now anyway, so she bustled around making sure
there was enough to drink in the taproom and the girls had their beds
made and were all where they were supposed to be. She'd taken over
from Shartsetseg as madam of the house, so she didn't have time to
stop over that much.

Anyway it was pointless trying to talk with me.

I didn't care how many new girls came in and out of Divaajin, while hashing over Dolgorma with me again and again got on Nara's nerves. Nairamdal was tired of it too. A couple of months, all right, but after that he only came when I needed something done. He'd come, help, and be on his way.

When Dolgorma came back, I was out.

I turned the key and her trampled shoes were sitting there inside. I thought I was going to faint. The whole place was quiet. I wanted to shout *Dolgorma!* but the tears streaming down my neck had washed away my voice. I was afraid to move for fear of scaring the moment away, for fear Dolgorma's shoes might disappear again, for fear I might wake up. A girl's head peeked out of the kitchen and ducked back in again.

She wouldn't talk to me. Not even after a couple of days.

How happy all those long months were compared to this. I'd been waiting for my sun to come back, and every single one of my thoughts ended in her embrace. Once we hugged, nothing in life could ever hurt me again. I was willing to forgive my daughter everything, and even say some unattractive things about myself, but this knocked me for a loop. Not a word. She avoided my eyes. She sat in the kitchen listening to the radio, washed her clothes, brushed her hair, left in the morning, and came back at night. Undressed, threw her clothes over the chair, and slammed the door to her room. Nothing, not even a twitch of the lip. She looked through me like a shop window. I could act the fool or act insulted, either way it was in vain.

I didn't mention it when I went back to my family. Whatever else Oyuna's like, she always minds her manners, so no one pressed me for my reasons. They took me back in like a fold of sheep encircling a wayward lamb. No big questions.

The last thing I decided to try before I left was Nara. I invited her over to our place and then went out for the evening. Let her talk it over with Dolgorma and let me know how it goes.

When Nara came to take me to the station, I bought some gifts to take along. You can't go home without them. Flashlights, candles, dishes, some hairpins, and a knife sharpener. Nara said not to bother giving anyone her greetings and to keep an eye on my things during the trip.

Whatever talk the two of them had, it didn't bring Dolgorma back to me. She was lying on the rug in front of the TV when I got home. Even the stupidest program was more important than me.

I sat in the kitchen, turning a knife in my hand. I stayed that way all afternoon.

The knife grew warm, twisting in my hands like a living thing. I ran a finger along the blade, turning the grip in every direction. The wood was reddish brown, polished to a shiny black from all the hands that had used it to scrape mutton tendons with. It was left here from the little old lady that Shartsetseg had put out. She had the place signed over to her, then took the lady's key and packed her off to her relatives. The lady toddled off like an obedient child. All the evil *mangases* would go chasing through Yellow Flower's eyes whenever she got to that part. Don't tell a soul, she'd say. My aunt was a smart one; she'd always been smarter than everyone else.

Mergen had also gripped this knife in his fist. My aunt used it for mutton *khuurag,* and in his moments of rage he would rake it across the table. His spot was as grooved as the face of a seasoned old countryman, as his face was the last time I saw it. When Dolgorma came in, I was holding the knife to the sun. She must've seen the flash. She ducked into the next room, the bed creaked once, and then wrenching silence again. I laid the knife on the table, but my hands went on playing with it.

When I lifted my head from the table, Dolgorma was on her way out again. It was morning. I called to her. The door clapped shut.

I can be at peace, I don't deserve any blame. If my daughter had shown even the tiniest sliver of willingness, I would've moved mountains for her. I would've smashed the meat plant's windows, painted every seat on the trolleybuses red, her favorite color. I would've climbed to the top of the radio tower and brought her down the red flag. And that would be just the beginning.

Only this was the end, so I went back to where the rocks and flowers had long since forgotten me and children garbled my name. Where the horizon was boundless and the rocks in summer long after dusk were warm and smelled of lizards.

I left Dolgorma a note taped to the closet in the entryway with some money and a good-bye. I told her everything, but the whole time her gaze was coiled up like a snake in a corner, and I wondered whether her ears were shut as tight as her heart, which beat only when I wasn't near.

Nara walked me to the station. We carried my bag between us, each holding one of the handles. The rolled-up money was pinching my feet and my *del* was all hot and uncomfortable. Nara promised that she'd keep an eye on Dolgorma and the next time Nairamdal came that she would tell him I was gone and if he still felt like fixing the leaky faucet and the toilet, he could do it for her from now on, because the place belonged to her.

Two days before I left, a thin, crumpled envelope arrived in my mailbox. Mergen was dead. The crinkled Chinese writing told the story. A signature that said nothing to me and a big red stamp saying KITAI. I could've gone to our spot in the mountains where the dead are left and whispered those strange stilted words to the rocks. But Mama had already passed through the stomachs of the wild beasts, and it had nothing to do with Oyuna's family. I told Nara. She laughed and said she doubted she'd ever get a notice like that for the fish *naimaachin*.

Nara said she'd sink in shame if she had to do something like that.

She didn't think I was serious about going back after all those years. Taking up a bed in Oyuna's *ger* without a man, without a decent reason. Showing up with just one bag like a little girl, while my gray hair bespoke an old lady with nowhere else to go. That would kill me, she said.

Even if I'd had somewhere else to go in the City, I still would've left. All the noise and the fast cars had started to get to me. I'd actually made up my mind before Dolgorma came back. Whenever more than one big car at a time drove by, the glasses rattled in the kitchen. Before Dolgorma left, we used to talk all day long. Morning, noon, and night, nonstop, so I didn't notice. Now that it was quiet, I noticed all sorts of noise. Every tick of the kitchen clock, the rustle of worms in the oatmeal jars, the constant drip of the bathroom sink. The silence with Dolgorma there had been so loud it hurt, and I'd exhausted all my options. And I wasn't just thinking of me.

Nara had one little room at Divaajin. I had an apartment I hated. I couldn't stay here, sprawling around my spacious abode, when the only piece of furniture that fit in my sister's cell of a room was a sweat-stained hooker's settee. That was the main thing. And that's why I wasn't walking away with an aching heart. Forget about me.

My sister deserves a place of her own after all these years. And once I'm out of the way for a while, my daughter'll have a chance to get over her silly grudge and everything can go back to the way it was before.

Dolgorma came down with jaundice once. I told her not to eat *khuushuur* from those little *guanzes* in the passageways. She said Inkhe made her. She said Inkhe said if she didn't, she would find herself another friend who wasn't such a priss. They were little.

Dolgorma spent a good few weeks laid up in the hospital and another couple weeks at home after that. I bought her whatever she wanted. Russian illustrated magazines for children, tons of ice cream and cuddly toys. She must've had at least five shaggy dogs and a whole heap of expensive dolls stashed beneath her pillow. One of them even walked and talked. I'm sure we'll be able to smooth things out when she remembers that. Or the television. No one else in her class had a set as big as hers, and Japanese no less. She talked me into it when we went one day to buy leggings at the department store.

Or New Year's. Every year we'd celebrate both the Russian and the Mongolian one. More fun and good food for us. I can count on my fingers how many people in the City do that. How many people there are in the City who bring their little ones so much joy. Back when I still looked halfway decent, and it's that spoiled little girl's doing that those days are long gone, there were some nights I didn't go to Divaajin. I'd just not go. It wasn't often, and Shartsetseg turned a blind eye, but still. How many women do that for their kids? The ones running around the streets could tell you a thing or two. Papa at home with a belt or permanently bent over a pool table with the guys, and Mama out of the picture or tanked. Why those kids run away is obvious to me. That I can understand.

Maybe Mama was right when she said I didn't push Dolgorma to work enough. That girl of mine never had to do a thing. The boiled lambs hopped straight into her stomach.

When I got to the *somon* center I happened to run into Naima. Oyuna had sent him to pick her up some sewing things, so he took me with him. The jeep was full of cigarette smoke, and with all the dust floating around you could smear a line on the window. I drew a *ger* and showed it to Naima. He just raised an eyebrow. It looked silly. The rest of the trip dragged on in silence.

I thought back to the first time I ever rode in a car. Or should I say I was old enough to remember it. Probably because it was with Khurem, the father of my classmate Khurem, who I had a crush on— the big one, not the little one. Old Khurem wore a felt hat and his belly spilled out from under his *del*. It seemed friendly to me, and when he laughed it shook like a tablecloth when you shake out the crumbs. I always wanted to see that belly naked.

I told Naima. He asked how old I was then. I said maybe eight or nine.

Naima raised his eyebrow again. I noticed he only did it with one, and so he had two deep, uneven creases across his forehead. I made a note to myself to mention it to Oyuna.

Naima took my bag and strode quickly toward the *ger*. I couldn't keep up and he didn't wait. He must've thought I was just dropping in for a visit. Summer was here.

Right off I noticed some things had changed around the *ger*.

Some of the rafters had a fresh coat of paint. I also didn't recognize the saddles hung by the entrance, and the photos of our parents that used to be next to the Burkhan on the table facing the door were as crinkled as the metal on an Ulaanbaatar fence. Oyuna said Anra had dropped them in the washbasin on her last visit. Anra's hands always start to shake when she talks about children, and Oyuna knows it too, so I don't see why she let her go anywhere near the basin with them. Our parents deserve more respect. Now their faces are shrunken and they look fat, which they never were in real life. Those are the only pictures of them we have. I gave her a piece of my mind. I am older, after all. Naima lifted his eyebrow again.

If he was going to do that a lot, it wouldn't be any better here than in the noisy silence of Sansaar.

Still, I didn't tell them. I went all day without telling them that this time it was for good. Mama's *ger* was still up, they hadn't taken it down. They moved it a little closer to theirs and left it there for me. Like sort of a guest *ger*. Little did they know, I wasn't budging.

A metallic chill was seeping up from the ground when I woke in the morning. It takes an old woman time to get used to it again.

ZAYA

187

▾

When I first moved to the City, the lights at night confused me. Every time a car drove by it woke me up. Dolgorma always found the rumble of engines soothing. Mornings in the City are never as piercingly blue as they are on the steppe. Here, the shine is so bright your eyes burn. In the City the daylight is muffled. The buildings block the sunshine, and what's left of it diffuses in the car and factory smoke into a soft, round glow. On the steppe, nothing stops the sun. Or the starry deep-blue chill. That's how it was my first day back after all those years in the City. I stayed in bed a little longer that first glorious morning.

Some of my parents' things were still there. The tin cracker box that had once seemed so big to me, some oily blankets folded up, a few blue dishes on the shelf—the ones Mama called festive—and some papers wrinkled the same way my parents' pictures were. It was never that great a *ger*. It was hard to set up and heavy as a waterlogged blanket. Papa bought it because it was cheap for an eight-sided *ger*, and then railed on it every time we moved. It was a dark circle amid the steppe. Inside, murky as half a black balloon at night, in daytime gloomy and smelling of skins. Only two beds were left. Batjar had taken one for himself, and the fourth ended up in the fire.

Naima said he wanted to make it a *guanz* for passing travelers. But any stranger plops his bottom down on Papa's stool and slobbers noodles on Mama's table, I will slap him out the door. This is a *ger*, not a snack bar.

When Papa breathed his last, they say it kicked up such a storm the *ger* walls rippled like an insatiable beige lake. Mama wouldn't have made such a fuss if there hadn't been any signs. A dish fell off the shelf too. One of the festive blue ones.

But my first morning there was peaceful. Except for the orange door decorations changing colors and shifting shapes. That was one thing my wallpaper flowers in Sansaar didn't do. I searched the shapes for the mosquito from Dolgorma's bedtime story, but instead I saw Mergen's massive paws and Nara's pouting red lips.

I felt my face. It was bumpy.

Patting around my belly, I found a mound as soft as aspic. When I grabbed at a fly, I could feel the loose skin flap on my arms.

Rubbing my hands on the blanket to warm them, I thought about the smells and colors fixed in my memory. First, the smell of all my sisters' hair. Including Magi's. Then the smell of Papa when my sister died and all he did was drink. The smell of my blood the first time it flowed between my thighs, and the smell of gasoline and cedar seeds that wafted into my Divaajin room when a man was done and I opened the window and let the fresh air in.

I left the colors for later, since Oyuna was raising a racket outside and I knew she would just scream louder and louder till I got out of bed.

Right away I told her about Naima's two creases over his right eyebrow. She seemed surprised. I ladled myself a bowl of morning soup and took all the yellowy chunks of fat and laid them out on the table. In case someone got hungry later.

Oyuna said not to do anything else, and next thing I knew it was nighttime again.

Before I went to sleep, I had another talk with Naima about the *guanz.* As in what did he think he was doing. He said not to worry. I know he used to go out to the rocks with Dolgorma and look at *risunki.* Maybe he thought I'd forgotten, but when he married Oyuna he married our whole family with her. That's the way it always is. It wasn't like he was born yesterday.

The sun blazed all morning, right from the break of dawn. You couldn't raise your eyes even. I brought something to eat with me and went to have a look around at a few of my favorite spots. What if the snakes were swarming again? Tsetsegma runs around barefoot all over the place like a maniac. She's fully grown and still hasn't learned to go easy on her elders. The way she comes flying through, it's a wonder she doesn't knock the stool out from under me.

And next thing I knew it was nighttime again.

The next morning I thought back to the colors. The whole time I had this feeling there was something that hadn't come to me yet, and then on the third day it hit me. The *khataks,* Kulan's eyes, Mergen's couch in the kitchen, my bed at boarding school, Erka's *del.* All of them blue. Like the sky, dropping little by little. Red was the color of Shartsetseg's angry days and Dolgorma's cheeks when she caught a fever. Her forehead was blazing like a stove on New Year's Eve and the doctor just sent us home. This was after I stuffed some bills and a bottle of booze in his pocket. He let them drop into the pocket of his white smock, and still said he was busy. Dolgorma hung in my arms like a shot chamois. Withered and limp like Mama must've been that time in the back seat.

Oyuna would never admit a mistake. If they hadn't driven Mama to the hospital, she might've been around still for another couple of winters.

They knocked the soul out of her.

Rattling around in the back of a jeep is the last thing anyone needs when they're hanging by a thread. When their last words die in the roar of the engine, what've we got to pass on to the next generation? Who's going to tell the story of the mosquito to Tsetsegma and Zula's children? And they won't get anywhere in life without pride in their ancestors. Blind as milk glass. That's how the eyes of the dead are. Gray as the panels on the concrete buildings in Sansaar, as my hair, as Hiroko's favorite horse that Nara told me about. Gray was also the color of the newspaper stands in the City.

On the third day I cut my hand. My head was somewhere else and my hands were absorbed in their work. If only Oyuna didn't sharpen her knives every week. Who ever heard of that? I felt a warm trickle and looked down to see what it was. My hand looked like it had done something bad and I'd caught it in the act. It didn't hurt. It was like it wasn't even mine. I cut my hand in the winter once. The blood had come streaming out and hardened into a pink icicle. Like a precious gem or the long claw of a witch.

Oyuna ran right over. She was frightened. When you pour vodka on blood, it stinks like a drunkard's fists. That's how the ones at Divaajin who didn't pay ended up. Also gray. Faceless and full of sperm.

On the third night they asked me how long I was going to be there. I said I didn't know, took off my boots, and handed Oyuna my money. Later that night, I discovered another ten thousand *tugriks* still tucked away in my left boot. I snuck back to Oyuna's *ger,* where everyone was fast asleep, and put a bill under each tea bowl like a colorful little placemat.

The next morning Oyuna's shouting woke me up again.

The dogs had gotten into a sack of entrails that Naima forgot to put inside for the night. Torn intestines lay splayed across the grass while the beaten dogs whined in pain a little ways away. I was ready to stick Oyuna on top of a camel and yell at it to run away and never come back. Oh, those blissful days when I could slap my hands over her mouth and hold her till she gagged.

I sat down on my bed and wove my hair into two decorative braids and tied them with girlish blue ribbons. Even an old crone doesn't always have to look ugly. I gulped down some soup and went to go sit on the stone.

The stone was a legend throughout the region. It was the biggest one for miles around and was worn smooth from being rubbed. By the little fingers of children, stretching up from below but unable to reach without a push; by men leaning against it when they found a moment for an afternoon smoke; by women sitting on its rough, warm surface, discussing their husbands and children. It looked like a bowl. Climbing in was hard, but once she was inside, a woman was well protected from the wind and biting sand. And if two people got together and put something soft on the bottom, they could have sex in there, and as long as they were quiet, there could be someone five cow tails away and they wouldn't even know.

I wrapped my arms around my knees and felt like I was in a butter tub, an impregnable *ger* with a view. I'll never feel a man on top of me again.

His strength between my legs, his hungry lips on my cheeks. If I had any say, I'd like to do it at least once more. Just as a reminder. Say, with Biamkhu. By now he must be even older than me, so my cracked skin and flabby hips might not be as disgusting to him as they would be to somebody younger. Last night I was changing my clothes when suddenly Batjar came barging in. My breasts, my crotch, it was all right there. Only for the blink of an eye, but I saw the look he gave me when we sat down to supper. Curling back his lips like a dog over rotten meat. He didn't even apologize.

Oyuna keeps on pushing me to do some work. She's always managed on her own, so I know it's not that she needs the help. And I told her so too. My money was there on the table. Those round rolls of bills that allowed me to have my pride even here. I've broken four bowls. Three by accident, one on purpose. Oyuna can spend all afternoon figuring out where they're cheapest. She even factors in the money for gas and the fact that the cheaper ones don't last as long.

So long as it's summer I'm fine just sitting around and basking in the sun. I'm like ice. I'd like to have a talk with Naima. But he's avoiding me. Three times now I've nodded to him to step aside with me, and three times he's nodded back no. I often notice him sizing me up with that raised eyebrow of his when I'm doing or saying something. Like when I took my parents' picture and put it between two heated stones to flatten it out, and spent all day keeping watch to make sure no one kicked it over. He also frowned when I finished the leftover *aaruul*. It must've been there on the shelf for a century at least. It didn't have any taste left, so getting it down was a struggle. It was a sacrifice on my part.

I've finally given up on Naima, once and for all. I ruined it. Not that I meant to. I took up knitting and made a coverlet for their Burkhan. Sort of a sweater, like. Naima turned red as a sunset when he walked in and saw it. He flung it at my head, and afterwards I heard him telling Oyuna about it outside. Traitor.

Erliiz, erliiz, erliiz, I say to myself when the rage comes over me. Everything I've done in my life has been clouded by that. I go off into the mountains and come back with an armful of herbs. I drop them in front of Oyuna's *ger* and hope it'll make things better.

The Red Mountains are incredibly old. The oldest ones in all of western Mongolia. It used to be the whole world was as high as their peaks. The world didn't used to know any such thing as mountains. Then came disaster and the earth was flooded with giants. Whole herds of them, pouring in. They trampled over everything. People crunched under their feet like fleas, *gers* and herds vanished forever under their soles. The sky disappeared for a few thousand years, a gigantic wolfskin clouding the horizon. The giants went by wolf names, and as they roamed the earth, the echo of their thunderous howls was everywhere. Their voice battered people's ears. Anyone who heard them from too close bled to death from their ears. When the giants wanted children, they would pluck out a hair thick as a tree and stab it into the ground. The next day there was one giant more. The Red Mountains are the only place the giants never set foot in. Everything else was trampled flat. Where the Red Mountains are now, supposedly there once grew stinging killer flowers. Even a giant couldn't survive their burn. And so the mountains remained. The only ones from the old world left.

That was Papa's best story about our *aimak*. He had five of them.

Whenever we had visitors, he would talk about our region like it was some kind of remarkable place. He got that from Grandma Dolgorma. I knew the Red Mountains weren't the only ones, so I couldn't figure out why he said that. One time he heard me arguing about it with Nara and said, Listen, girls, those other mountains didn't grow until later. Like steppe tulips after the first rain that fell to earth, after the fire dog strangled all the giants.

I don't think Naima knows that one. He might like to hear it, since everyone knows he goes hunting for *risunki* in the mountains, and he brags that he knows every stone there is up there. Oyuna sometimes calls him in vain.

Whenever Naima knows he won't be needed for any work, he just doesn't come home. Oyuna scolds him, but he's used to it by now. It happened just the other day. I offered to warm him up some food. He just threw his hand in the air.

I still can't bring myself to say it. That I'm not leaving. I keep waiting for a moment that won't ever come. It's not like they're going to give it to me.

Yesterday, I embroidered Tsetsegma's *del*. I'm not trying to bribe her, but it beats scraping caked-on grease out of bowls. I suggested we don't even bother. We always eat the same thing anyway. And besides, when you eat three times a day, the leftovers don't get a chance to stink. *Zalkhuu,* Oyuna said. Then, with a spit: Lazy cow. Let her wash them herself then. Numbskulled for all time.

Tsetsegma thought my embroidery was too wild, too childish and colorful. I took her *del* when she wasn't looking and then brought it back as a surprise. *Ma-meee!* she screamed. I didn't think grown women cried to their mothers for help. Oyuna came flying over, and the two of them laid into me. They said I did it on purpose. But I only did one thing on purpose and that was that bowl I smashed. That was totally serious. I remembered long ago how Mama had shown me the embroidery on her sleeve, saying with pride that her aunt had done it, a long-dead woman with one glass eye. I wanted that too. To make something for someone that they could show off.

Yesterday, though, something I'd thought for a long time turned out to be true. I started out for the bowl stone to sit and watch the sun, but I never made it. Batjar had said he was going into the center, but that was a lie. He was in the stone bowl making the moves with a woman. I recognized his breathing. Every now and then a hand or the curve of a bent back peeked over the edge, and the sound of a woman's groans carried to me on the wind. Zula was gone all day too.

That evening the two of them came home together. Zula's face was red and flushed.

When a woman's got someone you can't always tell. She goes about her business, carrying happiness in her heart. When a man's got someone, he shoots his mouth off left and right, calling for toasts and puffing up like a stallion that's become head of the herd. That was exactly what Batjar was like the whole time I was there.

Naima, on the other hand, is grumpy all the time. At least he is with me. I've given up trying with him. I never could see through that man.

A man learns all the skills he needs as a little boy in his *ger*. He goes to school in the *somon* center, has a wife, then children, and, if he's fortunate, a son that he can pass on all his knowledge to. Then he dies and the animals eat him. That's the kind of man Naima is. But not all men are like that. Papa, for instance, knew what it was to raise bastards. To answer all their silly questions, watch that they don't go near the stove, and hold their horse so it doesn't bolt when they clamber onto its back. Papa knew what it was to hit a woman out of grief. I saw his fist in Mama's face more than once.

Mergen, on the other hand, knew what it was to do nothing at all. To get a stiff butt from years of waiting. To wear a dent in a chair from sitting. Even Naima's own son knew something Naima never knew. What it is to say nothing and lie, and pet a woman's privates in secret.

I've been here long enough now that Oyuna's getting antsy. Asking me about my plans and what about the City. She said she knew a man who was driving into the City from the center next week to go and see relatives. She could set it up for me. I told her I liked it here. The City is crazy, and besides, all of the people closest to me are here. For the first time she smiled a little.

I think she knows I'm smart. I think she has the feeling that that's also the reason why it didn't turn out so well for me.

It's obvious my sister thinks my life has been a failure. But maybe she doesn't hold it against me. She's the type that gets everything over and done with right away. She's always got something handy.

ALL THIS BELONGS TO ME

194
▾

Whether for animals or for people. The only thing she can't do is get her daughters out of the *ger*. She harps on them constantly. She can't see that they're cursed by Uregma. Hardworking but incredibly unattractive.

A woman in the center told me she really felt for Oyuna and asked me to tell her she said so. But you don't say that to a woman with children. Nobody has that right. Least of all her *erliiz* sister from the City.

The days are all alike. Except for the grass turning yellow and the animals little by little shedding their summer coats. There's less and less light every day, and the bowl stone isn't even warm at midday anymore. The mountains glow red with the setting sun before supper, and Naima doesn't get home until dark. Time to trade in the summer *del* for sheepskin. My legs are so cold they feel naked, and yesterday, for the first time, I spent all day inside by the fire.

When I sit out in front of my *ger* I feel like a khan princess. My *del* full of balmy wind, blowing up like a bubble. I know it here. The grand steppe with bumps spreading out in every direction. At my back, the only mountains of the old world left, and beyond them, and dozens more like them, our proud City.

So what if my hair is cracked and gray.

So what if any little kid can outrun me.

Because all this belongs to me.

Zaya of Bashkgan *somon*.

■ □ ■ □ ■

WRITINGS FROM AN UNBOUND EUROPE